T0113604

RIDGES FOR THE WISE

THE BERASCULATAN CRISIS

JOE LITAK

Edited By: Joe and Steve Litak

Author's note: This story deals with the economic, social, geopolitical, militaristic, intellectual, and religious aspects of today's society in a science fiction format.

Archway Publishing books may be ordered through booksellers or by contacting:

Archway Publishing
1663 Liberty Drive
Bloomington, IN 47403
www.archwaypublishing.com
844-669-3957

ISBN: 978-1-6657-1845-5 (sc)
ISBN: 978-1-6657-1844-8 (e)

Library of Congress Control Number: 2022901801

Print information available on the last page.

Archway Publishing rev. date: 02/07/2022

AUTHOR'S NOTES

1. The story centers around the idea of will happen when it comes time to select a new monarch for the Berasculatan people as their so to be their late and or previous leader and or king Volerick Lobberstein I has no more biological descendants left because he has outlived them all and the only truly legitimate heir comes from the bloodline of youngest surviving brother Temerick, Duke of Lecavestria of whom is the was the most loyal of his i.e., Volerick siblings and subjects. Volerick I was in power for a total of 80 years (10) as both vice regent and regent of the kingdom and (70) as king of the kingdom.
2. The contenders for the throne of Berasculata come from a wide range of countries from around all of the planet Mulizan and Mulizan is in a system that is 820 quintillion light years from Earth.
3. The Grand Duke of the Grand Duchy of Portville, Kiverold Fleishenberger III, long reigning leader of the Grand Duchy of Portville is trying to destroy and thus confiscate the lands of the Viecke people in the Grand Duchy for his i.e., Grand Duke Kiverold III's own purposes.
4. Viecke people, a group of citizens of the northeastern part of Berasculata and southwestern part of the
5. Grand Duchy of Portville seek an autonomous state free of any political affiliation
6. Kakoria – Werpistan, a joint nation of symbiotic peoples of which the Kakori dominate the Werpian people via technological knowhow but which the Werpian people live longer than the Kakori, the nation is just a few thousand miles from the nation of Vistrabia.
7. Dolvan, a trilaterally genetic constructed robot of Kakori, Werpian and Vistrabian DNA that commissioned under the orders of Furistahl Bauspeirada Sr. but was officially inaugurated into service by Furistahl Bauspeirada Jr. and his son Furistahl Bauspeirada III.
8. Ulstanagard Hantabolvia IV, a Vistrabia count of whom has no chance of succeeding to the Vistrabian throne due to his aunt being the current queen of Vistrabia but can make a claim to it through a marriage between him and his Berasculatan cousin Duchess Maeve Lobberstein – Hantabolvia of whom is also sought for marriage by her Gorgadalian cousin Gleckerhambeck Hantabolvia, a Gorgadalian

viscount of much wealthy and property due to fact that he is a son of the current queen of Gorgadal.

9. Prince Phillip Lobberstein III, murdered nephew of Volerick Lobberstein I, and grandfather to potential king Volerick Lobberstein II, of whom was 3 years old at the time of his i.e., Prince Phillip Lobberstein II's grisly death and 4 years old at the time of his i.e., Volerick Lobberstein' great- great grand uncle King Volerick Lobberstein I's sudden death.
10. \Duke William Nivecoat, an ageing agent of King Volerick Lobberstein I tasked with both protecting the remaining Lobberstein royal family from untimely demises like the late Prince Phillip Lobberstein II and the unequivocal death of King Volerick Lobberstein I not all unexpected but still tragic, but also one of the chief ministers of the B.S.S. or Berasculatan Special Intelligence Service of whose primary duty at the onset is to find out who had been involved in the plot against Prince Phillip Lobberstein II and thus bring them to justice.
11. Yolanda Yorenaski, a female B.S.S. agent assigned to make contact and thus try and apprehend those that may have been involved in the death of Prince Phillip Lobberstein II.
12. Cyrus Ajukalani Wagglesmont, a Machu Primean soldier fighting in the armies of the Madrigald Coalition who after which would be assigned to help negotiate the terms of reconciliation between the Madrigald and Fatavan Coalitions thus ending the Berasculatan War.
13. Thaddeus Posler, a male B.S.S. agent who is caught up in an accidental Kakori quantum space -time trans dimensional portal which transports him and several other individuals i.e., Fatavan prisoners of war whom were in the process of being return to their home countries but were instead transported the Remigarian by accident, he is the great nephew of Duke William Nivecoat by marriage.
14. Oscar Veritos Maesis: opening narrator of the book and a Kakori mystical space-time time jumper.

AUTHOR'S ACKNOWLEDGMENTS

For this I would like to acknowledge and thus thank these people for their help in framing me and giving me the drive to work on and thus complete the book.

First, I'd like to acknowledge and or thank my mom and dad for giving me life and the foreknowledge to know that I can be whoever I can and me be in my life.

Second, I'd like to thank my brothers and sisters for giving their love and friendship when they did so and for also being there when I need them to be there for me.

Third, I'd like to thank my aunts and uncles for being kind to me when I need there help in doing certain things in my past stages of my life.

Fourth, I'd like to thank my friends and classmates of whom gave me hope and care of when I need them to accomplish the certain tasks, I need to get done during my school years.

Fifth, I'd like to thank some certain teachers of whom taught me how to be a good citizen and also gave me sense of how to have fun.

Sixth, I'd like to thank those of whom gave me care in school when I was in need of medical care.

Seventh, I'd like to thank although I have worked with and who gave me purpose when I couldn't find comfort at home.

AUTHOR'S DEDICATIONS

For this part, I Joseph Peter John Litak dedicate this book to the following people.

I. My mom and late dad
II. My brothers and sisters, first cousins, second cousins and third cousins on both sides of my extended family.
III. My aunts and uncles, and family friends, friends and neighbors both past, present and probable future ones.
IV. My little nephew Ryan Jacob Ronquillo, his little love whomever that maybe, my little friends Giovanni Suszynski, and little Axel Leniham.
V. My friends and former classmates from both Pride Alternative School and also all of my friends from all of the Evergreen Park area schools I went to.
VI. My current and former coworkers in the Village of Evergreen Park.
VII. The love of my life, the little "Dolphanic Swan" of the southside of Chicago

Dedicated to my young nephew Ryan Jacob Ronquillo and also for my young friends, Claire Corley her brother, Giovanni Suszynski, Claire Ferrin and her sister, Sophie Lovato and her young brother and both Axel Leniham and Matthew Palenik.

CONTENTS

PROLOGUE

(850 DAYS BEFORE THE BERASCULATAN WAR)

It is a very crisp April morning. There is a flock of bluish-green hummingbirds moving about the grounds of Iskelvimbarkien Palace. Coming out to view these birds up close is Her Royal Highness, the Duchess Maeve Lobberstein. She is the youngest daughter of Princess Elaine Lobberstein and Count Vladimir Hantabolova. Maeve is eighteen years old and fairly beautiful, with many freckles on her face. She has had a lot of suitors come to call for her hand in marriage, and she has turned them all down.

After having a conversation with one of the hummingbirds, she notices someone coming towards her. It's her uncle, Prince Phillip Lobberstein. Maeve answers him in a cool tone. He acknowledges the hostility she has for him, but he has something important to ask of her. He wants her to speak with his daughter, Sarah. It seems that Sarah will not talk to him or her mother. He feels that out of all the royal family members who can reach Sarah about her problem, it is Maeve.

Maeve agrees to do what her uncle has asked of her; she says she'll do it after she gets off work that day. He is ecstatic that Maeve will speak with Sarah. However, before he leaves, he asks her how her mother, his sister Elaine, is doing. She tells him a half-truth, and before he realizes it's not the whole truth, she has left the terrace.

Not wanting to call his niece a modest fibber, he heads for his uncle's study. He knows that he can call his wife from the study, because that phone has not been tapped by the news agencies or the legislature. After fifteen minutes, he reaches the study from the terrace. He checks to see if any of his uncle's attainders are around. Prince Phillip doesn't want them knowing what he is doing, because they will probably bother his uncle with the details of what he is discussing. Any mention of how his uncle's health is to anyone curious might show that the king of Berasculata is of a weakened state, both physically and politically. When he sees none of the attainders around, he slips into the study. It will take him forty-five minutes to make a phone connection with his wife, Agnes.

Lady Agnes Lobberstein responds to her husband's phone call with utter joy in the hope of re-establishing a link with her youngest daughter, through Phillip's niece, Maeve. She tells him that when she gets home from work, she'll make the most extravagant dinner that the children still at home and he have not eaten in years. He tells her that he will be glad to eat the meal but he has to get off the phone, because his uncle is coming. Phillip expresses his dear and deep love for her. She responds in kind to him. Suddenly, the phone goes dead on his end, and he realizes that she had to hang up too.

With both phones hung up now, Prince Phillip Lobberstein approaches the side door to the study. It is opposite of the door he used to let himself in. Before he makes his way out of the study, he sees William Malushingham, his uncle's chief advisor and a pain in the neck towards Phillip.

"Oh, good morning, Prince Phillip," Malushingham says. "How are you doing? How's the family?"

"Very well, William. How's your wife and children?" replied Prince Phillip Lobberstein.

"They're all doing well. I hope to take my son, Gerald, off to college in the fall."

"That's good to hear. Well, I must be on my way, you know."

"Ah yes, be on your way then, and I hope to see you later," remarked Malushingham. "By the way, did I see you coming out of your uncle's study just now?"

"Yes, William, you did. However, rest assured, I was only making a phone call to my wife about a personal matter."

"May I ask why you thought to use your uncle's study to make a personal phone call?"

"Well, if you must know, I thought my phone was being bugged, and since I know my uncle's phone would not be bugged by the legislature or the press, I used it."

"Oh well, I guess you have a legitimate reason then. Just don't let me catch you in your uncle's study again, because you know he only gave his staff permission to use his study for governmental matters. Understand?"

"Alright, William," Prince Phillip said. "This will be the last time you see me in this house for a long time."

"I am fine with that," Malushingham replied. "Don't get me wrong; I don't hate you, Prince Phillip. It's just that if your uncle needs anything, I am very capable of handling it myself."

"I understand, William. It's just sad that you have more respect for my brother, Terry."

"I don't respect Terry that much, Prince Phillip. It's just that we have the same goals for the monarchy."

"Well, I'll tell him that the next time I see him; he'll be glad someone has the same ideals for the monarchy."

"Oh, don't do that. That will add to his ego, and he already has a large ego. He'll make my life even more intolerable."

"Well, I don't care, William, because I'm leaving now."

"Alright, you can stay for a little bit," Malushingham conceded, "but you have to be gone by the time your uncle arrives, which will be in twenty minutes."

Twenty minutes pass by like the sands in an hourglass. After meeting with other people during this period of time, Prince Phillip again sees Malushingham.

"Did you hear about my run-in with Monsignor Rondel Makerhalth?" Malushingham asked.

"Yes, William," Prince Phillip said. "So, I'll be seeing you later. Okay?"

"Well, at least you can give him my apologies and salutations. Also, tell him that if they want restitution from me personally, he can have it."

"I will tell him, William. Be assured that you will be made ambassador, if I'm become monarch of this wonderful country."

"I am thankful for that," Malushingham said. "I'd be willing to represent you at the bishop of Total City's religious and political conference."

"No, William, I think I will do that in person, because the bishop and I have a lot of things to discuss."

After he left his uncle's residence, Prince Phillip headed for Easer House. When he got there, he is greeted by Rondel Makerhalth, Dilavestan's ambassador to Berasculata. He returned the greeting with as much pomp and circumstance as had been shown to him by the Dilavestan ambassador. After their initial greeting, both men went their separate ways. It was at this point that Prince Phillip was to plan for new trade negotiations between the two countries. It was to take him at least two and a half hours to fully prepare for the meeting with the Dilavestan ambassador and his entourage.

The meeting started at two thirty in the afternoon and lasted for hours, with very little breaks in between. When it finally ended, Prince Phillip and Rondel signed a trade treaty that was to last up to the time of the Berasculatan War. Noticing that he had missed dinner with his wife and younger children, Prince Phillip Lobberstein decided to get some flowers for Agnes and some toys and models for the children.

After the meeting, he headed east towards the Briber Street Commons. Once inside the main store, he went towards the toy section. It will take several minutes to find what he wanted to get for his and Agnes's seven young children. Upon leaving the main store, he went to the flower shop in the Commons. He bought seven dozen roses and four dozen daisies for Agnes. He paid twenty-three dollars for the whole lot.

However, Phillip didn't make it home that night. On his way home, while going through Stringhoff, the town near his uncle's estate, he was assaulted by a pair of brutes. They beat the prince and kidnapped him. A search was set up with the local police and military in the area. The search, however, ended in despair.

After combing the countryside around Stringhoff, the local police and military unit traced the prince's whereabouts to a building near the Berasculata and Portville border. After a long standoff with the prince's captors, the local army unit stormed the building.

In the ensuing melee, a squad of troops found the prince's body near by the two original captors.

The army unit took three of the captors alive. An extensive and intense interrogation of the surviving captors took place. However, despite the best efforts of the interrogators, nothing of real value was learned from the captors. Subsequently, the captors were given very speedy trials and convictions.

At each of their trials, the code name "Beriguron" was brought up. It was assumed at first that Beriguron was an alias for William Malushingham. But after an extensive search of his personal files, there was no mention of Beriguron on any of them. So, there was a cold trail into the whereabouts of who Beriguron was, until the code name came up as the owner of the Vistrabian Ionized Coal Company.

The company's chief executive officer, Reginald Kiswather, was arrested on the morning of August 2. The charges were conspiracy to commit the murder of Prince Phillip Lobberstein and financial misconduct of funds for said murder. Reginald adamantly denied the charges but hinted to the prosecution that someone in his inner circle might be responsible for Prince Phillip's murder.

Janus Verimbecker, the lead magistrate, questioned him at length and told him that if he told them this person's name, the person would have the same thing done to him as he did to Prince Phillip. Then Janis remarked that his government's special witness section could protect him and his family from the person and his minions, if he only told what he knew about the young prince's murder.

Reginald then said that his uncle, Sangeld Kiswather Sr., ordered the murder of Prince Phillip.

"You mean to tell me that your uncle ordered the prince's murder?" Janis asked.

"That's exactly what I am saying to you, Mr. Verimbecker, and I'm willing to testify to that in court."

"I am so glad to hear that, sir. Now, if you could tell us where he might be found so that our special police force can make him pay for his crime," Janis replied.

"I don't really know exactly," Reginald said, "but I know someone who might know where my uncle hangs out."

"Who is this person you speak of?"

"Her name is Tabitha Haeluki; she is sort of his special companion in a manner of Vistrabian state business."

"So, you're saying that she is an escort for your uncle? Am I hearing you right?"

"You might call her that, but she is more his fiancée. Ever since his wife died, he has been seeing a lot of women. However, he has become very close to Tabitha lately."

"If you're telling us the truth, we have to act quickly," Baron William Nivecoat chimed in.

"Do you know this Haeluki person, William?" Janis asked.

"Well, not exactly, Janis, but I know her father," William said. "He is an old classmate of mine. Tabitha is his oldest daughter."

"So, she about twenty-four years of age, and Sangeld Kiswather Sr. is about fifty-two years of age?" Janis guessed.

"No, she is twenty-six years old, and he is fifty-four years old. He is also rumored to be quite unpleasant."

"Unpleasant? What kind of unpleasantness are we talking about?" Janis asked.

"Well, I am not really sure, but I heard that he beat up on his past female companions, not including his wife, for small infractions against his rules," Baron William said.

"So, he abuses any female who doesn't measure up to what he deems appropriate?" Janus asked. "Am I hearing you right?"

"That's correct. I think we should find her to make sure he hasn't hurt her."

"Well, I agree with you. I'll have Terry call her home because he seems to know her phone number."

Five minutes go by. "I am not receiving an answer from her home," said Terence Verimbecker, Janis's brother. "I think we should head right over as soon as possible."

"Alright, Terry," Janis said. "You and Baron William Nivecoat can lead the way while I ask the office to put out an all-points bulletin to arrest Vistrabian prime minister, Sangeld Kiswather Sr."

As they approached Tabitha Haeluki's residence, Sergeant Thomas Olienaker told them the Vistrabian prime minister's personal aide, Atergeld Ruminage, had been in a major traffic accident, and the premier may have been killed.

Soon after that news was relayed, Baron William Nivecoat said, "I don't believe that old wolf is dead, and besides, we haven't even found Tabitha yet."

"We'll call some of her friends from high school," Janis suggested.

"What if they don't know where she is?" Terence asked.

"Then I am sure the baron can check out the Vistrabian embassy in Iskelvimbarkien's western district for clues to the young lady's disappearance. Right, Baron Nivecoat?" Janis asked.

"Right, Janis, and I'll also follow up on the status of the Vistrabian prime minister," Baron William said.

Soon the three of them were to head in several directions. Baron William Nivecoat went to Deiker's Pub. The two Verimbecker brothers left each other's company after reaching Hepphaertis Square. Janis went into Zwieschler's, an all you-can-eat restaurant. Terence was seen going into the Gitzerhoffbrau. It took them less than an hour to get the information they needed. They all went back to report what they found. Terence went first in revealing what he had learned.

"I have learned that a certain Hiram Uselanksi has been seen with a woman named Tammy Fitzhogan," Terence said, "and this Ms. Fitzhogan is an alias for a Vistrabian mistress, whose phone number is almost exactly similar for Tabitha Haeluki."

"So did you call this phone number, Terry?" Janis asked.

"Yes, and I learned that this phone number was purchased by a man with the initials S.K. This same person was seen near Pizani Point. So, I called the hotel in Pizani Point and spoke to Tabitha for a few minutes."

"Well, I am glad you heard from her. I thought I saw her at Gwendolyn Jisper's restaurant with someone who claimed to be Sangeld Kiswather Jr."

"I'll tail the younger Kiswather, if Baron Nivecoat agrees," Janis suggested.

"You know, I agree with the idea of the tailing him," Baron William said, "but we have to use someone who won't be recognized. Otherwise, the mission to trap his father will be for nought."

"So, who should we use on this very special assignment?" Janis asked.

"Well, it would have to be someone young and beautiful," Baron William said, "with a decent personality, and who is not too sure of herself."

"That precludes anyone of our relatives, but maybe we can use one of the Berasculatan Special Service's female operatives," Terence suggested.

"Who do you have in mind?" Janis asked.

"A woman called Yolanda Yorenaski," Terence replied, "and from what I've been told, she isn't a personal appearance operative."

"How do we contact her?" Baron William asked.

"I can contact her handler and tell him that she is needed for a special assignment."

"Fine let's contact him and get her in, the field immediately," Baron William said.

"I'll do so", said Terence Verimbecker.

CHAPTER 1

DEATH OF A KING

It had been at least two hours since she got the special assignment from her handler, and she had barely washed the taste of soda out of her mouth. After she got dressed for the assignment, she headed for the Triple Rockets café, where she usually met with her contact. It was only a few minutes from her apartment in the Filawacker district. She was to positively identify her "cat" by his "purr."

She sat down at a table, and a young man approached her. It was Sangeld Kiswather Jr.

"Hello, beautiful, what's your game?" he asked. "How can I make you my friend tonight?"

"Okay, well, you can put a breath mint in your mouth to cover the smell," Yolanda Yorenaski said, "and after that, you can buy me a glass of mucojuice, doll."

"Done and done, sweetie pie. So, what's your name, and who's got their cellphone on buzzer?" Sangeld asked.

"My name is Xenox," Yolanda replied, "and it's my law partner calling. He is going to scream at me for something, I bet. So, you may want to walk away while I take this call."

"Okay, but you had better tell me later, because I don't like being caught in the middle of any unpleasantness, honey cheeks."

"Oh, don't worry," Yolanda said. "I'll be sharing with you all possible information at a certain time, I'm sure."

"What is it, Simon?" she asked, speaking into her phone.

"Simon? What are you talking about? My codename is Felix the Mailman," said Jason Greiker.

"Just play along, Jason," she replied, "and respond to the name Simon."

"Alright, I'll play along, but you'll have to respond in code about the mark."

"That's exactly what I'm talking to you about right now."

"What are you talking about? Okay, I am sorry I brought it up." She turned towards Sangeld, who looked puzzled, and asked him, "Where were we? I'd like to get a better picture of what you are really like."

"Sure, doll! I'm a hard-working exchange student, and my father is the Vistrabian prime minister."

"It must be hard living up to what he stands for," Yolanda said.

"Oh, it's quite hard. Every time I try to get close to my father, something or someone pulls us apart. We have to try new ways of communicating with one another. We don't talk all that much, not since Zara came into his life."

"Who's this Zara person, if you don't mind me asking?"

"Not at all. Zara is Zara Reinaskert, a reporter for Channel 745 News."

"That's interesting to me," she said. "One would think he'd want to date someone a little closer to his own age."

"Well, he doesn't, and I admire him for it. because no one is ever going to replace my mother in my father's life, or in mine. Understand me, Xenox?"

"Oh, no one can replace your mother. I get that, but I was mainly trying to get you to open up more, because you seem to be in a daze about something else."

"Well, I'm not in a daze," he replied. "I am just more worried about my father's safety."

"Why should you worry about your father's well-being? If he is as important as you say, he'd have bodyguards up the yin yang doing their best to protect him from whatever came his way."

"I wish that were true, but my father has made his share of enemies over the years. The only person he trusts more than Zara is Furistahl Bauspeirada Sr., the Vistrabian High Commissioner for the Verigula District of Vistrabia."

"You mean he is a close personal friend of Bauspeirada?" Yolanda asked. "Well, that's very interesting to hear. I don't suppose you could introduce me to him?"

"I think I could do that, but you have to understand that my father's friendship with the count only goes so far back."

"Well, maybe you don't want to start our friendship on a good note."

"Oh, but I do want to start our friendship on a good note. I'll make the call to make sure the count is home and receiving visitors. By the way, do you happen to have change for the phone booth?"

"Why, did you leave your phone at home?"

"No, I didn't. It's just that the Vistrabian embassy here in Berasculata frowns upon its citizens using their embassy -issued phones for non-governmental purposes."

"Fine," Yolanda said. "Here's some coins. Make your call on the public phone."

"Thanks a lot, Xenox. You won't regret this. I'll make sure the count talks to you if he is up to it."

Sangeld called his father's mentor and friend, Count Furistahl Bauspeirada Sr.

"Hello, this is Sangeld Kiswather Jr. Can I speak with someone about the count?" he asked.

"Hold your horses, young man. I'll be with you in about five minutes". It was Henry Jaenolisker. "Come on, Frobisher. Get outside. You know how the master of the house doesn't like it when you slobber all over his newspapers. Okay let's go back and pick up the phone. Hello, young man, what are you calling for?"

"Hi again, sir. My name is Sangeld Kiswather Jr. I was wondering if the count was up to having visitors, because I have something to show him, and there is someone with me who wants to meet him."

"Well," Henry said, "I'll check with the count and be back in a few minutes with a response."

Henry came back to the phone after half an hour.

"I'm very sorry to have kept you waiting on the line, but I've got good news for you, sir: The count says he can fit you into his schedule at around 4 p.m., provided you will be properly dressed for a round of tennis before dinner."

"Don't you worry about me and my date," Sangeld said. "We'll be ready at one o'clock and then head over."

"Good, sir," Henry said. "I'll expect you at the house at four, which will give you plenty of time to get properly dressed and be here."

"You will have someone outside the count's residence to greet us, right?"

"Yes, sir. Slyvester Hockenweiller will be here to greet you and your friend."

"Fine. We will see you in a little bit. Don't rush the count to speak with us. I'm sure he will be in conference with his nephew, Valeutin."

"Oh, I'm sure he will be done talking with Master Valeutin, well before you arrive."

"Well, goodbye for now. See you at four."

After he hung up the public phone in the café's foyer, Sangeld returned to talk with Yolanda.

"In a few hours," he said, "you and I will be having dinner with Count Furistahl Bauspeirada Sr."

"Oh, that will be nice," Yolanda said. "But I've got nothing to wear to the dinner with the count."

"Well, don't you fret, Xenox. We can go to Three Apples Shopping Center and find something for you to wear."

"Okay, that's great, but how are we supposed to get there? Neither of us has a motor vehicle."

"Don't worry, we'll hitch a ride on the Iskelvimbarkien Express hover train system; the shopping center is just a short walk away. Then we can walk another three blocks to the count's residence."

After the hover train transported them to the area, they walked to the Three Apples Shopping Center. When they left the sporting goods store, Sangeld ran into an old friend.

"How are you, Sangeld, old boy?" Tobias Leiferman asked.

"Oh, I'm fine, Tobias," Sangeld said. "How are you, old pal of mine?"

"I can't complain," Tobias replied. "I just got wed to Ursula about three and half months ago, and we were buying gifts for her kids. They're my step kids now."

"Really? You got married three and half months ago, and you did not invite me to the bachelor party. Why not you, old dog?"

"Well, I would have, Sangeld, old man, but my new father-in-law, Kurt, is a pious old gentleman, and he did not want to have his new son-in-law to get into a drunken stupor before the wedding. You, see? I didn't want him getting mad at me."

"Well, if my dinner with Count Furistahl Bauspeirada goes well, I will try to put in a call to the Portvillian embassy in Vistrabia; I could speak to the grand-duke on your and your father-in-law's behalf if you like."

"I'm sure he'd like that very much, Sangeld, and I'd be very grateful to you and your household forever."

"Okay, then I will call the embassy after the dinner, Tobias. I'll call you to tell when and where it is to be. Alright?"

"Fine with me, Sangeld, and thank you very much for doing this for me. My wife and her father will also appreciate it."

"What are friends for, Tobias, if not to help each other out with their problems?"

"Again, thanks a lot, Sangeld. I hope you and your young lady friend have a nice time with the count."

"Oh, I'm sure we will have a good time."

Sangeld retrieved Yolanda from her conversation with Ursula Leiferman, and they headed out towards the residence of Count Furistahl Bauspeirada Sr. of where they were greeted as expected and thus led to the residence's clubhouse to change into their tennis attire.

After they changed, they were led to the residence's main tennis court, where they were met by their host for the evening, seventy-year-old Count Furistahl Bauspeirada Sr., his wife, Sophie, and the couple's nephew, Valeutin. After much fanfare, the tennis matches began. After the last match ended, dinner was served to the five of them.

The dinner was very sumptuous; each of them was filled with delight. After a couple of drinks of mucojuice, the three men and their womenfolk played a game of gin rummy. That's where the real conversations got cooking. Yolanda began talking to Countess Sophie, and Valeutin joined into the conversation. When they asked why he was interfering with their private conservation, he gave them a very cryptic response.

"I'm sorry to butt in like this," he said, "but my dear Aunt Sophie, where is the teleprompter's slide monitor?"

"It's in the closet by the stairs," his aunt answered. "Why do you ask?"

"Well, I'm going to show my dear uncle what I've learned here," Valeutin said. "I might be able to help him and you out with your stock portfolio."

"Well, that's good to know," Countess Sophie said, "but if you don't mind, I was trying to talk to Xenox about her future in the high-stakes game of elementary school teaching."

"Oh, well, if I knew you were trying to convince her to be as competitive as you are, Auntie Sophie, then you'll probably ruin any chance of my getting to know Xenox later."

"Oh, I'm sure you'll get to know me better," Yolanda said, "without the use of your auntie as an excuse."

As she was heading towards the guest bedroom, Countess Sophie Bauspeirada saw the light in her husband's den go dim, which meant that he had finished his conversation with young Sangeld Kiswather Jr. As the den's door opened, the men came out, thanking each other for speaking about an important subject. Count Furistahl looked up and noticed his beloved wife Sophie in the distance, walking down the hallway to the guest bedroom. Then he saw his nephew approaching him. Valeutin told his uncle every word that his Aunt Sophie had told him.

Count Furistahl was in a sour mood after hearing what his nephew had told him; the count sauntered off towards where his wife had headed off to sulk. Meanwhile, Sangeld returned to talk with Yolanda, who was getting bored of Valeutin. He told Yolanda that rather than returning to their individual residences, the count had invited them to stay overnight there as the count and countess's private houseguests.

Yolanda went past the guest bedroom to thank the count and countess for allowing her and Sangeld to stay the night. They appreciated her gratitude and invited her to eat breakfast with them the next morning.

The next day, after eating a wonderful breakfast with the count and countess, Yolanda thanked the couple and went out the door. Once outside, she caught a hover bus heading towards the Berasculatan Special Services office.

Once she was inside the BSS main office, Yolanda went into room G1176-A, where she met her handler, Jason Greiker, Terence and Janus Verimbecker, and Baron William Nivecoat. The men quizzed her on what she had learned of those major conspirators in the murder of Prince Phillip.

She told them some very interesting anecdotes, which were used to expel some people who lacked diplomatic immunity, including Valeutin Bauspeirada. Upon learning that he had been ordered to leave Berasculatan, Valeutin vowed that he would appeal his expulsion with as much vigor as was humanly possible.

After losing his appeal, Valeutin left with his pride hurt and his children in utter dismay. This dismay would go on for some time, thus leading King Volerick Lobberstein

I to remark that if individuals who distorted the causes of the functions of government should be returned to their country of origin, with very little fanfare.

When the king heard who had brought this information to his attention, he said he wanted to meet Yolanda and the others. He ordered a simple banquet be formed for him and those responsible for bringing the treason against him to an abrupt end. The banquet was King Volerick's final act as king, because he was to die before it was over.

The king gave a speech at the banquet, which went like this: "I am so glad to know all of you, because you helped me and my family shine a light on the tragedy that has befallen the court. For that I will be eternally grateful. I am also pleased with the fact that you were able to discover the fiends trying to discredit me and the finance minister in this hard economic time."

After they all accepted His Highness's praise, they went silent as he went further with his remarks.

"As you all know, my late nephew, Phillip, was meeting with the Dilavestan ambassador before he was murdered by those same fiends. I've decided to set up a new meeting to continue negotiations with the Dilavestan party but on a larger scale than before. You five will take the lead in the renewed negotiations. Do you accept?"

Yolanda and the other four responded to the king's question with a resounding yes.

This was followed by the king saying, "Good. I am glad to hear that."

As he was taking a sip from his goblet to further toast the quintet about their new duties, the king grabbed his chest and started to fall back onto his chair. As his royal courier tried in vain to help steady the old king, he slumped down and sat still. He was dead.

Not wanting to cause mass hysteria over what had just transpired in the great royal banquet hall, Count Vladimir Hantabolvia Jr. called for a special council meeting for two weeks after the wake and funeral of the most revered monarch in Berasculatan history. He would still have the quintet do their new duties, but he would have a tighter security presence, so that none of the quintet was murdered.

After leaving with the late king's corpse in tow, those responsible with the functions of government saw that the late king's remains were brought to the funeral parlor.

The funeral parlor was run by Thomas Jerilason. He prepared the king's body for burial and hired a special security detail to watch over the king's coffin, so no one could steal it. His special assistant organized the Requiem Mass at St. Martha's Church, with Reverend Geoffrey Prinwinkle presiding.

After the Mass, the coffin was taken to St. Jude's Catholic Cemetery for burial. After the burial, those in the funeral party headed to Briken House for a memorial banquet.

During the banquet, William Malushingham, chief advisor to King Volerick I, was killed by Duchess Maeve Lobberstein.

It had been seen by many associated with the late King Volerick I as a minor victory for their agendas, but for Abner Malushingham, the untimely death of his father was to hamper the special council's meeting on January 13, 2456, because Abner sought retribution for the murder of his father by seeking the harshest punishment for Duchess Maeve Lobberstein.

The punishment was begun when the duchess was placed in the custody of Vice-Admiral Jesse Alscord for a term of four weeks until the meeting was convened, then she would join her mother in Blienbourg Mental Hospital.

CHAPTER 2

RUSH TO PEACE

The major members of the special council were meeting in the main chamber of the Lobbersteinium to discuss how to run the government now that the Berasculatan throne was empty. Someone suggested the monarchy be dismantled, until such time that a suitable replacement for King Lobberstein I could be elected by the nobility. This was turned down immediately by the council. Soon after the first break in discussions, a better proposal was made: for Berasculata to be governed by an intermediary who was to rule until the youngest of the Lobberstein heirs was able to govern the country. This proposal was accepted by two-thirds of the members of the special council.

With the intermediary proposal accepted, the next task was to nominate between them who was to be the chosen intermediary head of state. After fourteen ballots, Eric Teirolagus was selected as the intermediary representative of the Berasculatan government. He governed for seven weeks until he was assassinated by his own bodyguards, because he was seen as a tool of Abner Malushingham. He was immediately replaced by Timothy Yankering. Now Timothy Yankering was more vigilant in the post as intermediary governor than his predecessor and he used fewer bodyguards and carried a blaster on his person. He felt this would be more of a deterrent than not having any personal protection at all.

This was to prove very effective to a point, because on April 3, 2456, after Yankering had been on the job less than a month, Theodore Mackerly, a very disgruntled citizen of Berasculata, pulled a Swiincher dagger and attacked Governor Yankering with it. The governor was only slightly wounded, but it made him really question his family's security. Thus, on April 5, 2456, Governor Timothy Yankering resigned from the post.

He was succeeded by his unscrupulous deputy governor, Thaddeus Hazzerone. Now while he was not a good choice for governor. Hazzerone was able to keep the people under his thumb for three months without much incident. However, on July 7, 2456, Hazzerone would find himself in a dilly of a pickle when the Humpier Revolutionary Front decided to undermine his statutes and began holding militant protests outside the Lobbersteinium, and thus Governor Thaddeus Hazzerone would ask the M.A.C.R.E. confederation for help in dealing with the rebel group.

Unfortunately for him i.e., Governor Thaddeus Hazzerone, the leaders of M.A.C.R.E. confederation would turn down his request for military aid, however then Gregory Istelmar, chief executive officer of the International Welfare Society (IWS), a nonprofit organization, would thus decide to take part in the actions against the rebel groups, if asked and so Governor Thaddeus Hazzerone would ask him i.e., Gregory Istelmar for help from him i.e., Gregory Istelmar in dealing with the rebel groups. In secretly recorded communications cables, made public by the Berasculatan News Agency Channel 45, Istelmar told Hazzerone that his organization would help subdue the rebel group. In the recordings, both men keep their remarks very short and to the point. Here is what one of the newly released recordings said:

"Oh, don't you worry, Governor Hazzerone, my organization is fully prepared to handle any threat the group makes towards you and your government."

"That's good to know, Mr. Istelmar. When can you get here?"

"My organization can be in the region in about a week."

"That will make things easier on my limited security personnel."

"Well, my volunteers will be very happy to be welcomed in your country."

"I'm glad you feel that way, because I'm going to arrange that you are met by the Posler Committee."

"Okay, that sounds intriguing. Who is the Posler Committee?"

"Well, if you must know, Mr. Istelmar, the Posler Committee is the committee administered by Wainwright Posler and managed by Baron William Nivecoat."

"Thank you for telling me that," Istelmar said. "I thought the Posler Committee was a subterranean rat you guys had."

"No, they aren't rats, but they have been giving me mentoring troubles. So, you have to work with them with kid gloves."

"I'll make sure to do that so you know can trust me, Governor Hazzerone."

"I trust you explicitly, Mr. Istelmar, by the reputation you have made for yourself and your clients. But I cannot, in good faith, trust any of your volunteers until I've met with them personally."

"You'll meet them in good time, Governor Hazzerone, when we arrive in Berasculata."

"So, you when your ships arrive at the end of the week, I will meet them all at Krevelingshire?"

"Yes, you will meet me and my volunteers at Krevelingshire on July 15."

"I was just making sure that I heard you right the first time."

"Nothing wrong with being thorough, but this seems overanalyzing by you," remarked Istelmar.

"What you call overanalyzing, I call preparing for an easy transition of policy management."

"Well, we hope to see you well prepared to greet us at the hydro port on the morning of July 15."

"My top aide and I will be at the hydro port to greet you," Hazzerone said.

When the IWS craft arrived at the hydro port on July 15, it was met by a long limousine from the provisional Berasculatan government. As the door to the IWS craft opens up on the hydro port's main launch sloop, the door of PBG craft's door opened across the way. As the aides to the two main allies reached over to greet each other, their bosses stepped up beside their respective aides. Others from the IWS craft head over to the PBG craft. It was when Istelmar and Hazzerone spoke to each other in person.

"How was the journey here, Mr. Istelmar?" asked Governor Hazzerone. "Not too rough, I hope?"

"Oh, it was not too rough for us," Istelmar replied. "In fact, we were quite pleased to see some of the people we have here to help in their skiffs."

"Well, it is good to know that the journey wasn't too rough for you and your volunteers. Now, if you and your volunteers wouldn't mind, my aide, Theodore Kriskelstone, and I would like to show you where you'll be living for the next few weeks."

"Well, since I speak for the group in general, I say that it would be most generous of you and your aide."

"Well, then I suppose we should head for the ship provided by the PBG and head for the Zincolorus Repository Center."

A few seconds later, the large group got on the *Slippery Slope*, the craft provided by the PBG. Once everyone was settled into their seats, the captain of the Slippery Slope turned the engines back on, and the craft headed to the Zincolorus Repository Center. After they docked at Zincolorus Repository Center's main pier, the crew members disembarked and headed for the Pythagoras Medical Hospital to get inoculated, in case they came into contact with various diseases. After the PBG crew was fully inoculated from the primary diseases that were running rampant in the area now, they were led to the building where the Posler Committee had its offices.

They went inside the building, which had very dim lighting. The IWS volunteers were shown to where the Posler Committee was. Angela Meusen told Istelmar that the space was too small for her needs. He responded that she would have to make do until they found her a better working space. She replied that she also wanted to find herself separate living quarters. He agreed after some discussion.

Angela Meusen started looking for a place of her own to live, while she worked with the group on the behalf of the people of Berasculata that the group was supposedly helping. After a couple of hours, she found a residence an apartment building. She became very good friends with Thaddeus Prizweiller, the janitor of the building. They talked at length about subjects important to the two of them. Thaddeus told Angela about some of the political dealings that he knew of by reading the *Dewinster Times* newspaper.

When Angela asked Thaddeus about the *Dewinster Times*, he told her that the newspaper was published by a man named Frigulest Ganker, a Manchu Primean journalist who had been exiled from his homeland for reasons of morality. It was at that point that Angela asked Thaddeus where she could contact Frigulest Ganker.

Thaddeus told Angela that Frigulest could be found at the Raushenhagger Hotel for the criminally insane. She thanked him for that information and headed right off to see him. As it turned out, he was her long-lost maternal uncle.

After Angela reached the Raushenhagger Hotel, she headed over to the main desk and asked the head nurse where she could find her uncle, Frigulest Ganker. The head nurse, Belinda Baskerfield, told Angela that Frigulest was in the R-Wing of the hotel. Angela thanked Belinda for the information and headed down to the R- Wing.

When she found her uncle, walked over to him gently. As she approached him, she could sense someone else coming up behind her; she turned around to acknowledge the person, but they rushed past her.

When she got to her uncle, Angela could see the weary scars of old age on his face. She began to speak to her uncle but was told to be quiet. She ignored this and spoke softly to him.

He acknowledged her with a nod and led her to his room, where they were free to discuss his sister Wilma, Angela's mother. They spoke about Angela's mother for about thirty-five minutes. After that, Angela asked her uncle about the political situation in Berasculata and how he was able to write about it without the authorities knowing. He told her one whopper of tale, which he claimed was a fact.

"Well, Angela, my young wonderful niece," he began, "I know you are not going to believe this, but what I am going to tell you is the honest truth."

"Okay, Uncle Frigulest, I am here to listen to everything you say. I've got all the time in the world to hear it."

"Well, you know how the old king, Volerick, died of a heart attack?"

"Yeah, I heard that, Uncle. So, what does that have to do with my mission here?"

"Well, it fits in with your mission because the intermediary governor of Berasculata is working on a plan to remove the royal family permanently, and he needs your advocacy group to help quell the people who could prevent that plan from going forward."

"Why would Governor Hazzerone do that, good Uncle Frigulest?"

"Well, Angela dear, it's because he is the unofficial lackey of Abner Malushingham.

"You mean he is working with Duke Abner Malushingham?"

"No, what I said is that he's the unofficial servant of the duke. He is currently doing what the duke wants; otherwise, you and your associates would not have been called into this travesty of political injustice."

"Uncle Frigulest, are you suggesting that my associates and I should leave without helping these people?"

"No, I'm not suggesting that at all. But I ask you to work with the Posler Committee and help them bring back some semblance of honor and integrity."

"Alright, Uncle Frigulest, I will do as you say, but first, I'd like to know why you gave me that bit of advice."

"They are all good people, Angela, and I have a good relationship with committee's head."

"Is that the only reason for that particular advice?"

"No, but the other reason is not really important right now."

"Alright, Uncle Frigulest, I'll do it for you and for my mother, your sister's, sake. It will be a glad day when you get out of here."

After completing her visit to her maternal uncle, Angela decided to head for the Swing restaurant to eat. Then she went back to her apartment so she could sleep; she would have a lot of soul searching to do the next day before she went off to work. She planned to call her mother and tell her that she had made contact with her crazy uncle. By the time Angela got back to her apartment, it was about 2:30. She slept for the next six hours before she was paged by Yolanda Yorenaski.

The conversation between the two women went like this:

"Hi, Angela, this is Yolanda Yorenaski. I am calling to inform you about the changes to the provincial policy. Could you come in soon to work your magic on it?"

"Okay, Yolanda. Sure, I'll work my magic on it, but can I have a few minutes to get some breakfast before I come into the office?"

"Sure, just make sure you show Bartholomew your work pass."

"Alright, I will," she said.

After hanging up the phone, Angela headed for Charles Steak Room Restaurant. Baron William Nivecoat had recommended the place to her. After she got inside the restaurant, she ordered her breakfast, and it only took the waiter five minutes to get the food to her table. After she said a blessing over the food, she began eating. The food was alright for the price of the meal, and she left a generous tip for the waiter. She walked out of the restaurant with a half-smile on her face and then strolled the three blocks to the Posler Committee's building.

Once through the sensor-laden doorway, she walked over towards Bartholomew Rooster's checkpoint. Bartholomew scanned Angela's work pass with his security wand. After confirming her identity, Bartholomew directed Angela over to hydro-elevator shaft # 3. The hydro-elevator arrived a little late because of a slight malfunction in its sequencing node. When Angela arrived at her cubicle to start her day, it was 12:15. To her amazement, she had a number of policy files to modify. It took two and half hours to create invoice programs for each of the seventy files. Then she input each keystroke pad command file to everyone working in the Posler Committee building. This took her until 8:15, when she finished work.

Around 8:30, she headed to St. Anne's Mission to help her friend, Allison, with the IWS's soup line. While there, she met Maxwell Nivecoat, the baron's son, who was working with sick and destitute citizens of Berasculata. Maxwell helped her put on her vest. She fed 125 poor people in three and half hours and then returned to her apartment at 3 a.m.

Angela then slept for eight hours, and when she got up, she had a nice brunch. After brunch, she got a voicemail message from Yolanda, telling her to report for a special training session. She got to Yolanda's office at 1:45, just in time for the session. A couple of other people took part in the special session, which lasted until 4:55. After it was over, Angela had dinner with Roger Talbert, and then they headed over to the soup line again. After serving meals, they went to the children's hospital to help care for the kids.

After helping the children, Angela and Roger went dancing at a nightclub. They danced until around nine o'clock, then they went their separate ways. Sixteen hours later, they met up again in the presence of Terence Verimbecker, who was assigning them to a special duty. This assignment would take four weeks to complete and was run through Yolanda's office, but it was managed by Yolanda's handler, Jason Greiker.

Greiker put them through a rigorous mission schedule that was to begin on August 4, 2456. This was to start from the Pageldorf Rustoria at 3516 W Good Hope Boulevard. The committee had reliable intelligence that a target of the investigation into Prince Phillip's death had been seen in the area several times in the last couple of months. The committee wanted Angela and Roger to apprehend the target before he got away. When Angela and Roger pressed Greiker for further details about the assignment's target, he only said it was vital that they apprehend him without incident.

With just that minimal information, the new investigative pair of the Posler Committee took their assignment with some dismay. However, they were determined not let their new employers down. They made their way through some tough crowds and went into the Pageldorf Rustoria. Angela and Roger signed in to the apartment as cousins Ashley and Robert Vandek of Dilavesta. The manager of the apartment building gave them the key to apartment 1522-A. Once inside the apartment, Ashley and Robert got down to the business. To their amazement, two high-resolution bio-scanners sat on the coffee table.

As they looked over the bio-scanners, the phone in the apartment rang. It was Jason Greiker. He was calling to give them further details about the assignment. He told them to make contact with the committee's main informant, codenamed Octopus Rainmaker.

When Angela asked Greiker how to identify the informant, he said Octopus Rainmaker would be wearing a trench coat with a squid lapel.

"Well, Mr. Greiker, that helps us some," Angela said, "but we need more information to go on. So, if you would provide it, it would be very much appreciated."

"Sorry, Angela," Jason replied. "I'd give it if I had more to go on myself."

"We understand," Roger said. "I guess we can do what we can with the little information we have."

At that instant, Angela and Roger began officially working for the Posler Committee. They decided to head for the apartment building's massive dining hall, looking for their contact. While Roger walked towards the dining hall's southeastern wing, Octopus Rainmaker (actually named Oliver Reesewind) made himself known. To make sure that it was really their contact, Roger asked him some identifying questions.

After confirming that he really was their contact, Roger led Reesewind to where Angela was sitting. Angela asked Reesewind about the Posler Committee's target. Reesewind told them the man the committee wanted was in apartment 467. When pressed further about the identity of the individual in the apartment, Oliver said it was none other than Sangeld Kiswather Sr. Oliver then said that he would go to the apartment with them to arrest him.

The two of them welcomed his help, and then Oliver told them they could go to the apartment after he finished his lunch. They said that that was fine, since they had to go back to their apartment and retrieve their handcuffs. After Angela and Roger retrieved the handcuffs and headed over to apartment 467, Oliver was waiting for them at the apartment; he picked the lock to Kiswather's door.

After opening the door, to their amazement, they saw Furistahl Bauspeirada Sr. sitting in a chair, bleeding from a knife wound. When they asked the count what happened, he only said that he hadn't expected to be attacked, but he was glad he was, instead of Kiswather, his old student and friend.

Oliver pressed him about where Kiswather was. Bauspeirada told Oliver that he was going to the home of Henrietta Narestton.

"Count Bauspeirada, are you sure that Kiswather is at Narestton's home?" asked Oliver.

"Yes, I am sure that's where he is. He sent me a wire communication from there a couple of days ago."

"Well, what in world are we still doing here?" Angela replied. "Nothing left for us to do here, so let's get over there before the suspect slips through our grasp again."

The three got on a hydro skiff going towards the Oglethorpian Causeway. Once they reached the end of the causeway, they disembarked from the skiff and proceeded directly to Narestton's residence. Angela knocked on the residence's main door, and the door was answered by none other than Henrietta Narestton herself.

Henrietta asked the three people standing outside her door what they wanted. They told her they wanted to see Sangeld Kiswather Sr. on a very private matter. When she pressed the three further on the reason, they said they would only speak with Kiswather. She then waved her servant girl, Mildred, forward.

Mildred approached her mistress, who told her to show the trio to where the Vistrabian prime minister was staying. She nodded and led them to a shabby-looking log cabin in the farthest corner of the grounds. The trio then asked to see the inside of the cabin.

Mildred opened the log cabin's rusty door, and the trio stepped in. They found some very interesting items inside, including a rudimentary transponder radio, a blood clotting bag, and a box of fake IDs and masks. After looking at the IDs, Oliver said Kiswather was traveling under the name of Boris Kansander and working at a supermarket in the Hebonglizer Region, near the border of Portville.

Angela asked for a sonic synthesizer phone so they could call the Posler Committee and tell them what they had found. The phone was brought to them, and Roger hooked it up to the rudimentary radio. They then left the residence with the modified radio in their possession.

Oliver suggested they could place the modified radio near the supermarket and listen to conversations at Sangeld's residence. He then called for a cab to take them to the Hebonglizer Region. The cab driver, Aristotle Grinhammer, said they could use their credit cards for the high fare, but someone had to reimburse him for the fuel he used. Angela said she would get an associate of theirs to reimburse him when the journey was finished.

They got into the cab and embarked on the forty-four-block trip, which took two hours to complete, due to heavy traffic. Angela and Oliver paid most of the bill, leaving the remaining part to Roger. Grinhammer dropped them off at the Silver Cove Supermarket on Elk Street and Tenth Avenue.

Once inside, they looked through the supermarket until they came upon the elusive Sangeld Kiswather Sr. Oliver told Kiswather he was under arrest for the murder of Prince Phillip Lobberstein.

Kiswather angrily denied the charges and said he doubted the authority of the Posler Committee because they should have arrested him several months ago and not now. Ignoring his protests, Oliver put the handcuffs on Kiswather and said he was bringing him to the committee's headquarters to face justice. Not wanting to create a more public scene with the trio, Kiswather decided to go with them quietly.

As they were leaving the supermarket, Kiswather's boss asked them why they were taking his best employee away in handcuffs. Roger told him his "model employee" was a cold, calculating killer who was wanted for murder by the provincial government. After that, the trio took their prisoner and left.

After leaving the supermarket, Oliver put in a call to the Posler Committee. The person who answered was Baron William Nivecoat.

"So, you and your team finally accomplished what many others could not do, Oliver," said Nivecoat.

"Yes, sir," Oliver said, "and we are hoping that someone will come help us bring the prisoner back to headquarters."

"Don't worry," Nivecoat said. "We will send Alex to meet you. He will have Squad 14 there to transport Kiswather back to headquarters. Good job."

"Thank you, sir, and send my best wishes to Yolanda," Oliver replied. "Tell her I have some special gifts for her when I get back."

"Will do, Oliver, and hope to see you very soon," replied Nivecoat.

Alexander Petrosine and Squad 14 soon arrived at the supermarket. Alex greeted Oliver, Roger, and Angela, and then he motioned to his aide to take personal charge of the prisoner, Sangeld Kiswather Sr. The squad headed for the Dragon Hill Train Station, where they caught a specialized bullet train, which took them back to Posler Committee headquarters. When the specialized bullet train pulled up to the platform, the squad got on with their prisoner; they stashed him in a highly reinforced crystalline cabin.

The bullet train pulled out of the station at 5:30 p.m. and arrived at the Posler Committee headquarters' station at 10:30 p.m. After arriving, the squad took their prisoner to the offices of William Nivecoat.

Nivecoat looked on Kiswather with bemusement, for he could not believe he had brought him to justice, after so many months of trying to capture him.

Before he could speak to the prisoner, Kiswather made an inflamed speech. He said, "As there is life in this vessel of humanity, I will not give you the satisfaction of seeing me in dire despair. I promise you, sir, that before the current year is out, I will be back in Vistrabia, tending to my government's business at hand, and you will be nothing more than shivering duck ready for plucking."

Nivecoat responded with these words: "I don't know much about Vistrabian rescue protocols for felons of your stature, Kiswather, but as for me being a shivering duck ready for plucking, I can promise you that my associates will not let me fall into any trap that you have planned for my downfall."

"Your downfall from office has already begun, Nivecoat," Kiswather said. "You just don't realize it yet."

"What do you mean by that?"

"I mean that your citizens are getting tired of the way your government is handling the people's growing poverty and starvation."

"So, Kiswather, you decided to act for the betterment of our citizens by plotting the murder of Prince Phillip Lobberstein, who was a staunch support of the people's best interests."

"No, I merely speeded up the process for getting things done. I am not ashamed of what I did."

"So, you are saying that there's no way of stopping the kind of chaos you have wrought upon us as a society. Am I hearing you right, Kiswather?"

"Yes, you are hearing me right, Nivecoat, and my execution will not endear you to those among your citizens who feel the same way I do."

"I am getting tired of your argument that civility cannot be returned to the classes of Berasculatan society. I only hope that the heavenly Father looks favorably on you."

"Let's be clear about a couple more things, Nivecoat. I have no fear of dying for my beliefs, and your society will tumble when I am gone, because my corporation was keeping many of your citizens employed, leading up to the death of your beloved Prince Phillip."

"Those two facts are without merit, because we have seen some growth without your corporation's influx of funds. So don't try that ploy with me, Kiswather, and as for the prince's untimely demise, it has caused some deep scars in our country's national fabric."

"You may be right on that score, but it only really matters to those individuals who want to restore the Lobberstein monarchy without a truly reformed constitution."

"No, Kiswather. It matters to everyone who feels they are truly Berasculatan, and not a phony Berasculatan."

"What's your definition of a phony Berasculatan?"

"True Berasculatan work hard for a decent wage and have pride in their country. Phony Berasculatans have no real pride in their country."

"That doesn't really answer my question. Would you care to elaborate, Nivecoat?"

"No, Kiswather, I will not elaborate my answer."

"Well, we can talk further on it, Nivecoat, once I am back in Vistrabia."

"Oh, but you aren't going back to Vistrabia," Nivecoat said. "You will be sent to Drognau Prison on the Isle of Glinger for the remainder of your life."

"So, you have already pronounced judgment against me, before I've had a chance to defend myself in a court of my peers?"

"No, you will get your chance to defend yourself in court. I am just saying what is most likely to happen if you are convicted."

"So, when will I have my chance to defend myself in court, may I ask you?"

"During the next week to ten days, you can make a formal request for a lawyer to defend yourself."

"Can you find a proficient judge willing to prosecute me in that time period?"

"Don't worry. I'm sure Judge Marcus Hibbletopper will preside over your trial for murder and embezzlement."

After Kiswather selected his legal team, he heard that the honorable Judge Marcus Hibbletopper would be presiding over his trial. But before his trial for murder, he hit the talk show circuit. These appearances were very low key, and none of the hosts were allowed to ask about his personal life.

CHAPTER 3

FAULTY ALLIANCE

The trial of Sangeld Kiswather Sr. opened on September 7, 2456; many people who admired Kiswather protested outside the courthouse. To deal with the protesters, the provincial government's police force set a five-mile-wide barrier wall around the courthouse's access road; the number of protesters was limited to only 250. The police also used a type of neural agent against the protesters, infuriating their families. Many of the protesters became paralyzed.

The trial stretched on for more than a month. By the fifth week, even the impartial reporters were being targeted by the riot police, because they were seen as rousing the public's opinion of the trial.

In the sixth week, several mysterious packages were delivered to the courthouse. They were sent to Sangeld Kiswather Sr.'s lawyer. When the lawyer showed the contents of each package to his client, Kiswather smiled. He told his lawyer the packages were his "Get out of jail free" card. When his lawyer asked why, Sangeld explained that the scraps of paper pieced together formed a highly sensitive document that implicated the Grand Duke of Portville, Kiverold Friesenlenburger, in an act of genocide against the Viecke tribal people.

His lawyer said that would be a good case for M.A.C.R.E.'s human rights committee, but it had no bearing on this particular case. Sangeld insisted that it be entered in evidence, but his lawyer said it might hurt them with the jury. Sangeld said as long as they had the document entered as evidence, they had a slim chance of swaying the jury.

The document was entered into evidence after forensic tests were made to confirm it was authentic. The prosecution team objected to the judge for allowing such evidence into the proceedings. They asked the court of appeals to override Judge Hibbletopper's decision to allow the document, which they claimed was hearsay. The court of appeals ruled that, even though the document was entered into evidence, only certain issues could be used by the defense team to prove that their client did not act alone in his criminal actions.

In response to this ruling, the defense team asked Judge Hibbletopper to file a petition for the detainment of Grand Duke Kiverold Frieslenberger of Portville, until such time that he could be called to testify for the defense.

Andrew McWorwicker was given the task of detaining Kiverold Frieslenberger, the Grand Duke of Portville, so he could testify. Judge Hibbletopper told McWorwicker to make Frieslenberger feel like a witness to a crime, not a defendant, until they were able to charge him with genocide. McWorwicker would do this unpleasant duty on the morning of January 3, 2457.

On that day, Frieslenberger stopped being a hostile witness for the Kiswather defense team and became a defendant himself in a human rights trial. Frieslenberger paced in the defendant's box, not knowing what the M.A.C.R.E. prosecuting team would say about his actions. Quentin Balmer, the head of prosecution team, exhibited well-defined eyewitness testimony and even played a recording detailing the plot to dehumanize hundreds of thousands of Viecke people.

When he directed several pertinent questions at the defendant, Frieslenberger just nodded and looked away. Eventually, Frieslenberger's lead attorney, Edwin Theusinler, began to rip into Balmer's case against his client. Theusinler mentioned Kiswather and asked how the police could believe a convicted murderer's story, when there was only circumstantial evidence of genocide?

Balmer objected to Theusinler's assertions that investigators were misled by anyone and explained that they had been building their case for some time. He also stated that the evidence provided by Kiswather was only the icing on the case's cake.

Judge Hiram Caelonish asked both attorneys to approach the bench and asked them some very direct questions of his own. After getting the answers that he expected, Judge Caelonish told the attorneys to get on with the business at hand, or he would call for a recess for the day.

Balmer and Theusinler prattled on for an hour each, without making any progress, so Judge Caelonish called it a day. He said he would give each attorney nine days to plan for the remainder of the trial. Balmer and his team decided to seek more witnesses to testify to the human rights violations committed by Frieslenberger and his associates. Theusinler and his teammates looked for anyone who could back up their claims that there were no human rights violations committed by Portville troops.

Balmer got his witnesses assembled in a secret location, so the defense team could not harm them. Meanwhile, Theusinler tried in vain to find anyone willing to testify on his client's behalf, so he decided to shadow the loved ones of the witnesses. Unfortunately, Arthur Vanderloessen, one of his paid surveillance technicians, was arrested for driving a hypercar while intoxicated. After bailing out Vanderloessen from jail, Theusinler had to deal with an injured client.

Theusinler visited the holding center's medical wing to check on Kiverold's physical condition; he had been brutally beaten and stabbed. When he went into the medical room, Kiverold was being helped onto a gurney by several strong nurses. Theusinler walked up to the gurney and asked if Kiverold wanted go back to the judge and accept a plea bargain for the charges against him. Kiverold told Theusinler he would not consider a plea bargain of any kind. Theusinler asked him why not, and Kiverold said he was a fighter. He would rather fight the charges against him and win the case, unlike Kiswather, who accepted a plea bargain and was allowed to serve his prison term back in Vistrabia.

Kiverold's reply astounded Theusinler; now he had to find someone willing to testify for the defense. This was going to be very tricky, since he only had two more days until the trial resumed to try to find anyone with the courage to stand up with his client against the human rights violation charges.

However, his hopes gained some traction when Clarisse Reugarfeld, a disgruntled widow who lived on the Berasculatan/Portvillian border, agreed to testify on the defense's behalf.

The trial resumed on January 12; after listening to the prosecution present evidence of genocide against Kiverold, Reugarfeld shifted in her seat at the back of courtroom. After the prosecution presented testimony from its principal witnesses, Theusinler vehemently cross-examined them. When it came to the defense's chance to rebuke Balmer's charges against his client, Theusinler got up from his seat at the defense table, walked over to the podium nearest the judge, and called Mrs. Clarisse Reugarfeld to the stand.

Clarisse rose from her seat and headed to the stand. After she was sworn in, she gave a very astute account of what her life was like in the Grand Duchy, claiming the current grand duke had made things a little better during his early term in office; she also said she wished people would stop picking on her favorite, Riesling Hoffer.

Balmer and the judge were both taken aback by the statement. In fact, Balmer was so enraged by Clarisse's statement that he asked for a postponement, so he could collect his thoughts on the matter of the case. Judge Caelonish granted Balmer his request for a postponement until 1:45, when he would be able to cross-examine Clarisse.

Balmer cross-examined Clarisse and found her to be an angry old woman whose only claim was that she had some trouble with the Viecke.

The trouble was because a couple of them had squatted on a large piece of her land and turned it into, as she put it, a den of ill repute, from which she would have to clean off the stench of the Viecke who had settled there. After she was done testifying, Clarisse went back to her seat at the back of the courtroom. Judge Caelonish told both legal teams that he would make his ruling on the human rights violations' charges in the morning. The judge then told the bailiff to clear the courtroom.

Balmer and Theusinler and their legal teams left the courthouse that afternoon, preparing for the worse-case scenario. The next day, Judge Caelonish called them back to the courthouse at 7:45 a.m. He told them some of what he would say was good for both, some was bad for both. The rest was in between.

Here is what he told both groups: "After careful consideration, I find Kiverold Frieslenberger, the Grand Duke of Portville, guilty on all charges of genocide. However, I also find that since there was no clear-cut evidence of physical genocide, I sentence the Grand Duke to be incarcerated for the remainder of his life in Thrinker Prison".

Tobias Leiferman, now a leading member of the Provisional Viecke Council, filed a grievance against all those he felt took part in the genocide against his family. One of the first ones to be sued was his so-called friend, Sangeld Kiswather Jr. When he heard that he that he was being sued by his old schoolmate, Kiswather was somewhat taken aback. He referred the matter to his lawyer, Richard Laggerhorn. Laggerhorn made inquiries into how much Leiferman was seeking in financial compensation.

After a few weeks, Laggerhorn began negotiating a settlement with Leiferman's legal counsel, the Honorable Gerald Tansolovick. Tansolovick and Laggerhorn held lengthy negotiations on the Berasculatan island of Hiskelhaven.

The two counsels negotiated until March 2, when a very tense critical impasse occurred. At one point during the negotiations, it seemed that the two men were about to come to blows over the legal proceedings. There was little communication between the two lawyers for the next two weeks. Then, on March 17, at behest of their wives, the negotiations started over again.

The next time the two legal counsels met, it was on a yacht that was anchored in the Gulf of Zaperbaldis. They held discussions for several days before reaching a tentative agreement, in which Kiswather would pay Leiferman $125,000 per month for three months. Kiswather and Leiferman signed the agreement on March 25. With one legal battle over and done with, the next lawsuit had to be dealt with delicately.

This next legal battle did not involve Kiswather, but he knew he could advise the defendant in how to handle being sued by Leiferman and Tansolovick. This defendant was Jeremy Yankering. Yankering had been the budgetary director of the Portvillian Cabinet and had counseled the grand duke to eliminate the duchy's debt by getting rid of the Viecke people.

After being virtually destroyed economically by the lawsuit filed against him by Tansolovick, Yankering took his frustration out on Gwendolyn Vadelin, an unsuspecting foreign worker. Vadelin's Gorgadalian brother was to further complicate Yankering's life, when he trailed him up until the two-year anniversary of Prince Phillip Lobberstein's murder. When he asked Gerald why he was following him, Vadelin told Yankering it was because Yankering had physically abused his younger sister.

"So, you want to avenge your sister's honor?" Yankering asked. "Is that what you are trying to say to me?"

"Yes, I am, sir," Vadelin said. "I demand restitution for the shame you have done to her."

"Well, you are just going to have do your worst to me, because I will not apologize to you or your sister for what I did to her. I was just blowing off some steam, and she got that the gash to her face by her own fault."

"I do not believe you, and I will never believe you. I still demand you provide restitution."

"I repeat my previous statement: You will have to do your worst, because I will not give you or your sister any apology."

"Then you leave me only one recourse left, which is to challenge you to a duel."

"Fine with me," Yankering said. "If that's how you want to do it, then I accept your challenge of a duel."

"Good. You have accepted my challenge because it is the only other way of avenging my sister's honor. Where and when shall we meet to duel?" asked Vadelin.

"Well, why don't we have the duel tomorrow morning at eight o'clock?" Yankering suggested. "It should be in a public place, with many witnesses, to make sure no one is able to accuse either of us of cheating."

"That seems reasonable by me," Vadelin said. "How about having the duel at Raverdam Park? It's the most public area I can think of."

"Fine. I will meet you at Raverdam Park at exactly 8 a.m., by the statues."

The next morning, at eight o'clock, Jeremy Yankering, distant cousin of Timothy Yankering, provisional governor of Berasculata, was waiting in the far corner of Observance Point in Raverdam Park for Gerald Vadelin.

Vadelin arrived, with his seconds right behind him. After getting the rules of the duel straightened out, Wallace Pinsolderick, the official timekeeper of the duel, told both combatants to step off twenty paces, turn, and then fire. They began to walk, but before they reached the twenty paces, Yankering could see out of the corner of his eye that Vadelin was already preparing to fire his ion laser blaster at him. He knew he had to turn a split second earlier than expected. As he turned, however, Yankering could see that Vadelin had been struck down, seemingly by a blow from his own blaster.

Not wanting to be accused of murder, Yankering rushed past Vadelin's party at a quickened pace and went out the park's east entrance; he could see people rushing up towards him, shouting and calling him a cheater and a murderer. He headed for the Falapin Embassy, where he sought an audience with the Falapin ambassador to see if he could get asylum. The Falapin ambassador, Theodore Maserditorah, told Yankering that he would grant him asylum if he signed over a promissory note on some property Yankering owned in the north of Cavolerin.

Yankering agreed to do this, so the ambassador had his secretary give an asylum note to Yankering, so that Yankering could avoid justice by hiding inside the Falapin Embassy's grounds. Yankering used the asylum papers until May 5, when he faced a wrongful death lawsuit by Gerald Vadelin's widow, Natasha, who asserted that Yankering had murdered her beloved Gerald in cold blood.

Yankering's attorney, Abraham Ustermond, told the judge that his client had acted in self-defense. The lawyer for Natasha Vadelin argued that Gerald had been bullied into an unlawful duel by the defendant, who was a cold-blooded fiend whose only purpose in life was to cause misery to Gerald Vadelin and his family.

To protest this slander against his client, Jerome Yeisler objected to the accusation and denied that his client was a cold-hearted individual. But that approach did not sway the jury, which awarded Gerald's family a large sum of money.

After hearing the judgment in their favor, Natasha's attorney, Robert McTolberg, asked the judge to make sure that Yankering paid his client as soon as possible. The judge agreed to require Yankering to pay Natasha and her family in increments of two thousand dollars a month.

After that order, Yankering filed for bankruptcy. He would thus take a job counseling troubled youths at a hostel, where he also lived. He did this for three weeks but then was fired after screaming at an eleven-year-old girl. After being fired from his counselor job, Yankering became a bouncer at a nightclub. That gig led to some more trouble for him, because he got into a fight with a Manchu Primean college student who was on vacation.

The college student, Arnold Wagglesmont, called his cousin, Cyrus Wagglesmont Jr., and told him that he had been insulted by a bouncer at the Wild Hawk Nightclub.

Cyrus told his cousin, "Well, Arnold, I don't know what went on between you and this bouncer, but I'll make an inquiry into how the nightclub does its business."

"Thanks, Cyrus," Arnold replied. "I really appreciate this very much. If there is anything I can do for you and Marla, you just name it."

"Don't mention it, Arnold. I would do anything for my young cousin, you know that. So don't worry. We'll come by the next time I'm in the area."

"Okay, I'll tell Laura so her sister can set aside a room for you, Marla, and the kids. Alright?"

"Fine by me. I'll tell Marla that we'll being going to Berasculata the first day we can get away from our jobs."

So, on June 25, Cyrus took his family to Berasculata for their vacation. While he was there, Cyrus checked in with the Manchu Primean Embassy to get a guidebook to see where his quarry was located. Once he learned the address, he went to the Wild Hawk Nightclub.

Once he was inside the Wild Hawk, he walked over to the bar and spoke to the bartender, Max, who told Cyrus about the altercation that had occurred between Arnold and the bouncer, Jeremy Yankering. After hearing what happened, Cyrus went to find Yankering. When he found him, Cyrus told Jeremy that he had to been corrected in his demeanor towards young college kids like his cousin, Arnold, to which Jeremy said to Cyrus was that he had been told not to pick a fight with any of the college age kids of whom visited the nightclub but that he that is Jeremy did what he did because of what he Jeremy saw a way of keeping a steady paycheck to pay back what he owed Natasha Vadelin for what the court had told him to pay her i.e. Natasha for her lost income i.e., Gerald's paycheck and also because he felt that he owed Judy Juperiskendendi for the kindness she had shown him i.e., Jeremy since he had been hired there at the nightclub and because he thought Arnold Wagglesmont was harassing her i.e., his friend and co-worker Judy

In the meantime, even as he that is Jeremy was all but done dealing with the particulars of the issue with the Wagglesmont cousins about what had transpired at the nightclub on that particular night, the governments of both Vistrabia and Gorgadal were also pursuing for him i.e., Jeremy Yankering as well but for different reasons. The Vistrabians wanted him to use his military background in the training of their young recruits, while the Gorgadalians sought him for the money that was still due to Natasha Vadelin and her family.

Now after he that is Cyrus has finished conversing with Jeremy about the situation, Cyrus has realized that Arnold and Jeremy had been unable to communicate their feelings in a civil manner, and that led to their misunderstanding. Later, he had his cousin Arnold meet with Jeremy at the Wild Hawk to reconcile their differences. Once that was done, he and Marla took their three children to go the Vesney Theme Park, to spend some quality family time.

Before their vacation was over, however, Cyrus received word that instead of returning to Manchu Prime, he had to head for Aeripal Air Base to talk to his boss, General Thomas Buricavi, eldest cousin of his friend Colonel Reginald Buricavi.

This is what they discussed:

"Good morning, General," Cyrus said. "How is your family?"

"Oh, they are fine," Thomas replied. "Now look, Cyrus, Command wants your squad on high alert in the event we have to go to war here."

"War? What do you mean?"

"The Vistrabians appear to be massing troops near their border."

"Understood, General. Don't you worry, sir; I'll have them ready and willing in the next week."

"That would be great, Cyrus, but I don't think we'll need them that quickly."

"Well, people say it's better to be prepared for the worse before it happens than throw things together at the last minute."

Neither of them knew this at the time, but there were forces at work to bring the war to bear sooner than expected. War was officially declared on the morning of August 4, 2457. The political firestorm had been brewing for more than two years; two coalitions had been set up, the Madrigal Coalition and the Fatavian Coalition. The Madrigal Coalition was made up of the countries of Manchu Prime, Dilavesta, and Gorgadal, and their Kakorian allies. The Fatavian Coalition was made up of Falapia, Taeruga, and Vistrabia, and their Portvillian allies.

CHAPTER 4

RESILIENCE TO FIGHT

As the first units of the two coalitions mobilized, there was little doubt that there was no going back. Madrigal launched their first troops from the Vieslick transportation region in Manchu Prime. The troops included 132 brigades of light cavalry, eighty corps of elite Manchu Primean marines, seventeen divisions of armored paratroopers, seven units of Manchu Primean Naval Seals, three squadrons of the Manchu Primean Air Force, and two units of heavy infantry troops. They were paired with a smaller Dilavestan force of thirty royal light cavalry, fifteen units of Dilavestan Naval Seals, eight divisions of armored paratroopers, two squadrons from the Dilavestan Air Force, and a unit of heavy cavalry. The Gorgadalian military supplied a larger portion of the Madrigal Coalition in the first three weeks of mobilization of the Berasculatan War.

Their adversaries on the Fatavian side of the conflict were more spread out. Of the Fatavian Coalition forces mobilized before the first battle, the Vistrabian military contingent had the bulk of the troops. Their number of troops was similar to the Gorgadalian contingent of the Madrigald Coalition. The next strongest contingent, the Taerugans, who had more troops than the Madrigald's Dilavestan contingent. Also joining the Fatavians was the Falapin contingent, which merged with a small Taerugan outfit under the leadership of Colonel Bernard Nawanki and his younger brother Captain Stanley Nawanki.

It took two weeks for the Fatavian transport ships to reach Berasculatan waters. When the Fatavian fleet came into view in the Sorgen Straits, Admiral Nathaniel Thanderbrook of the Madrigald Coalition ordered his gunners to open fire on the coalition's lead ship, the *Horned Beetle*. In response to his ship being fired on, Admiral Thomas Vieslenlanger returned fire on Thanderbrook's *Sea Maiden*. As both ships fired upon one another, the Madrigald and Fatavian air forces took potshots at each other.

Thus, the Battle of Sorgen Straits was fought; it lasted ninety-six hours. When it was over, seven ships had been sunk, eight ships were badly damaged, and forty-five aircraft had been destroyed. Once the damage to his task force had been fully assessed, Admiral Thanderbrook asked Chaplain Arthur Quesmandon to lead the crews in prayer. The chaplain accepted this assignment with a modest heart, as he spoke over the *Sea Maiden's* intercom.

After giving his blessing over his fallen and wounded comrades in arms, Chaplain Quesmandon asked the admiral if he could travel with the forces heading ashore. The admiral told the chaplain he would discuss it with the other Madrigald Coalition commanders. On the morning of September 14, 2457, Chaplain Quesmandon was allowed to go ashore with the first Madrigald Coalition forces.

About 3 p.m., the boat carrying Chaplain Quesmandon and the 34th MC Army Battalion, commanded by Colonel Reginald Buricavi, hit the beaches near Sorgen. The battalion was to secure a machinery factory and a food storage facility.

The 34th MC Army Battalion was welcomed by the town of Sorgen; the citizens housed the troops for three weeks without incident. On October 5, a Fatavian battalion, under the command of Sylvester Thewenherrogan, attacked the town. The Battle of Sorgen continued for nine days before Buricavi soldiers overwhelmed Thewenherrogan's men. When the battle ended, 5,468 troops had died.

Buricavi ordered Thewenherrogan held in prison, and two weeks later, he decided to have Thewenherrogan transported back to the *Sea Maiden* in ionized irons. Despite being held in irons, Thewenherrogan continued his mission, trying to decimate the ship's ability to continue its part in the war. Thewenherrogan had moderate success at this, because on the morning of November 1, a fire broke out in the ship's brig and spread to the aft engine room. It took several days to repair the damage to the engine room.

On November 12, a new battle began, one that was to last for several weeks. It was mostly a land battle, but the *Sea Maiden* had a supporting role. They kept Furistahl Bauspeirada Jr.'s forces from landing on the Zigurana Marshlands before the Buricavi-Hasopwarich defensive line was fully prepared. The *Sea Maiden* did its best, but after twenty-eight hours of constant combat, the Bauspeirada brigade eventually found its way to the Zigurana Marshlands.

When Bauspeirada saw Sorgen, which he and his men had fought so badly for, he was to remark to his adjutant Theodore Gresson, "What a slummy place this is, Lieutenant Gresson."

"Yes, sir," Gresson replied, "but I am sure we'll be able to make something of a headquarters here after we drive the enemy out, sir."

"Well, I don't doubt that, Lieutenant, but before you begin that task, I'd like you to do two things for me."

"What do you need, sir?"

"First, I want you to have some men ascertain the enemy's strength and position on the hills directly facing us."

"Done with that, sir; what's the second thing you want me to do?"

"I want you to have my youngest son, Furistahl III, set up his troops for a sneak attack on the far left of Buricavi's main line. Clear?"

When he heard what the second thing was, Gresson became somewhat suspicious. He felt that the viscount could have relayed the orders to his son himself. Nonetheless, he did what he was ordered to do and told the younger Furistahl what his father wanted him to do.

Gresson found the younger Bauspeirada a bit of a snickering fuss bucket, and he was about to say this to him when the young man beat him to the punch, as it were, and reiterated what his father ordered.

"So, my father has ordered me to attack the general and his young cousin on the left," Furistahl Bauspeirada III asked, "while Kiswather Jr. attacks the cousin's right flank? Do I hear you right, Lieutenant Gresson?"

"I suppose so, sir. He feels that Kiswather can hit the young Buricavi's brother-in-law, Benjamin Hasopwarich VI."

"Oh, so we are to make it easy for Kiswather to remove his old adversary from the international war college from the field?"

"Well, if you are going to be so uncivilized about the whole thing, I'll just ask your father to change his orders."

"No, don't do that; I know how much the viscount would frown on my disobedience to his wishes. I will do as I'm commanded to do. I just don't like the idea of kowtowing to an officer who has his own personal agenda in this war."

"Nor do I, sir, but those are the orders. So, I suggest you get your troops moving in the direction of the Buricavi forces. Do you agree?"

"Yes, I do think I should do that, but I must wait until my deputy commander, George Dorno, rejoins his artillery units. You can go right away but you'll suffer heavy losses. Do you understand me, Lieutenant Gresson?"

"Yes, you can attack the Buricavi forces when he's back with his artillery units. When do you think that might be?"

"He should be ready to attack in half an hour. I'm just waiting to hear from his aide de camp, Captain Michael Seiswan, to know when he's ready for combat."

"Well, as I can see, a young trooper with artillery colors is coming towards us now."

Captain Seiswan approached them and said, "I am here to tell you, sir, that my commander has linked up with his artillery units and says that he will start firing them at the enemy's position just as soon as you are ready."

"Very good, Captain," Bauspeirada said. "Give your commander my compliments, and tell him to commence firing in ten minutes. Have him keep firing them until we fully engage the enemy."

"Yes, sir, Colonel, sir. I will return quickly and tell him. May I inquire as to the precise target area, so as to know where to tell him you want the artillery fired?"

"Yes. The target area for his ionized laser guns is the point just beyond those hills yonder. Do you see them, Captain?"

"Yes, sir. I do see them. I will tell Lieutenant Colonel Dorno to fire on that point with everything he's got."

"Exactly. Now, return to your commander before he wonders what happened to you."

After he watched young Captain Seiswan head back towards the direction he had arrived from, Bauspeirada ordered his soldiers into their formations. Once they were lined up, he waved his sword and had them march off from their staging areas. As they headed out, Dorno let loose with a barrage from his 188-millimeter ionized laser guns. One of the casualties from the barrage was General Thomas Buricavi. Although he was only slightly wounded, Buricavi was out of action for the remainder of the battle. He assigned his duties to his friend, Colonel Cyrus Wagglesmont Jr., effective at 3:46 p.m. on November 15, 2457.

After hearing that he had been give command of the 78th MC Army Battalion, Cyrus decided to place his old battalion under the command of his brother, Captain Atergeld Wagglesmont. Next, Cyrus ordered his troops to pull back to a safer distance from Colonel Reginald Buricavi's troops, but to reinforce the direct center of the colonel's line. This maneuver was designed to give Buricavi a stronger reserve force to use, should he require it.

As Bauspeirada main element approach his left flank, Buricavi told his adjutant, Wayne Tiblerson, to swing his left flank down and snap the neck of the advancing Vistrabian force.

Sensing the worst possible outcome of his front troops, Bauspeirada deployed his remaining troops south of the center line, where they were hammered by Buricavi's artillery units. The remainder of Bauspeirada's force had to slither back to base, inflicting minimal damage to Colonel Buricavi's command. They reported that there was no possible way of capturing North Sorgen from Madrigald forces without aerial and ground battery support. The younger Furistahl even told his father, Furistahl Bauspeirada Jr., this fact on the morning of November 18. His father told him to stop complaining. Realizing that he was not making much headway with his father's stubborn attitude, Bauspeirada decided to lead his troops even further off the proposed plan of attack against the Buricavi-Hasopwarich defensive line.

He led them to a point directly facing Wagglesmont's new command troops. This was to be the younger Bauspeirada's swan song, if his new point of attack was repulsed. This time, he headed farther down the line, instead of being in the back of the first column of his troops. He led from the very front of the column. As it would turn out, the young man earned a purple heart for his bravery in combat.

After some rest and the refitting of his unit, Bauspeirada got another assignment from the desk of Prince Mortulakin Hantabolvia of Vistrabia. He was to attack his latest adversary on the plains of Thippermaux. His father would give him all available support in the field, and Silas Stoerinhaffer was to draw the elite of the Buricavi-Hasopwarich's defense to him and his squadron of troops. As it unfolded, however, the Fatavians suffered a total loss.

For all of the military strategizing involved in the operation, there was no well-defined plan. There was no cohesion between the Fatavian commanders involved in the fight. First of all, it started on the evening of December 9, in the dead of winter. They trudged over heavy mounds of snow and ice, and it took them sixteen days to reach the area of attack. By the time they arrived, they were tired and hungry. On New Year's Day 2458, it was a battle between weary Fatavian units and fresh and well-fed Madrigald units. The battle continued for the next six days.

After the battle was concluded, soldiers from both sides gave some graphic (but sometimes vague) details of how the battle was waged. The soldiers who gave their opinions about the battle were treated by their commanders in varying ways. The Fatavian soldiers who spoke about the battle were cruelly reprimanded, whereas the Madrigald soldiers who spoke out about how the battle had been conducted were temporarily reassigned to different posts and slightly reprimanded.

The two sides rested until January 29, when the Battle of the Jaded Grove began. It was to be fought over a period of twenty-nine months.

Now of the several battalions from both coalitions of whom were amassed in Swiegarone, at the southern and eastern edges of the Winvarduen Forest. They began to harass each other with high proton turbo laser fire. This lasted until February 16, by which time hyper tanks had joined the fray. On February 21, the battle started to take shape. The fight included the older cousin of the crowned prince, Hiram Matthias Maerovich, of whom who was slightly injured in the fight. After becoming incapacitated, Maerovich turned over command of the MC 132nd Army Battalion to his aide, William Waturichan, whose cousin, Jeffery, was commanding the MC 164th Army Battalion on White Leopard Hill.

The two Waturichan cousins were attacked by Captain Ulstanagard Hantabolvia. For his part in the battle, Hantabolvia had lost the use his right eye and suffered a partial loss of use of his left hand. All in all, the Battle of Swiegarone was a modest Fatavian victory, because their forces gained access to the Swiegarone River. However, Hantabolvia would not have much time to celebrate his victory, for by March 5, the Waturichan cousins and the newly recovered Maerovich were preparing to give him a proverbial hot foot.

The hot foot lasted until March 29, when Hantabolvia ran low on food and ammunition; he could not fight any longer. As he left the battlefield of Osuerim, he remarked to his aide, Lieutenant Ebenezer Niwendale, "What we have done and seen in this region has been good for our coalition, don't you agree, Lieutenant Niwendale?"

"Yes, sir, Captain Hantabolvia," his aide replied. "I certainly agree with your assessment of the situation."

"Well then," Hantabolvia said, "since we are both in agreement about how we conducted ourselves and the men in battle, let's head north and east to give our brothers in arms some help in disposing of their foes, as soon as our able-bodied troops are back in camp."

Unlike their Fatavian foes, after the battle, the three Madrigald commanders decided to rest awhile, giving each of their chaplains the opportunity to say Mass over their dead and dying troops. They took two and a half hours. By then, Hantabolvia was on his way north to the city of Hueverad. But when word got back to them about the raid of Hueverad, the trio led their slightly weakened armies north of Hueverad, so as to keep the young captain off balance.

By this time, the Battle of the Jaded Grove had been going on relentlessly for some time. On April 15, the Battle of Vieserlam began. Hantabolvia eventually concluded why he and his troops ended up on the battlefield there.

They were there to be slaughtered, to a man; however, the captain and his inner circle were removed to a field hospital by Fatavian medics. Surgeons from the field hospital spent twelve and a half hours repairing the damage to Hantabolvia's body. While out of action, the captain heard that his protégé, Sergeant Major Abraham Clienotarum, gained some ground east of the mining town of Vieserlam.

When Hantabolvia returned to the battle, Clienotarum showed him the field he attained in battle, which he used as a field headquarters for his advance towards the tributary that led to the Jaded Grove battlefield. Hantabolvia readily accepted the land Clienotarum gave him and made him his new aide (Lieutenant Niwendale was assigned to Prince Mortulakin Hantabolvia's staff). Clienotarum accepted the new job and requested that his nephew, Isaac, be made a special survey scout.

Scout Isaac Clienotarum continued his survey work until May 25, when the Battle of the Crow's Horn was to begin. The Battle of the Crow's Horn lasted until June 15. Six of the army units fighting in the battle were totally destroyed. It ended in a stalemate, because neither coalition achieved its objective.

In one very memorable instant, General Paul Thanderbrook, the Madrigald commander who was in charge of combat operations for the coalition, remarked, "As we can look upon the enemy from its hiding place on the battlefield, we can determine that they have the fighting spirit of fire ants and the ferocity of horned buffalos. Therefore, it is with great animosity and utter contempt for their character in this instance that, I, General Paul Thanderbrook, order the troops under my direct command to burn a deep hole in their collective backside."

Later on, the general was reprimanded for his overly fiery style of speaking. The reprimand gave the general time to contemplate his strategy for the next battle that he and his troops were to take a much more subdued role in. Just days after the reprimand ended, on the morning of June 25, Thanderbrook led his men to Wild Rock Creek to take on the combined forces of Brigadier General Henry Hougmen and Colonel Wilhelm Yaspanwick. Joining up to fight with Thanderbrook were Colonel Edmund Waturichan and Captain Edward Greiker. The Battle of Wild Rock Creek ended in a victory for the Madrigalds. For the next week, Greiker heard that his younger cousin Jason had enlisted to fight on the Madrigald side.

On July 8, Jason Greiker had joined the Madrigald Coalition; because as he had been part of the Berasculatan Special Services for a time and was on the Posler Committee for the past two years, but he decided the committee had been too downgraded and thus was absorbed into the Berasculatan Civilian Worker's Party (BCWP). Jason believing the BCWP was inept because its head, Wendell Thieslicker, had handed the provisional government's operations over to a friend of the Fatavian Coalition (the friend Thorgan Threseson had kept Thieslicker on as an advisor).

When Jason's cousin asked him about the other Posler Committee members, he said they were mostly undecided, but if the Madrigald Coalition needed help, they could be trusted to fight for them. On July 17, a small strike team of special operatives planned to free Yolanda Yorenaski and the old council, who were being held captive by the newly created BCWP. The strike team was led by Jason Greiker and Thomas Reinhardt, a mixed martial arts expert. The nineteen-member strike team's first official mission took them to Yingbarius Station, a mining town with a recently constructed prison, a cruelly designed structure. The team attacked the dimly lit cell block, manned by at least forty guards. They set off a small explosion as a diversion and then extracted Yolanda and the other council members.

Once the strike team succeeded, Jason ordered the diversion to be stopped and called for a covering run from an MC R-34 bomber.

With Yolanda safely removed from the Fatavian complex, the strike team led her back to the rendezvous point, where Edmund Greiker debriefed her as to what was going on with the fight against the Fatavian Coalition. When the captain heard what she had to say, he called the general and colonel together to plan a military operation north of where she had been confined. After consulting with their superiors, the commanding officers in the field asked if Yolanda and Jason could help the strike team scout the enemy's strength around the city of Hawanerouse.

The strike team, Yolanda, and Jason agreed to assess the forces gathered near Hawanerouse. On August 3, the scouting mission began, and it took three weeks and four days to complete. By this time, the combined troops of Thanderbrook, Greiker, and Waturichan were approaching the city. As the new MC 225th Army Battalion came to within sight of Hawanerouse, the three Madrigald Coalition commanders could not wait to attack the Fatavian forces.

On the morning of September 1, the Battle of Hawanerouse began with light battery fire from both coalitions' guns. For the next eleven weeks, Thanderbrook's combined

Madrigald Coalition forces pounded the Fatavian Coalition's defensive lines. When they finally broke the lines on the morning of November 24, they faced a Fatavian force commanded by a young military officer who had the aura of a much older man.

The Fatavian commander was none other than Valeutin Furisthal Bauspeirada, brother of Furistahl; Valeutin was not a man to be trifled with. Even though he had fought in thirty-six military engagements during his early military career, he didn't look a day over twenty-five years of age. The reason for his youthful appearance was because he had been in a hyperbaric chamber for the last five years. So, even though he was really forty-five years of age, he looked half his age. When Thanderbrook learned this, he changed his strategy.

While the general changed his strategy, Lieutenant General Valeutin Furistahl Bauspeirada was devising a more sinister plan for his own troops, which was to speed up a special project his father had authorized, which involved the use of bio-mechanical creatures.

Meanwhile, back at the Madrigald Coalition main headquarters, Prince Phillip Mauwoerkin, the chief of staff, was getting briefed by his adjutant, Yuri Buricavi, youngest son of Senator Carl Lutanus Buricavi.

Here's what was said between the two men:

"Well, sir," Yuri began, "I've got some good news for you, and I've also got some not-so-good news to tell you."

"Okay, Yuri, let's have the good news first," Mauwoerkin said. "Once you've given me the good news, then you can give me the not-so-good news."

"Alright, sir, here is the good news: We have won a majority of the ground battles, and we are doing okay in other battles still going on, but there is a downside to all of this due to staffing."

"If I am hearing you right, Yuri, we are being successful most of the time, but we have a staffing problem, is that a correct assessment?"

"Yes, sir, that is accurate, but it's not the whole thing; it seems that the Fatavian Coalition is working on a secret bio-mechanical program that could do a great harm to our troops in the future."

"Do your intelligence agents know when this weapon could come on line?" asked Mauwoerkin.

"Not yet," Yuri replied, "but we finally were able to crack their codes, so we could have that information soon."

"Well, good job, Yuri. Keep me advised on this, and I'll advise the chairman of the MC."

"Yes, sir. I'll get right on it."

"Goodbye for now, Yuri. I hope to see you tomorrow," Mauwoerkin said.

"Goodbye to you, sir. I also hope to see you tomorrow."

CHAPTER 5

ARCHWAY TO DOOM

As the morning began on December 2, 2458, there was an eerie calm running through the ranks as Thanderbrook got to his feet to address his troops. He told them that as they approached the next stage in the Battle of Hawanerouse, they were to do it without him for a few days, as he had been sent for by the Madrigald Coalition high council. He told them they should not worry, because it was only a strategy meeting. The meeting was to take place over the course of several hours.

The strategy meetings finally ended on December 10. Thanderbrook did not have any time to sit and rest; he was overdue back at his headquarters. He asked Sergeant Timothy Guidecker for a ride back to the bluffs overlooking the city of Hawanerouse. The sergeant told the general that his troops had won the battle for Hawanerouse and were pressing forward to take the town of Cascapurimadia. When the general heard this news, he told Guidecker to take him quickly to where his brave troops had been fighting for their lives. They arrived at the site where a makeshift field headquarters had been set up.

The crew transport dropped them at the tent where Colonel Jerome Uskelinder had laid out a huge field map with allied and enemy troop movements. After they came into the tent, he turned to face them and described the military operation taking place just three and half miles down the road from them.

"Well, as you can see, sir, my aides and I have devised a more diverse plan of attack to drive those Fatavian troops out of Cascapurimadia."

"So, what's the problem, Colonel?" Thanderbrook asked.

"Well, sir, it seems that the commander of the Fatavian forces, Lieutenant Colonel Ulstanagard Hantabolvia, has decided to dig in. He's called up all the reserve troops he can muster and thrown them into the pocket we were in the process of creating."

"So, we'll just have to find a weak spot in their proverbial armor and exploit it to the best of our ability, that's all."

"We might need a heavy dose of prayer to pull that off, sir," Uskelinder said. "We just don't have resources or men to pull it off."

"Nonsense," Thanderbrook replied. "All we need is sixteen highly dedicated troops and a leader to guide them to the area we need surveyed."

Just then, Major Henry Yorenaski entered the conversation area and volunteered to lead the surveying team with his company of fifteen men. They asked him why he sought this particular mission, and he told the general it was a personal matter, claiming they could do the job in the timeframe allotted and be back before the battle.

Thanderbrook agreed and wished them all good luck, as he knew they'd be crossing dangerous terrain. Yorenaski's company made the journey to Cascapurimadia in three days. One of the team members spotted an ionized laser gun turret and pointed it out to Yorenaski. They passed the turret and cautiously made their way across the east end of the city towards Mount Akariz, to get information for the general.

They found a sensor security post with a small detachment of troops stationed there. Once the team made its way through the security post, they walked down a wide passageway running down to the base of Mount Caourilag. Three and a half hours later, they reached the summit, where the team found the fortified headquarters of Colonel Hantabolvia. Yorenaski assigned his two best demolition personnel to set up charges to blow the exterior walls of Hantabolvia's main living quarters, so they could capture him.

Corporal Oscar Hendricks and Private Timothy Saunders set out to accomplish their task; first, they had to sidestep a motion-capturing sensor at the back of the processing center. After successfully dodging this sensor, the two men entered the building and began setting the charges. As they were finishing their mission, the major told them to speed it up because he didn't want them to get captured. So, they increased their speed, set charges, and left the area.

But before they could activate the explosives, they were alerted that some of their gadgets had been discovered. They hightailed back over to the others in the unit, so they could leave quickly. When they got back to the rendezvous site, the Special Forces unit decided to take a different path back to friendly lines.

The unit marched a circuitous route back to the Madrigald lines at Hawanerouse. They traveled the long way back, mostly under cover and in the dark, arriving on December 24. After having a good dinner, Yorenaski went to bed in his tent. The next day, he briefed Thanderbrook of what the unit had observed.

The general would tell Yorenaski to go and get some caffeine in his system, because he was going to brief the Madrigald Coalition high council about the information he gathered and ask for input before presenting his plan for the forthcoming battle.

For the next nine days, the council debated Thanderbrook's plan, finally agreeing to it. After his plan of attack was ratified, the general told his subordinates they should prepare for battle. On January 5, 2460, the lead columns of Thanderbrook's army made their approach towards the city of Cascapurimadia. They were to be met with fierce ionized blaster-cannon fire from the gun emplacements to the northeast.

They suffered modest casualties in the early going. However, as the fighting progressed, Hantabolvia's forces started to take on more casualties than Thanderbrook's forces. By the third day of the battle, some twenty-five thousand casualties were reported. The battle raged on for another fifteen days. Hantabolvia was rumored to have remarked that he would not be able to get back to Hawanerouse without substantial military support. He received some replacement soldiers to continue his battle.

On January 24, the last day of the Battle of Cascapurimadia, the battered armies of both coalitions crawled back to their camps after gaining modest amounts of territory for their prospective side. Both coalitions wondered who would sustain their willingness to fight a war, as they were losing the support of the citizenry. To prove that fighting the war was a necessary evil, both coalitions held forums to show how their side was winning.

CHAPTER 6

CLOSE TO EMPATHY

With the fighting for military control of Cascapurimadia ending in a virtual tie, both the Madrigald and Fatavian Coalitions had to devise new ways of continuing hostilities between their governing councils. On February 7, a battle began that would change the demographics of the war forever. Captain Atergeld Wagglesmont Jr. and Colonel Abraham Waturichan presented their plan for attacking the Fatavian forces at the nearby town of Gliverborg. Gliverborg was strategically important because it was the main access city for the Fatavian forces entering Berasculata from the southwest. It was also the headquarters for Colonel Roger Niwendale Jr. In his view, holding the city gave the Fatavian forces control over the Gawesin Valley.

Wagglesmont claimed that if the Madrigald Coalition controlled the Gawesin Valley, they could control the flow of wheat in the area. This wheat was vital to the Fatavian military, which needed it not only for food but also for feeding their animals back home. He ordered his soldiers to attack anyone who tried to take the wheat that the Fatavian troops had secured.

On March 3, a special meeting was convened to discuss the practicality of isolating the Fatavian forces in the Gawesin Valley by sending a modified flotilla down the Weunawick River. After the special meeting, Captain Thaddeus Waturichan was assigned command of the flotilla unit. He was in charge of a force of 1,250 men, traveling on armor-plated ships. The modified flotilla started for the Gawesin Valley on March 11 and arrived a month later.

The first battle in the region lasted until April 28. Half of the 1,250 troops of the flotilla contingent were killed or wounded. Those men were flown to the Madrigald Coalition field hospital north of Hawanerouse for treatment. On May 15, the other men were refitted with replacement troops, led by Sergeant Timothy Quagander. He marched the replacement troops forty-eight miles to their unit's location.

When they finally arrived, they headed over to their designated areas. Waturichan was only too grateful to have them under his command. He told his top aide-de-camp, Lieutenant Olaf Reinagorn, to welcome the men and feed them well, because a major attack was expected within the next few days. On the morning of June 3, the Madrigald Coalition attacked the tiny village of Shacakija. The battle continued for forty-eight days.

On July 25, a peace summit between the two coalitions was arranged. The negotiators met on the Yagmash River. They met in a two-room house owned by a Mr. Jeremiah Towlings, a preacher, who had some input on the terms being discussed. After nine days, the negotiations broke down. So, on August 11, a new battle began. This battle continued for sixty-five days, and after it ended, there was hope that new peace negotiations might be in the works.

However, after losing badly at the Battle of Sterling Creek, the Fatavian Coalition was in no mood to discuss terms of peace. In fact, Mortulakin Hantabolvia decided to enact a take-no-prisoners policy. On October 17, he issued a bounty on any Madrigald Coalition commander. This bounty system was to begin on October 22.

He did this because Thanderbrook was planning his next military offensive, centered on the city of Kiscauleigh. By the time the offensive began on November 3, he had survived at least four assassination attempts on his life. By November 25, he decided to take a more cautious approach after being injured in combat. He sent Colonel Reginald Buricavi a note informing him that he was to be his replacement. The note reached the colonel on December 8.

Buricavi arrived in Kiscauleigh on December 23. On January 3, he achieved a small victory over the Fatavians at the Battle of Pirsch, just south of Kiscauleigh. Not long after that, the siege of Kiscauleigh began on January 9; it ended on the morning of March 2. When he and his troops entered the city, they were welcomed by throngs of war-wearied individuals. One of the city's high-ranking officials begged Buricavi to give the city better protection.

Buricavi pledged to do just that, but first he needed to set up a regional fort. He selected Mount Gaskunder as the site for the fort. Buricavi then hosted his brother-in-law, Colonel Benjamin Hasopwarich VI, for a general briefing. The two colonels discussed the planned assault on the Heights of Eskelinhavern.

Hasopwarich telling Buricavi that the assault should be launched in several phases, so as to give the Fatavians no direct point of defense. Buricavi thus knowing how important the taking the Heights of Eskelinhavern from the Fatavians was, he would thus ask Hasopwarich to draw up some illustrations as to show the high council of the Madrigald

Coalition, as to how the assault on the Heights of Eskelinhavern should go. The designs were very detailed, with such scope. Thus, after studying the illustrations, Buricavi sent his formal proposal with the illustrations to the Madrigald Coalition's high council for approval or disapproval of the assault on the Heights of Eskelinhavern.

The Madrigald Coalition's high council approved the plan on March 25. The battle for control of the Heights of Eskelinhavern began on the morning of April 3. It was to begin very sluggishly because of miscommunications between Buricavi and his subordinate commanders. Buricavi rectified that by having Thanderbrook's son, Isaac, set up a mobile relay station. On May 9, a small skirmish was held just below the Heights of Eskelinhavern; it was a modest Fatavian victory. After the victory, the Fatavians did not expect the Madrigalds to launch a counteroffensive.

The counteroffensive took place on the morning of May 11; it was led by Captain Cyrus Wagglesmont Jr. He marched his men four and a half miles down the Trongan Boulevard to the town of Veggars. Once in Veggars, Wagglesmont came into contact with Major Ivan Kiswather. Now, Major Kiswather was not as experienced at strategy as his cousin, Sangeld Kiswather Jr., but he could hold his own.

When they came into close quarters combat with one another, Wagglesmont was slightly disadvantaged, because Kiswather blocked almost every blow he threw his way. For the next nine days, the men fought each other, and then the Battle of Veggars ended in a draw.

On May 23, Wagglesmont reported to his superiors that the Fatavians were on the decline. This statement was rebuffed by Senator Robert Viskers.

The senator questioned this claim and complained that he had not been allowed to see the official transcripts that dealt with the war for some time. On June 9, Wagglesmont was summoned to the Madrigald high council's administrative offices to comment on his report. After answering all their questions, Wagglesmont returned to his duties. When he returned to his tentative headquarters, his aide-de-camp, Lieutenant Arvin Nivecoat, asked how the meeting went.

He told Nivecoat that they would be joined on the battlefield by an unofficial observer, who was to be accorded all of the privileges of an officer. On June 15, Wagglesmont's forces began a major attack against a much stronger and larger force than they had faced before in combat. Their numbers were somewhat downgraded after fighting the Battle of Vanuenila for forty-three days.

By August 2, Wagglesmont asked for a general military conference of all Madrigald forces. It was held on August 7. He told Thanderbrook his general opinion on the strategic situation that was creeping up on the Madrigald Coalition. The general gave him some advice and then passed Wagglesmont's concerns on to the other high-ranking officials of the coalition. On August 16, he returned to Wagglesmont with a reply from the officials.

After hearing the officials' response, Wagglesmont went for a short walk by himself, saying he needed to get some air. When he returned to the Madrigald Coalition's main headquarters, he was greeted by his nephew, Silas. Silas Wagglesmont was a corporal working for General Josiah Grenwirth. He told his uncle that he was relinquishing his duties to train a new combat unit. He trained the MC 2398 Marines for the next four months.

On January 18, 2462, he led them on their first active mission, a minor victory for the Madrigald Coalition. In hearing that his forces had been modestly defeated, Colonel Ulstanagard Hantabolvia told his aides that if he had the troops and supplies that Wagglesmont had, he would have attained an even bigger military victory than Wagglesmont had.

As it was, on January 26, he asked the new chief of the Fatavian Air Corps for an aerial bombardment of the city Nielese. The bombardment lasted three days and left a third of the city in ruin.

The Madrigald Coalition launched a counterstrike against Fatavian military installations, unlike the civilian targets the Fatavians had attacked. It began on February 3 and last eight days. After the successful counterstrike, they decided to go after Hantabolvia personally, seeking justice for their lost comrades in arms. They vowed to keep fighting until he was wounded or dead. The hunt for Hantabolvia began on February 19.

After trying to pinpoint where Hantabolvia might launch another attack, Yorenaski and Thanderbrook heard that someone was running a cocoa smuggling ring in Bawerdouidanian. Not wanting to dismiss the criminal complaints generated by the rumor, Yorenaski and Thanderbrook sent a special investigative team to look into the matter. The investigators talked with several eyewitnesses and obtained some crucial DNA evidence proving that a high-ranking Fatavian military officer had visited a local pharmacy, looking vitamin B supplements, according pharmacist Edward Dawlenhurst.

When pressed further by the Madrigald investigators, Dawlenhurst said that the man bought a hundred dollars' worth of sugar pills and then stored them in a warehouse in Vinslak; this was the home base area for the grand duchess of Himorelam, a highly astute cousin of the Lobbersteins, whose son was trying to regain his rights to the Berasculatan throne, through any means possible. On March 26, a fire broke out in the warehouse, destroying all the crates inside. It took fourteen firefighter units to put out the fire.

After the blaze had been put out, the Madrigald investigative team went to the home of Isaac Yendaford. To many people who knew him, Yendaford was a very adapt arsonist who worked for anyone with deep pockets. After waiting awhile, Yendaford arrived home, and the Madrigald investigative team moved in to nab him. Seeing that he was surrounded, Yendaford gave up. When the lead investigator asked him for whom had he done the warehouse fire for, he answered that he had been contracted by someone known as Trivantan.

It had been rumored in several military circles that Trivantan was the codename for Oscar Priscollen, who had been dismissed after several years as the Lobberstein royal family's gardener. The investigative team suspected Priscollen had fallen into the ranks of the Fatavian Coalition. After a very thorough search of his financial records, it was established that Priscollen had indeed joined the Fatavian Coalition. A warrant was issued for Priscollen's arrest, and he was apprehended on April 9.

When the Madrigald military police captured him, he had plans that had been stolen from the Madrigald high command. He was tried and convicted of espionage; to avoid the death penalty, he told the court about Patrick Kerlaundis, who had given him the plans.

Once the Madrigald investigative team had confirmed the information, Prince Phillip Mauwoerkin sent five Special Forces troops to apprehend Kerlaundis. These five troops searched for Kerlaundis but were instead drawn into a Fatavian trap. With no way of getting back to their own lines, the men decided to fight to the death.

As the five troopers gazed into the eyes of their potential captor, one of the troopers pulled out a bandolier and charged the Fatavian military commander with such ferocity that the bandolier almost flew from his arm. The trooper was shot dead but managed to wound the Fatavian commander. The other four Madrigald troopers began to verbally spar with the Fatavians. Their commander was quite amused with the gall of his prisoners. On the morning of May 19, he put the prisoners on display in a cage.

They remained in captivity for a month, and then the three of the captives died from starvation. The last captive perished on the afternoon of June 27. Five days later, new Madrigald troops arrived where the tragedy had occurred, and these troops sought vengeance for their dead colleagues. On July 11, they caught one of the Fatavian troops responsible for the tragedy. This soldier told the Madrigald troops that they were only following orders from Captain Oliver Yammerick, Hantabolvia's new aide-de-camp.

With this revelation, the Madrigald Coalition's high command knew they were on the trail of their prey. Arthur Resminki, the commander-in-chief of the Madrigald Coalition, devised an elaborate plan to nab the elusive Hantabolvia. Resminki ordered a highly secretive mission around Glifford's Gorge, where Yammerick was supposedly stationed. It was to be launched early in the morning on July 21. At 6:15 a.m., the trap was sprung, and the Madrigald Coalition was waiting for their Fatavian enemies. By 8:30, both coalitions came into direct conflict with one another.

The Battle of Glifford's Gorge was fought for 123 days. When it was concluded, several units were completely destroyed and would never rise to fight again. On September 25, a peace summit was called. This summit lasted for nearly two weeks, but no agreement was reached. So once again, hostilities resumed on October 12. The next series of battles tested both coalitions' willingness to fight a war of utter destruction. After the Battle of the Waking Falcon, a parochial conference was held in a nearby restaurant, as the local religious sites had been damaged during the fighting.

The ministers discussed how to bring the conflict between the coalitions to end. Each of the ministers met with a member of a coalition at varying times over the course of thirteen days. On November 5, the Madrigald Coalition asked for more spiritual advisors. The ministers were a little disheartened because they couldn't end the war, but they did their best to comfort their Madrigald flock with the utmost care. At a belated All Souls Day Mass on November 2, the ministers met their Madrigald chaplain brothers and began blessing each one of them for doing the heavenly Father's will.

On November 11, the ministers had their first official spiritual meeting with Resminki, the Madrigald coalition's leader. After the meeting ended, Resminki and Reverend Thomas Mordena sat down to discuss what the ministers' role in the field of battle would be and where they would be sent to guide the Madrigald troops as a whole.

They drew up a very detailed plan for placing the ministers in camps away from immediate danger. Reverend Mordena later told his fellow ministers where they were to be stationed for the duration of the hostilities. On Thanksgiving Day, the ministers were placed in their specific camps to give their spiritual guidance to their congregations.

After getting to know their congregants, the ministers faced their first major test in dealing with giving Last Rites in the field, as the Fatavian coalition launched its most daring military campaign yet in the war. On December 12, the forces of Furistahl Bauspeirada Jr. launched an amphibious assault against the MC-6113 Armored Marines unit. The marines were harassed for twenty-two days. As Bauspeirada prepared his troops to move on to the heights where the MC-6113 Armored Marines were located, he found that the marines were willing to hold their ground to the last man.

On January 4, 2463, the Battle of Tortoise Hill took place; many in the rear echelon of the Fatavian Coalition believed that this campaign was the beginning of the end of their war. After the fighting ended on the afternoon of January 13, the Fatavian Coalition's Furistahl Bauspeirada Jr. boasted that the moral victory resulted from a new fighting strategy.

This attitude changed on the morning of January 24, when Major Henry Yorenaski decisively defeated the braggart at his own game. However, not long after his defeat of Bauspeirada, Yorenaski was evacuated from combat duty in the Berasculatan War for medical reasons. On February 5, he was replaced by Lieutenant Colonel Cornelius Hasopwarich Picaloy. On February 9, Picaloy led his troops into the Battle of Lions Gulf, against Lieutenant Colonel Alexander Nawanki Jr. The battle raged on for forty-seven grueling days and concluded in a draw. One of the casualties was Chaplain Reverend Albert Cooleson, who died giving Last Rites to a soldier. He was buried on March 31. Picaloy gave him a stirring eulogy.

Once all the mourning had run its course, Picaloy got his troops back into their training regimen. They finished training by April 9, and their next combat campaign was against Nawanki's cousin Ogurant. The MC-6678 Armored Calvary fought a combined force of Nawanki and Ogurant in the Battle of Yurgalos; after three weeks, the Madrigalds claimed victory, but it was a costly win. The battle taught Picaloy a lot about the Fatavians' resolve.

Picaloy asked to meet with the high council to discuss how to completely defeat the Fatavian Coalition. He heard back from high council on the afternoon of May 13. Their response was that they'd meet with him after his next victory. That kind of response really roiled the normally modest and calm Picaloy.

Two hours passed before he wrote in his journal to air his frustration. He felt the Madrigald Coalition's high council was dragging its feet on meeting with him. After that, he wrote a personal letter to his wife, Maria. In the letter, Picaloy asked his wife how she and their five children were doing. After concluding his letter to his wife, he asked his most junior officer, Corporal Thaddeus Kinger, to mail the letter when he went into town.

At which Corporal Kinger said he'd only too be glad to do so, for he was going in to town to see his girlfriend, Olive; while in town, he would mail the letter home to Gorgadal. Picaloy sealed the letter with his family's seal and handed it to Kinger, who headed for the Iskelvimbarkien Post Office. The walk to the post office only took seventy-five minutes.

As he walked up to the Iskelvimbarkien Post Office, he saw someone harassing a woman he knew, his girlfriend Olive's sister, Patricia. He went quickly inside the post office and handed the letter to the agent, Max Jawaller. After dropping off the letter, he came out of the post office to see if the individual was still harassing Patricia.

Sure enough, the man was still up to it, so Kinger decided to get involved in the matter. He called over to Patricia, and the guy yelling at her turned towards him and told him to mind his own business. Thaddeus replied that this woman was his girlfriend's sister, adding that he didn't like strange people bothering his friends.

The man, Norbert Hazzerone, told Thaddeus to buzz off and go back to where he had come from. Thaddeus said he would stick around until Norbert stopped harassing Patricia.

When he heard that, Norbert swung his fist at Thaddeus, who raised his hands to defend himself. Patricia backed away from the two men, and their fight turned into a real brawl.

Eventually, the sheriff of Iskelvimbarkien arrived and stepped between the two now-bloodied brawlers. As fate would have it, the sheriff, Angus Pormossie, bruised his eye in the brawl. After finally separating the two men, Pormossie charged them with disturbing the peace; he locked them up. After they each paid their bond, both men were released from jail.

After receiving paperwork with his court date, Thaddeus went back to work, where he received counseling from Reverend Arthur Castergarden. After several counseling sessions, they developed a close friendship. Unfortunately, the friendship was shattered by Reverend Castergarden sudden death at the age of forty-five. As he wrote his late friend's family about their lost relative, Thaddeus felt a calling to become a priest himself, but he quashed those dreams because of how he felt about Olive.

So, on the morning of May 30, after they had gotten involved in another battle, of which was to continue for fifty-four days. After this battle, Thaddeus decided to leave the military service and thus decide to become an Orthodox Christian minister, after taking

Olive as his wife. Not long after this particular personal decision by the now Orthodox Christian minister in training and former Corporal Thaddeus Kinger, did Picaloy begin to search for a new clerk. Now it was just about to take him i.e., Lieutenant Colonel Cornelius Picaloy, a little over a couple of weeks to find Thaddeus's replacement. By which time things were beginning to "heat up on the frontier "again and of which there couldn't be any lack of preparedness by anyone on either side of the conflict i.e., Berasculatan Crisis, and so with that in mind Lieutenant Colonel Cornelius Picaloy would have to get his troops and new aide up to snuff on what the new military policies might be for the continuing crisis and or war, and so by August 10, Corporal Samuel Newcome, Picaloy's new military staff clerk, would thus begin to be put through his paces. Now of course it would Corporal Newcome at least another month to learn all his new duties However by the time he learned all of his duties which was on September 12, Picaloy would get his meeting with the Madrigald Coalition's high council. He was summoned to appear before Prince Phillip Mauwoerkin, who was the designated representative for the council.

They talked for about five hours, after which Mauwoerkin told him he would meet with the high council on September 15. With Mauwoerkin as his main supporter, he felt he could get approval for his plan to deal a decisive blow to the Fatavian Coalition and their allies.

As the meeting began, several members of the council seemed to be someplace else, while other members agreed with the lieutenant colonel's plan to virtually destroy the Fatavian Coalition, attacking their will to continue the war. Picaloy spoke for three hours and answered all the questions from the council. After defending his plan, he was dismissed, and the council began to debate in private. Nine days later, the members decided to approve the plan.

The council approved the plan by a wide margin, after making some changes proposed by Senator Carl Lutanus Buricavi of Manchu Prime. Buricavi suggested that the troops should not be divided during the attack. After agreeing to Senator Buricavi's alteration to his plan, Picaloy put his revised plan in motion. The attack began on September 26; it started with a concentrated bombardment of key Fatavian military installations around the city of Dragos. The bombardment continued for the next two months. Picaloy did not want to give the Fatavian Coalition's anti-aircraft hydroelectric turbo ion cannons easy targets. After assessing the damage reports from the bombing raids, he was optimistic about his land troops securing their specified objectives. However, because of a few less than tough -minded individuals in his land troopers' lead elements, they did not secure their specific targets without suffering some causalities, but after getting them i.e., the less than tough minded individuals out of his troop's way, they that is the rest of Lieutenant Colonel Picaloy take 7/10th of the Fatavian defense instillations around the city of Dragos.

CHAPTER 7

HOPE IS RISING

Now with approximately 70 percent of the Fatavian Coalition's military installations near the city of Dragos under Madrigald Coalition military authority, Lieutenant Colonel Picaloy decided to give Sergeant Abraham Waturichan a very top-priority mission. The later siege of Dragos began on December 2. After several key arteries to the city were cut off, the Fatavian commander surrendered to Waturichan. On December 11, Waturichan was given a much tougher assignment to handle, and the Madrigald high council assigned newly promoted Captain Morgan Hasopwarich to help him.

They linked up on December 19. After combining all their troops, Hasopwarich was put in command of the new corps, but Waturichan gave all the orders. His first order was to attack the Fatavian forces on Yipperhorn Heights. This battle began on December 27, 2463, and lasted until January 1, 2464.

By January 3, the new corps was just mopping up the last pockets of Fatavian resistance on the Yipperhorn Heights. That changed on January 7, when Furistahl Bauspeirada III arrived with a new Fatavian force. He did whatever it took to get his troops ready for a fight. In one particular instance, he had a Fatavian trooper who was not up to his standards whipped. This motivated the trooper to try his best not fail in the future.

However, this was not the approach Waturichan took with his troops. Waturichan gave his men a pat on the back once in a while. The two men led their respective corps against each other in the Battle of Jesnicki Flats, which ended in a draw. In the days immediately following the battle, Waturichan told his troops to expect further attacks by the youngest of the Bauspeirada Family.

On January 19, Waturichan's fears were realized. That was when he noticed that the Fatavians were assembling at a series of warehouses. He believed this meant that the Fatavians were bringing their robotic warrior program on line, and he could not let them do that, at any cost. So, on January 24, he formed a special demolition squad to deal with the warehouses, while he and the rest of his troops launched an amphibious assault against the enemy's new headquarters. That conflict was to be very costly for both sides.

After both coalitions recovered all of their respective dead, they moved on with their plans for their next battle. By this time, Waturichan had become a major figure in the Madrigald Coalition's planning meetings. The battle was fought over the course of thirty-nine days. After the battle, Furistahl Bauspeirada III took a much more definitive approach to handling his Madrigald foes, especially Waturichan, as he recovered from his more serious scars.

Once Bauspeirada healed, he sat down and wrote a letter to his beloved Anna Louise Reugarmen. In it, he expressed his love for her and said he hoped her father would send him some troops to continue his campaigns in the Berasculatan War, because he did not want to continually rely on people connected to his father or grandfather. The letter was mailed, but it was intercepted by the Madrigald Intelligence Service.

The MIS dissected the letter, to see if there were any hidden messages about Fatavian troop movements. This proved fruitless, but the MIS warned its allies of a Remigarian intervention force. By the time the warning reached the Madrigald Coalition, the Fatavian Coalition was preparing to launch its Operation Spartacus.

Operation Spartacus was led by Captain Valeutin Furistahl Bauspeirada, who wanted to prove his independence from his famous father, brother, and cousin. Rather than rely on familial help, he sent his staff away on other tasks.

On the afternoon of May 5, Valeutin and some of his elite troops were under assault by forces of Lieutenant Colonel Miles Buricavi, the youngest cousin of Colonel Reginald Buricavi. They battled one another throughout the month. The assault by Lieutenant Colonel Miles Buricavi was so resolute that on the morning of June 5, Captain Valeutin Bauspeirada was forced to capitulate to his much younger adversary. On June 9, Count Furistahl Bauspeirada was made aware that his youngest son had surrendered to a foe who had only basic training. After receiving this news, he was left shaking his head in shame.

Over the next two days, Count Bauspeirada tried to find a diplomatic way to get his youngest son out of a Madrigald Coalition military prison. Colonel Sangeld Kiswather Jr., the son of his old friend, offered a practical solution to situation. He told the count they should attack the prison using a floating barge that contained a hollowed-out capsule carrying the android life form known as Dolvan. After thinking about the proposal, Count Bauspeirada decided to go along with it.

Work on the floating barge began on the morning of June 21. It took until August 16, by which time another battle had been fought. On August 21, the floating barge was mounted onto its launching pad. By the morning of August 25, the floating barge was launched into orbit.

The floating barge was not noticed by the Madrigald Coalition until it was seen by a radio station operator who was adjusting his antenna placement to get better reception for his news broadcasts. He informed the Berasculatan provisional government of Governor Hiram Rasnowski, who told the Madrigald high command about it. On September 20, a special observation unit was established to track the floating barge and report on its activity, so they could decide if it was a military threat.

The unit observed the barge for two weeks, with little movement on the barge's behalf. But one evening, the special observation unit noticed slight movements on the barge and informed their superiors about it. Eventually, the Madrigald Coalition high command's high council declared the floating barge a military threat and issued orders to destroy it with an ion laser gun.

On November 5, the Madrigald Coalition gunners began firing at the barge. Sergeant Rufus Quayvish missed his opportunity to destroy the barge, but he told the next gunner the barge's proscribed entry angle. The next gunner likewise flubbed his opportunity to destroy the barge, but he nicked it. The third gunner also missed.

The Madrigald Coalition's high council came up with a new plan to destroy the barge. After discussing different types of countermeasures, they decided to use a manned drone fighter. Construction of the manned drone fighter began on December 1 and continued until January 2, 2465.

The high council had to find a qualified pilot to command the craft. They chose Captain Wendell Sawenderhaus for the job. His first task was to get acquainted with the functions of all the fighter's instruments. He learned its weapons systems very quickly, but then he requested a back-up pilot to assist him in case of an emergency.

The council chose Captain Rawlings Frimport as back-up pilot; the experienced ace had seventy-two air combat missions under his belt. After meeting each other for the first time, the two pilots became friends. They began hunting the barge on February 3. Their first flight ended after a couple of hours, with no sighting of the barge. They went off-duty and tried to relax, chatting about their favorite family moments and where they'd be if the war had not happened.

Sawenderhaus told Frimport he would probably be teaching junior high school, and Frimport told Sawenderhaus he would be probably be playing professional baseball. When he heard that, Sawenderhaus said he'd tell his wife to look for professional baseball teams when they got back home, so they might see one another at a game and hang out together. Frimport said he'd like that too. Not long after that, the two pilots were called back to duty.

Their second patrol was unsuccessful, like the first one, but they heard the shriek of an engine firing up in the distance. They flew their drone about half a kilometer from their air base to investigate the noise, only to find out it was nothing other than a hyperphone line going live. Not wanting to look embarrassed by having nothing to report to their superiors, they began a third patrol. During this flight, they discovered that the Fatavian Coalition was preparing a new offensive against an unsuspecting Madrigald Coalition force.

The two pilots reported this to their Madrigald comrades in the field below Nasolpam City. After receiving confirmation that their radio message had been well received, they headed back to their base. Several hours later, they received word that the Battle of Nasolpam City had ended in a draw, with the Madrigald Coalition suffering a few more casualties than the Fatavians. After grieving over their lost comrades, the two pilots began their fourth patrol.

At the beginning of their fourth patrol, Frimport and Sawenderhaus saw significant evidence that their quarry had been in the area they were searching. By their fifth patrol, they got a glance at the barge as it darted into a densely thicketed area. As they moved into position to try to get a better look, it pulled away with a hypersonic boom. Not wanting to get caught in the barge's wake, Frimport and Sawenderhaus broke off their pursuit. They pledged that next time, they would shoot the barge down, no matter what it cost them. After that, they flew the slightly damaged drone fighter back to base.

After a quick inspection and test flight of their replacement craft, Frimport and Sawenderhaus gave it a nickname, the Flaming Gulch II, after their first drone fighter, the Flaming Gulch. The Flaming Gulch II saw its first official action on May 11. Its first patrol lasted thirteen hours.

This patrol was not fruitful, but it did provide some promising information about the barge. They determined the barge's shielding was made of refined tungsten and bromide. To deal with this type of shielding, the Flaming Gulch II was equipped with a modified proton torpedo with a thermal heat sensor.

On May 19, at the start of its second patrol, the Flaming Gulch II passed by a Berasculatan science center that had been destroyed; it showed burn marks that suggested a large vessel had attacked it. After radioing their findings to their Madrigald superiors, the Flaming Gulch II pilots flew north of the science center. This region had also been hit, so Frimport decided to get a weapons residue specimen for analysis The specimen came from what had been an elementary school.

The specimen revealed traces of tachyons, so they decided to locate and destroy the Fatavian Coalition's science laboratory. The Flaming Gulch II could not do two separate operations, so a new squadron of drone fighters was unveiled, consisting of eighteen aircraft, and it was under the command of Colonel Wilfred Osselman.

Colonel Osselman was not like Sawenderhaus; but he expected his men to fly their crafts to the edge of insanity and back. During one of the early training sessions of the squadron's drone fighters, he criticized one of his young pilots for some tedious infraction. As a consequence, the pilot began drink off duty. When they were finally called up to deal with the laboratory, the young pilot crashed into the laboratory's defense turrets.

After the funeral for the young pilot, Sawenderhaus and Frimport told Osselman that he should be more compassionate with his young pilots. Osselman thanked the two Flaming Gulch II pilots for the talk, but he said they should be more concerned about the floating barge and let him worry about his squadron's young pilots. At that point, the matter seemed at a standstill, but that was to change when the squadron and Flaming Gulch II were forced by a stroke of fate to work together.

On June 11, the Flaming Gulch II and the new squadron came upon the barge. The Flaming Gulch II was in the lead, but the squadron began to shell the barge. They continued shelling the barge until the next evening; by this time, the barge had released its precious cargo, the capsule containing Dolvan. The Flaming Gulch II almost destroyed the capsule, but it slid out of firing range.

Sawenderhaus was seething from their inability to destroy the capsule. After a short debriefing meeting, the Flaming Gulch's crew were made part of the same flight group as the new squadron. The new partnership made Sawenderhaus and Frimport lose their lunches, but they followed orders. The new partnership was tested on the morning of June 26, when Osselman would not listen to either of Sawenderhaus's or Frimport's suggestions.

After a brief spat, the two commanders sat down and discussed their next mission; Sawenderhaus and Osselman came to an agreement about the chain of command. A week later, the joint flight squadron began their most dangerous mission. It lasted thirty-four hours, and nearly half the flight team was lost. In the end, however, the Fatavian Coalition was defeated and had to change their strategy before their next military expedition.

On July 13, the Fatavian Coalition high command's high council issued a new set of directives for their troops in the field of battle. This new policy was fully implemented on July 22, when they began their assault on the Madrigald Coalition's field command center near Heuristeram. The defenders of the command center fought valiantly to the city safe. After ninety-nine hours of fighting, the Fatavian troops gave up their quest for control of Heuristeram.

A week later, a meeting was held by the Heuristeram city council to ask their Madrigald Coalition allies to put a higher fence around the city; this would keep the city's residents safe from exploding debris. The command center's representative suggested revisions to the proposal and offered a small work crew to complete the task.

The mayor of Heuristeram agreed to the revised plan, and the work crew began to construct the concrete fence. Once it was complete, the fence was armed with turrets, which would give any further Fatavian troop incursions something to think about.

One day, the center's commander received word of a sneak attack on a Madrigald unit in the Threeper Valley. He decided to put the center on emergency lockdown and to have his chief advisors draw up a plan to launch their own counteroffensive to drive the Fatavian forces from the Threeper Valley. This plan called for an aerial bombardment of the Fatavian stronghold of Celiderhacern, followed by an amphibious assault. The operation began on the afternoon of August 13, and it was spearheaded by the Flaming Gulch II. The ground forces were led by Captain Simon Frickerhoff, who was a skillful and diligent officer of many campaigns.

When Frickerhoff gave his first orders in this particular campaign, the older, more veteran troops only had to look at his grayish mustache and brow to know he had enough experience to keep the younger, less knowledgeable troops in line. On August 22, as he moved forward to get a better view of his troops, Frickerhoff was wounded and evacuated to a field hospital. A week later, he was given clearance to return to the fighting area; by this time, his forces were facing the toughest resistance yet from an enemy force.

On September 4, during a close-quarters fight along the River Jawelush, Frickerhoff was mortally wounded and laid to his eternal rest. He was eulogized by his friend and young protégé, Major Morgan Hasopwarich, who said about his friend was a man of integrity and courage beyond his home and classroom.

After the memorial service was over, Hasopwarich gathered together his new battalion and prepared them for a battle he believed could last into the New Year. On December 1, officials decided that the fighting would continue until a peace agreement was signed; this meant that the constitutional monarchy had to be peacefully restored and that no one would challenge its authority. This decree had detractors among both coalitions, but more so in the Fatavian Coalition. Their high command was so disturbed by it that they decided to unleash Dolvan from his capsule.

On December 9, Fatavian authorities decided the time was right to release Dolvan from his capsule. A few days later, they turned on the frontal node of the capsule, opening the door of the capsule and freeing Dolvan from his temporary living place. After that, the troops who were in charge of bringing Dolvan on line rolled his magnetic cart down the ramp leading from the capsule.

On December 19, Dolvan was operational, and just before Christmas Day, he began his first mission. On January 3, 2466, Dolvan reached the Madrigald prison where Captain Valeutin Furistahl Bauspeirada was being held.

Dolvan activated his thermal imaging scanner to try to pinpoint where his boss's son was being confined. After locating the captain's heat sense, Dolvan switched over to his ionized sonic wave blaster gun. As he prepared to fire it, he detected enemy blaster fire coming straight at him; he switched to his quantum-fusion laser sword.

After several minutes, Dolvan found the source of the blaster fire and attacked the soldier responsible, Private Edgar Rinswork. Before Rinswork could recharge his blaster, Dolvan was in full combat mode. The private knew he couldn't survive, but he hoped to at least wound the unidentified combatant. The fight was over in less than a minute. As he lay dying, Rinswork could see that his adversary was a robot of some kind; he called out a warning to his fellow prison guards to be ready for the robot mercenary's next attack.

After hearing Rinswork alert the other guards in the military prison, Dolvan decided to shift tactics. Dolvan mimicked Rinswork's voice to lure his friends out of the prison. When Dolvan caught sight of another enemy soldier, he approached him. The soldier, Private Jerome Mederhogin, turned and fired at him, causing little damage to Dolvan himself, but giving himself a bad headache.

After Mederhogin was treated for his head wound, he told his lieutenant he had seen a strange creature came after him with a hammer in its hand. His lieutenant told him that he would not rest until they brought this creature to a quick and decisive end.

CHAPTER 8

THE RISE OF DOLVAN

Dolvan knew he had to free the young Fatavian captain quickly. He made it through to the second level of the Madrigald military prison before once again encountering more troopers. They spotted him right away.

As the three troopers prepared to fire their blasters at him, Dolvan blinded them with his smoke screen canister. Trying in vain to lock on to Dolvan's image, the three young troopers fired blindly at where the robot had been. Dolvan sensed that more enemy soldiers were approaching him, so he rushed up to the third floor, where the cells holding Valeutin and other Fatavian soldiers were located.

When he found the cell holding the young captain, Dolvan used his magnetic clasping arms and pulled off the grates holding the bars in place. Valeutin watched, amazed, as the bars to his cell were ripped from their hinges. Once he left his cell, the captain began to free the other troops who had surrendered in battle. After being freed from their cells, the Fatavian troops looked to return to combat.

Valeutin led Dolvan and his troops to the elevator that went to the corridor near the prison's exit. As they approached the corridor, a squad of hard-nosed Madrigald troopers began firing on the Fatavian troops. In the skirmish that ensued, several of the Fatavian soldiers and at least fifty Madrigald troopers were killed. Of those killed was Nathaniel Waturichan, the younger brother of Colonel Adam Waturichan.

When the colonel heard his younger brother had been killed, he vowed to go after the person responsible and make him pay for it. He set out for the prison on the morning of

January 14. He knew that he was risking his military career but felt honor bound, since his brother Nathaniel had saved his life when they were younger. When Colonel Waturichan arrived at the prison where Nathaniel had been killed, he recovered his brother's body and flew it back to Gorgadal for burial.

Once his brother's body was in the air, Waturichan began his search for Captain Valeutin Furisthal Bauspeirada. After following his trail for three days, Waturichan came into contact with a tribe who had done some business with the Bauspeirada's; but after getting shafted by the Bauspeirada family on a much newer deal of which would have been of benefit to both of them i.e., the tribe and the Bauspeirada family, the Bauspeirada family reneged on it and so after seeing him i.e., Captain Valeutin Furistahl Bauspeirada, they'd try to arrest him, but were thwarted by a laser blast of some kind, however not wanting to lose sight of their new intended target i.e., Captain Valeutin Furistahl Bauspeirada, the tribe would send Sylvester SoftPaw and his aide Tommy Claycorn after him i.e., Captain Valeutin Furistahl Bauspeirada, unfortunately both would be lost after coming into contact with him i.e., Captain Valeutin Furistahl Bauspeirada and his "entourage" of Fatavian troops and their eventually "rescuer" a metallic creature and or robot known as Dolvan as reported by Claycorn before he and SoftPaw died from their injuries, and that's what the tribe would report to Colonel Adam Waturichan. When he learned that Bauspeirada, Dolvan, and the rest of their party were nearby, Waturichan asked for a guide to show him where the Fatavian warriors were located. The chief of the tribe agreed to let his daughter Emily guide the young colonel, not only to help the colonel, in his quest for justice and revenge for the colonel's own lost brother but for seeking to bring back honor and justice for the loss of both chief's son and Emily older brother Sylvester but also help give the Claycorn family closure for the loss of their son, a friend and formerly possibly suitor of Emily.

After thanking the chief of the tribe for the kindness he showed him, Waturichan and Emily SoftPaw went into the city of Malenkier and sought out the local eatery; the colonel walked up to the clerk at the counter and asked if he had seen a man with a scar above his left eye and a tall robot. The clerk said he had such a man, but there had been no robot with him. The colonel then let Emily talk to the clerk to see if he'd be more cooperative with her.

Realizing that the colonel needed her cooperation in finding the murderer of his younger brother, she went over and talked to the clerk. After their detailed conversation, she told Waturichan that Bauspeirada was in a hotel down the street; he had come into the eatery with an older woman. They walked over to the hotel.

After conversing with the hotel's concierge, Emily and Waturichan learned that the young Bauspeirada was in room 1267, on the twelfth floor. They took the elevator up to the twelfth floor.

As they approached room 1267, they heard the sound of braking glass from inside the room. They went into the room and saw the bathroom door open; when they went into the bathroom, they saw the window had been broken. Waturichan and Emily looked out the window at their escaping prey and decided to climb through the window in pursuit.

When they got out onto the fire escape, he was nowhere to be seen, so they climbed up to the hotel's roof. Still not seeing him from the rooftop, they climbed back down to the ground and walked northeast of the hotel towards the Preigel River; a small crowd of people had gathered around some trees. They ventured over to see what the commotion was.

The crowd began to disperse, revealing an elderly gentleman sitting on the ground with a bleeding leg. When Waturichan and Emily got closer to the wounded man, they could see wires sticking out of his leg. He had been turned into a human time bomb. The colonel and his helper decided to do an impromptu medical surgery to remove the wires.

After finding some pieces of cloth to soak up the excess blood that was sure to flow from the wound, they began an improvised surgery. After cutting the wires out and cauterizing the wound, Waturichan and Emily brought the elderly man to the nearest hospital for further treatment.

They had hoped to get information from the elderly gentleman about his ordeal, but the doctor said they couldn't talk to him until he was fully recovered from his wounds. So, they were to wait eight days before they could discuss with the elderly gentleman. When they heard that, the colonel decided to go on leave. While he was away, Waturichan heard rumors of a military offensive in his vicinity. He decided to speed up the search for his younger brother's killer.

The elderly man told them a soldier and a well-built robot had accosted him in the park; they were there with a young woman. She was quite short and slender, with brownish hair and blue eyes; the soldier called her Madeline.

Waturichan and Emily began looking for the woman. After looking through some photo catalogues, they learned her name and address. Waturichan and Emily then went to where she lived.

When they arrived in her neighborhood, Emily spotted Madeline getting on a hyper train and signaled to the colonel that she had seen their quarry get on a train. After acknowledging her signal, Waturichan went to a ticket agent and asked when the next hyper train left. The vendor said the next train would be leaving in a few minutes. Waturichan bought two tickets and motioned for Emily to join him on the train platform.

They boarded the hyper train and settled in for a short ride. While they rode, they chatted and learned more about each other. They got off the train at the end of the line; Waturichan and Emily spoke to another ticket agent, who told them a skinny young woman had bought some food and left the station.

After leaving the station, they discovered one of Madeline's acquaintances and spoke with him for a couple of minutes; the gentleman, named Elias Poristerhoward, said he was going to a dinner party at Madeline's house that evening. When they asked if they could join him, Elias said he'd be glad to ask her. He pulled out his phone and began to dial her number.

Madeline answered his call, and they began to talk. After a short conversation, Elias said Emily and Waturichan could join him for dinner at Madeline's house. He then flagged down a hover taxi, and they all got in.

The hover taxi arrived at the residence. Elias rang the doorbell, and the young woman Madeline answered the door. The three guests were allowed to mingle further inside the apartment's front room while Madeline finished cooking dinner. After they had devoured the food, the four grown-ups chatted.

Eventually, Colonel Waturichan revealed to the young lady of whom he was and what they were looking for. Madeline broke down into tears and revealed everything that had transpired over the course of last few weeks. She had been forced to participate in the deaths of the colonel's brother and his comrades in arms. Waturichan believed Madeline's story and decided to call his superior officer and have him set up a listening post near the apartment building.

After his commanding officer approved the listening post, Waturichan waited at the apartment building to tell the leader of the unit, Lieutenant Jeremiah Clousier, what was going on. After positioning his men along the Viesalasa River, Madeline and Elias were escorted from the area.

Waturichan decided to tell his superior officer what he had been doing over the last fifteen days, when he had very little contact with his troops. The two men talked at length about what had happened, and the general could sense that his most trusted underling had been forced to do what he had done.

The general gave him a slight reprimand; he could have been punished more harshly, but the general understood he felt responsible for the safety of his younger brother. After this brief discussion with the general he that is Colonel Adam Waturichan begins to "put on" his "strategist hat" to see what might be in the offing. Now when he Waturichan learns that a huge Fatavian force is approaching the area north of Clousier's tactical unit, he begins to devise a plan to strike at the enemy before they reached the tactical unit's position. After getting the plan approved by the general, Waturichan launched Operation Scorpion, and after two and a half months of intense combat, the Madrigald Coalition gained a victory.

At this point, Waturichan asked for some much-needed time off. Assuming this request would be denied after getting himself in hot water with his commanding officer, Waturichan began working on another plan to deal with the Fatavian menace. However, a courier from General James Kitzelorn approached his tent. Waturichan asked the courier if he had a message for him, and he said yes, handing him a letter with many ribbons around it.

Waturichan slid the ribbons off the letter and began reading it. His time off had been approved. Waturichan decided to find Emily and have her continue their search for his younger brother's killer and the robot.

He and Emily began searching for the suspects of the fallen Madrigald troops; they found a store owner who said he had a confrontation with a soldier and a robot. Emily asked what direction the man and robot headed, and the store owner said they went west. Waturichan and Emily thanked the store owner and headed in that direction.

The path to the west stopped in the city of Kalosuis Minor. Waturichan and Emily noticed a huge military buildup in the city and decided to avoid direct contact with certain business owners, who might inform the Fatavian officers of their presence in the area.

As they went through the city, Waturichan found someone friendly to the Madrigald Coalition. Their new contact, Stephen Qactorishan, told them he had seen the soldier and robot near the barracks on the south end of the city. Waturichan asked Stephen if he could send a coded message back to the Madrigald lines so they could bring up a huge force to deal with Fatavian troops in the area.

Stephen said it was not really possible to do this without alerting the Fatavian military. While Waturichan wondered how he could get a Madrigald Coalition force to the area to launch a surprise attack, Emily devised a plan of her own and shared it with the two men.

After debating the pros and cons of Emily's plan, they agreed to modify it slightly and then put it in action.

Starting on the morning of May 6, Waturichan, Emily, and Stephen began one of the war's riskiest enterprises. They tracked certain Fatavian troopers for a certain amount of time and then switched off, confusing the troopers so they didn't know they were being followed. On June 20, they learned from a low-level mercenary enforcer that the Fatavian commander was preparing to strike the Madrigald force approaching from the east.

Hearing that a Madrigald force was nearby, Waturichan decided they had to get to their comrades and warn them of the Fatavian assault.

They headed for the Madrigald encampment, but it took them five more days to reach it. Waturichan told Colonel Reginald Buricavi that the Fatavians were planning to attack them. Buricavi thanked him for the information and told them he'd help them accomplish their mission.

Buricavi lent them a unit, which arrived on June 27. The unit consisted of twenty-two military personnel, led by Lieutenant Charles Soudermen, and three civilian contractors. Waturichan briefed the new men on the mission.

The first point of the objective was reached after thirty days. The commander of the unit that had been lent out to help Colonel Waturichan checked his radio for news on what had happened to Buricavi. What he heard on the radio was disheartening.

Although the general survived the Battle of Kalosuis Minor, many of comrades had not been so lucky. After giving them time to grieve over their dead and wounded comrades, Waturichan promised that their mission would help them seek justice for all of their comrades.

On August 19, there was a firefight near Wenashawloham City, and half the unit was lost. Soudermen suggested that someone had alerted the Fatavian troops about their presence. After reviewing all the facts, they decided that the lieutenant was right: There had been a double agent, but he had died in the firefight.

On September 5, a coded Fatavian message was intercepted and decoded. The message said that Grey Hornet needed to get Point Yancey in a hurry.

The person who could be the Fatavian Coalition's Grey Hornet must have had some connection to that coalition's hierarchical command structure. This was narrowed down to small group of individuals. After a detailed search for the Fatavian Coalition's double agent, it was determined that he was assigned to the Dilavestan contingent, one of the survivors of the firefight.

On September 14, the list of suspects was narrowed to three people. Each of them was given a task to perform to test their commitment to the Madrigald Coalition's desired cause, which was to restore the Lobberstein monarchy to its designated place in Berasculatan society. One of the suspects was cleared after completion of his task.

And then, the Madrigald Coalition narrowed the list to one person; Corporal Hans Herbert Zeliskand received a message that was determined not to have come from Dilavesta. When they approached his living quarters, Madrigald Coalition military police noticed that the door to his quarters had been booby-trapped. One of the troopers disarmed the booby-trap, and they went inside and found a letter addressed to someone named Cligger.

Trying to figure who Cligger was, investigators called together the fourteen survivors and started a search. On October, the investigators and survivors went on a long trek to the city of Jilaspondarim. They talked to several people who were on the payroll of the individual who went under the alias known as Cligger. The interrogations lasted two weeks, by which time investigators developed a sketch of the suspect.

On November 5, the investigators got a much-needed clue as to the whereabouts of Cligger. They found a crumpled-up bus ticket to the town of Apricoverlam, on the northwest border with the Grand Duchy of Portville. Some investigators were not enthusiastic about trudging into a far-off area that was not likely to help them apprehend the suspect, but if they had to go there, they were set to do so.

After reaching the town of Apricoverlam, the investigators checked in with the local sheriff and then went to the building that would be their worksite. On November 7, the next clue that was vital to the investigation came into their possession after some very intense negotiations. The man holding the clue said he'd only relinquish it for the right price.

The investigators stored the clue in a specialized folder, and on November 13, they learned that one of the suspects lived in a building not far from where their office. They had to act quickly if they were to nab Cligger, and that night, the team entered his residence after he fell asleep. When Cletus Louis "Cligger" Gerstenova heard voices in his outer chamber, he decided to go out and see who was there.

But when he went towards the bedroom door's magnetic lock, he heard an electrical drill running on the other side of the door. Gerstenova stepped back into the room, and the door fell to the floor. He could see the silhouettes of other soldiers and other individuals standing coming towards the outer chamber and as he tried to elude them, but even as he tried and failed, he was stung in the neck with a sort of sleeping agent.

When he woke up, he found himself surrounded by a dozen soldiers. He asked what they wanted and was told that he was to face a long and strenuous interrogation process. He promised to cooperate.

Over the next three hours, all that the Madrigald investigative team got from Gerstenova was his job title and the duties that came with it. After a brief rest period, the interrogation continued for a couple more hours before breaking for the day. The next morning, all they got was the same information, with some small things added to them, but it wasn't helpful. The second day of the interrogation yielded nothing useful.

But on the third day of the interrogation, investigators got more substantial information from Gerstenova. He told them what he knew about the death of Colonel Adam Waturichan's younger brother and then began speaking about a more insidious plot that was to take place very soon. He named Marvin Dascendo as someone involved in the plot.

Gerstenova said they could find Dascendo in the city of Ressing. The investigators went to the city and entered a local hotel to see if anyone knew Dascendo. The hotel's owner told Emily that Dascendo lived in the south side of town, along the Quisaleno River.

Waturichan chose four others to head over to the Dascendo homestead: Emily, Stephen, Jason Greiker, and Yolanda Yorenaski. When they arrived at the Dascendo homestead, they walked up to the main house but were fired upon by more than ten quadro-cannon laser pistols. They decided to take cover in some of the brush angling to the left side of the main house. Waturichan decided to call for reinforcements. Stephen sent a radio broadcast back to the others in the investigative team. Upon receiving the message, Captain Timothy Hasslend ordered more troops to support the team.

When Hasslend and the thirteen troops arrived, they could see the situation was dire. Waturichan filled them in on what happened. Hasslend ordered more reinforcements, and he and Waturichan set the team up to contain the hostile enemy fire.

When Dascendo saw more troops taking up positions around his residence, he ordered his family to continue firing on the interlopers. Waturichan ordered his men to start firing. In the ensuing conflagration that erupted, many civilians and soldiers were killed or maimed.

After forty-five days of intense fighting, Dascendo realized he had no hope of succeeding and surrendered to Waturichan. Dascendo asked if he could bury the members of his family who had been killed in the firefight. He spent the next twelve days, under armored guard supervision, burying his dead kinsfolk. On January 23, 2467, after the last grave was finished, Hasslend began his interrogation.

Dascendo was not much more helpful than Gerstenova. He was held in solitary confinement until he became more cooperative. On February 9, the team learned that Dascendo's daughter was ill. After giving him permission to see that his daughter Maria was being well treated, he told the investigators about the other members involved in the plot.

After giving up the names in his team in the plot, Dascendo was taken to a highly classified location, where he underwent further interrogation. Using information from Gerstenova and Dascendo, the team came up with a code name for the lead operative in the insidious plot: Sandwich Man.

This person controlled lots of land and was a major figure in the financial structure of the Fatavian Coalition's underground fundraising wing. The investigators assumed he was working in the Grand Duchy of Portville or was a member of the Fleischenberger royal house.

Not wanting to tip their hand to the new enemy, the investigators proceeded cautiously and set up a command center in the duchy's third largest commercial center. Moving in and out of the command center was rather perilous, and the team heard news reports that Portvillian Security Services (PSS) forces were patrolling nearby.

On May 15, the main PSS unit entered the area where the team was living, looking for the assassins of the old grand duke. The PSS unit began doing random searches and caught one of the conspirators in the assassination. Not wanting to be discovered in the area, Hasslend's team decided to depart.

CHAPTER 9

RETURN TO FIGHT AGAIN

As they began the next phase into investigating the insidious plot, Waturichan realized that the one-year anniversary of his younger brother's death had come and passed. He finished packing his things and joined the others in team as they left for the Portvillian capital of Hezerohofgarden. When they arrived at the main courthouse, the conspirator's trial was ending, and the team was awed by how quickly the death penalty had been handed down.

Upon learning that the conspirator was going to be executed immediately, Waturichan decided they should try to talk to him as soon as they could. Each member of the team spoke to the conspirator for a minute or two, to give them bits of information they could follow up after the execution.

They watched with amazement as the condemned man began walking to the pillar, where the executioner waited for his prey. As the young man knelt down, he yelled out that his friends would not rest until they got revenge for his martyrdom.

After yelling out that his group would avenge his death, the young man breathed his last. As they left the execution area, the team wondered who the young man's fellow conspirators were; where were they, and why hadn't they acted as their friend was being put to death? They realized that they were planning to act soon after Silas pulled a hidden capsule from the young man's body.

He showed the others in the team what he had found, and they realized it was a pathogen. Yolanda analyzed the capsule taken from the young man's corpse and determined it was a slow reacting pathogen; however, it was very deadly. They concluded that the executioner was in dire trouble, if not he wasn't dead already. They learned the executioner's name and where he lived, but when they went to the executioner's lodgings, the team found him convulsing on the floor, near death.

Not wanting to get infected with the same pathogen as the executioner, the team called in a Madrigald Coalition hazmat team to clean it up and find out if the pathogen had dissipated enough for them to create a vaccine. After the hazmat team determined the pathogen had dissolved, they inoculated the investigators. However, the leader of the hazmat team, Dr. Charles Truenardson, said that the executioner had a very slim chance of survival. When the investigative team asked him why, he said he had been too badly exposed to the pathogen.

After acknowledging Dr. Truenardson's analysis, the team told him why they wanted to know about the executioner's chances of survival. When Dr. Truenardson heard why they wanted to know if the executioner was going to make it or not, he began to wonder if the investigative team had gone off its rocker. Assuring him that their motives were both pure and logical, he filled out his report and got it ready for processing.

Just as Dr. Truenardson was about to leave for a much-needed break himself, Colonel Waturichan asked if he'd stay and help them with their investigation. Seeing no way to avoid it, the good doctor said he'd help with the investigation, but on a limited basis. After agreeing to this, Waturichan welcomed him to the team.

Dr. Truenardson asked the colonel what his specific duties were to be. Waturichan told the doctor he was to determine if a robot like Dolvan could be stopped by a pathogen. He also asked if Captain Valeutin Furisthal Bauspeirada was capable of using a pathogen to create an international incident by corrupting a protest group.

After taking in his new duties, Dr. Truenardson told the colonel that someone else may have been involved in unleashing the pathogen at the execution.

His conclusion was confirmed after the Viecke Liberation Front (VLF) claimed responsibility for unleashing the pathogen at the execution, and it promised to do something more drastic in the days that followed. Trying to gauge when the VLF's next attack would be, Waturichan decided to take the investigative team to the city of Quadonderawn. When asked why they should go there, he said he had a feeling they would run into the head of the VLF, and he suspected they were getting aid from the elusive Bauspeirada. The team agreed, not wanting to question him about anything having to do with the search for his younger brother's killer. On the morning of May 28, they began the two-week journey to Quadonderawn.

As they approached the city, the team saw a very large explosion. Deciding to investigate the explosion's denotation site, the team found that in the immediate wreckage, that there indeed was a slightly pungent tacos residue mixed in with the pathogen that the team had discovered at the executioner's residence. There was no doubt the VLF was indeed in league with Bauspeirada and his Fatavian compatriots. Hoping to finally determine his exact whereabouts, Waturichan, Yolanda, and Greiker went to a popular restaurant in the city. Finding nothing of note in their first surveillance job together, it seemed fruitless.

However, things picked up over the next few days. Starting on the morning of June 21, the three reported hearing that their quarry would be involved in something going down three days later. So not wanting to waste time in getting to the elusive captain and his mysterious partners in the Viecke Liberation Front, the team set up a base to surveil the reported targeted area for the attack.

When nothing happened on the morning of June 24, the members of the investigative team were subdued; however, their mood perked up as they began to see people setting up where the attack was reported to start off.

Determining that the attack would begin within thirty minutes of arrival of the elusive Bauspeirada, they set a trap for when he arrived. When the captain made his presence known to all in the vicinity, the team decided to move quickly and intercept him. They began yelling at him to get on the ground, spread his legs, and put his hands behind his back. He did not immediately comply with their instructions, and some of the teams were worried that Dolvan might be watching from an elevated position, waiting to strike down anyone who did harm to his head programmer's youngest son.

A few minutes later, Dolvan appeared. Bauspeirada suggested the team move back, so they would not be hurt in the melee that was sure to follow. Waturichan told the team members to back away from the captain. Pleased that the Madrigald Coalition investigative team followed his suggestion, he fired his blaster at an unoccupied structure, or so it seemed.

Dolvan sensed that the Madrigald Coalition investigative team wanted to make sure no innocent people were hurt in the blaster attack; he ordered them to get behind him and promised he would help them escape retribution by the Portvillian government.

As they got behind Dolvan to escape capture from the local authorities, they heard a loud scream coming from far off. A figure was running towards them and shouting at them; they noticed a Madrigald Coalition insignia on the man's shirt and then saw it was a colonel. It was Martin Oskellian, the stepson of new Viecke tribal elder Tobias Leiferman; he began talking to Waturichan and then said he wanted to join the Madrigald Coalition.

Oskellian informed the investigative team that he only joined the VLF because they promised a huge payout for any opposition protest to the old late grand duke. Deciding that this claim was true, the team sent a report on their activities to the governing council. As expected, the report came under intense scrutiny, since the Madrigald Coalition military establishment was not willing violate another country's territory without provocation. The governing council decided what the investigative team was doing was highly risky; they feared they might be killed as interlopers in a domestic dispute and decided to go and rescue them.

On July 10, the rescue team, led by General Patrick Callison, begin its trek to the Grand Duchy of Portville; it was just over two months after the murder of the much-beloved late

Grand Duke Kiverold Aloysius Fleischenberger I. After a week and a half, they reached the investigative team. After speaking with the colonel and other members of the investigative team, Callison told his rescue team to set up a perimeter of about two miles. Callison wanted to get the investigative team to safety, but he also wanted to deprive the Fatavians of their biological weapon. Callison knew this course of action could ruin his career, but it was essential. The combined team waited and hoped that Bauspeirada and his robotic mercenary would return to their vicinity. After they waited a few hours, before the elusive captain returned.

This was their opportunity to nab one of the Madrigald Coalition's most wanted escaped prisoners, and General Callison and Colonel Waturichan were happy to do so. They wasted no time to return Bauspeirada to prison, where he'd be reacquainted with Madrigald Coalition military justice. The combined team started back across the Portvillian/Berasculatan border.

When they returned from Portvillian territory, the teams were questioned by their superiors. Once this debriefing was concluded, it was determined that they acted in the best traditions of military conduct. However, they were warned to never overstep the chain of command again. After promising not to go outside the chain of command again, Callison and Waturichan received a mild reprimand.

Knowing they had gotten a huge reprieve from the Madrigald Coalition high command, Callison and Waturichan decided to take a more cautious approach in their next adventure. After consulting with military strategists, they proposed a plan to apprehend Dolvan and his new helpers. The Madrigald high command agreed to try their plan to capture the robot.

On August 9, the mission began with an assault on a newly constructed Fatavian military supply station in Girgandarios Heights. Awakened by the thundering of hydro-graded laser rifles, the Fatavian soldiers guarded the station with a defensive perimeter. Sensing that the Fatavian troops were baiting them to go into their kill zone, the Madrigalds began firing above the heads of the Fatavian troops. This alerted Dolvan that the newly commissioned MC-2960 Marine Unit was waiting to engage him in combat. Observing from his position on a hill above the supply station, Dolvan laid down a small wave of laser fire on his opponents.

Seeing the laser fire, Callison and Waturichan decided to turn their small force's attention on the hill just to the northeast of the supply station. The Fatavian commander of the supply station, Captain Marvin Reivelonseura, decided to march his troops in full pursuit. Reivelonseura believed that if he could trap his foes against the cliffs leading to the hill, he could destroy the Madrigalds en masse or force them to surrender.

Reivelonseura hoped his forces could reach the crest of the hill before the Madrigalds began their own assault against Dolvan; otherwise, the Fatavian Coalition's high command would hold him responsible for letting their prized archetypical weapon of destruction be destroyed itself.

A small group of the MC-2960 was tasked with holding off the enemy pursuers while the rest made their way up the hill. They built a small redoubt from which to fire at the approaching Fatavian troops. When the first Fatavian troops approached the redoubt, they were cut down by the Madrigald troops.

As more Fatavian troops approached the makeshift redoubt, the officer in charge ordered his troops to fight to the death; they planned to blast the makeshift redoubt to smithereens, thus giving their other comrades in arms a fighting chance to deal with Dolvan. Firing without remorse into the redoubt, the Fatavian forces could be heard singing gleefully at the destruction they were causing. However, this gleeful singing came to an end very quickly, as the last survivors of the redoubt pulled out their thermite detonators and blew the structure up.

In the chaos that followed, forty-five hundred Fatavian troops died, and fifteen of the sixty Madrigald troops survived to fight on in their task force's pursuit to bring down Dolvan once and for all.

Seeing the carnage from his hilltop hideout, Dolvan knew he had to leave if he was to survive himself. Beginning his descent from his hiding position, Dolvan could see that his pursuers were getting too close for comfort, so he decided to give them a flash show to watch as he left the scene. Hearing the long booming thud of a laser gun going off, the Madrigalds thought they would finally get rid of Dolvan.

As they approached where Dolvan had been hiding, the squadron could see that Dolvan had been leaking fluid. Tracing the fluid, the squadron concluded that he was heading in the direction of Cabburalighamshire. Before heading to Cabburalighamshire, they sent a coded transmission to the Madrigald high command, alerting them to their current course of action.

The Madrigald Coalition authorities told the squadron to follow Dolvan to Cabburalighamshire. Before they left, the squadron first honored the forty-five troopers who had courageously given their lives in the pursuit of Dolvan. After a short period of mourning, the squadron set off for Cabburalighamshire.

Unbeknownst to the squadron, the Fatavian troops were also on their way to Cabburalighamshire. The squadron arrived on the morning of August 16 and began looking for Dolvan after setting up their headquarters. By this time, the Fatavian survivors had arrived in the vicinity of where Dolvan was hiding.

Having no idea where to find Dolvan, the Madrigalds decided to start to in the industrial sector of the city.

They could not detect him with their wave detectors, and they assumed Dolvan had buried himself in some sort of preservation container to heal himself while someone got him the supplies, he desperately needed to refuel his motors. The Madrigalds wanted to find out who this person was. They wanted to find him and sabotage the Fatavian Coalition's ability to continue the war. The Madrigalds knew the Fatavians would want to find another backer like that of the late Grand Duke of Portville, Kiverold Aloysius

Fleischenberger I. The squadron soon learned that they had indeed found a new financial backer.

The squadron knew that with a new financial backer, the war could continue indefinitely. It was a challenge to both get a lead on Dolvan's whereabouts and figure out who the Fatavians financial backer was; they knew they would need more, if they were to put an end to the war. The squadron soon learned that a new investigative team would be joining them in the field. The new team arrived in Cabburalighamshire on August 25.

The new investigative team reported to Colonel Waturichan. He assigned them a search area, but they found no evidence that Dolvan was still in the area. On September 3, the colonel asked the head of the new investigative team if it was possible that Dolvan would return to the area; he said there was a slight chance of it. With that sliver of hope, Waturichan issued orders that if anyone heard anything over the next few days, he was to be told immediately. Nothing was heard for the next two months.

The lack of information was because the new Fatavian financial backer had muzzled the press. He did not want his new weapon of choice to be found until he was unleashed upon the helpless citizenry of Berasculatan society. Pondering why the new financial backer had wanted to keep Dolvan a secret for so long.

One day, Abner Malushingham appeared on a Fatavian Coalition-backed news outlet. In his opening remarks to the Berasculatan public, he said he had hidden Dolvan away because he did not want the Lobberstein family to return to the throne; he also offers shelter and aid to any Fatavian military personnel if they asked for help.

It was obvious that Malushingham could not be allowed to hurt the Lobberstein family when they return to lead the government of Berasculata. On November 22, the Madrigald Coalition put out a bounty for Dolvan, Malushingham, and Bauspeirada. The bounty led to a battle between individuals loyal to the Fatavian Coalition and individuals loyal to the Madrigald Coalition, and over eighty-three hundred people died.

After the bloodshed mellowed out in some parts of Berasculata, it got worse in others. The Berasculata countryside collapsed into chaos, and the three rebels had a good laugh at the misery they were causing.

Meanwhile, the squadron and the new investigative team were in the process of tracking the three fugitives down.

On December 1, 2467, their old adversaries renewed their assault against the MC-2960. The assault continued until January 2, 2468. With their old adversaries defeated and sent to prison, the road to bring the fugitives to justice was in full drive. After Abner sent a telegram to Bauspeirada, it was intercepted, and MC-2960 seemed on its way to nabbing the three fugitives in one fell swoop. However, this did not happen, but the squadron did apprehend the courier who had been used to deliver the telegram.

The investigative team questioned Martha Humeboyter, the courier, about where she had picked up the telegram; she only said that she had been told to pick up the telegram and deliver it to the address on the envelope. Assuming that she told them the truth, the joint task force headed to the address. When they arrived at the residence, Yolanda knocked on the front door. There was no response to her knock, so after a while, the task force decided to kick down the door. They quickly gained entry to the residence.

As they looked around the residence, the task force saw little evidence that the fugitive Fatavian captain had been there. Observing a fresh carton of milk in the refrigerator, they assumed he would be back soon. Callison and Waturichan ordered a stakeout of the residence, and the task force waited patiently for their quarry to return.

After several uneventful days, however, there was a small break in the pursuit of Captain Bauspeirada, as a hyper cruiser pulled up to the fugitive's residence, and a man and a woman got out.

Waturichan and Callison assumed the male lived at the residence, possibly one of the fugitive captain's relatives. He went to the front door and beckoned the woman to join him. As she approached him, he pulled a key chain from his pocket and opened the door. Waturichan told the task force to move into position after the two unsuspecting individuals made their way into the house.

Once the front door was shut, the joint task force members moved in. They knocked down the front door and were surprised to find young couple calmly watching a video. When the young man saw laser-tipped blasters pointed at them, he got up from the couch and demanded to know what was going on.

After explaining that they were after Captain Valeutin Furistahl Bauspeirada, the man said he was his cousin, Valeutin William Wyclef Bauspeirada, and that he didn't know where his cousin was. When Waturichan told the Madrigald Coalition high command that they had nabbed the nephew of the old Count Furistahl Bauspeirada, they told him to bring the nephew in for questioning.

They questioned Valeutin William Wyclef Bauspeirada for fifteen days and learned that he had been at the residence, but the elusive captain set up another rendezvous spot to meet with Dolvan and Malushingham.

After telling the task force what his namesake cousin was up to, Valeutin William Wyclef Bauspeirada assumed that he'd be released from custody. However, that's not what happened. Instead, the task force's higher-ups kept William and his female companion until they confirmed the information, he gave them. The task force planned to continue their search for the elusive captain. However, this plan hit a snag, when one of the conspirators who was giving the elusive captain a place to stay blew himself and many innocents up. This happened in an area far from where Valeutin William Bauspeirada had said the new rendezvous spot was.

The task force rushed to the scene to investigate. When they arrived, they examined the scene and concluded that the captain had been involved in the attack. They also found a thumb print on the device that carried out the detonation belonging to a local cell member.

This evidence led the task force to charge Abner Malushingham with genocide against his own people. The next step was to gather information on individuals who might be willing to help Malushingham in his twisted endeavors.

They came up with a long list of possible suspects in the harboring of Malushingham. They broke the list down into groups of thirty-five. After checking off dozens of names, the task force narrowed the list of suspects who couldn't be accounted for to five.

They talked to relatives of three of the five individuals and eliminated them from the list of suspects. Trying to get a lead on either of the remaining suspects led the task force to the city of Brantos, where one of the remaining suspects lived. They finally talked with this suspect and scratched his name off the list.

That left one name on the list of suspects: Brian Rasenowski, and the task force would have no trouble in locating him, as he was in the local jail for being drunk and disorderly. They asked the local sheriff if they could talk to Rasenowski, and the sheriff agreed.

Yolanda was chosen to talk to Rasenowski. She had a very short chat with him, and he told her where Malushingham could be found. As it turned out, he did not care about the younger Malushingham's politics, although they had the same dislike for the Lobberstein monarchy.

Yolanda asked what name Malushingham travelled under.

Rasenowski replied, "Zelwandishack."

Yolanda was decidedly taken aback when she heard that name.

"Do you mean that the little twerp has decided to dishonor himself by using the name of Zelwandishack, the Lobbersteins' loyal champion of old?" she asked.

"Yes, that what I'm saying to you, young lady," Rasenowski said. "He decided to use the name of the old king's champion of old, because it is his birthright's."

When they heard that, the task force decided to investigate further. After looking through tons of data files, the information turned out to be true. After leaving the jail, the task force went to Malushingham's ancestral home, but he was not yet there; the task force waited, and at five in the evening, Malushingham arrived in his most pompous regalia. Taking no chance on him slipping through their hands, Waturichan, Callison, and Yolanda took Malushingham into custody.

"Unhand me, you scoundrel, before I get really ticked off," Malushingham told General Patrick Callison. "You'll get a severe reprimand from your superiors."

"I may be reprimanded by my superiors," Callison replied, "but I highly doubt you'll take your claim to the court, since we have evidence that you committed treason against your fellow citizens. You are under arrest for crimes against the government."

"Alright, I won't press the issue against you," Malushingham said, "but mark my words: I will be laughing when you are unable to bring me to justice."

Malushingham was trying to bait him into a drawn-out battle of ideological word play, but the general would not respond.

On February 15, Malushingham was brought to trial on charges of trying to overthrow the provincial regency government. He pleaded innocent to the charges but was found guilty and sentenced to death. As he began the long journey to Klissermarcker Point to face his execution, there was an eerie feeling coming up from the south of the courtyard.

The MC-2960 squadron was observing the area, and then there was a huge boom that came from above the main parapet. It was Dolvan in the flesh, so to speak. He was holding a pair of sidewinder proton missiles in the barrels of his amplified blaster.

Jason Greiker thwarted Dolvan from firing on his primary objective; he wanted to make sure that Malushingham's execution went through, so he sacrificed himself for the good of the Madrigald Coalition's cause. Dolvan's proton missiles hit his body and exploded; the shrapnel that fell onto the courtyard had the desired effect that the regency government and the Madrigald Coalition wanted, for as he was trying to escape, Abner Malushingham, pronounced enemy of the state, was struck and killed by falling debris.

After she witnessed the unconventional ending of the traitor, Yolanda began to weep; she cried because of how barbarous in nature her country had become, and now she had to deal with the death of her close friend and colleague. To that end, she would not smile again until the stench of death had been wiped clean from the whole Berasculatan area.

Yolanda tried in vain to find Dolvan, but she soon gave up looking for the menacing robot. In the days that followed Jason's heroic and tragic death, Yolanda wondered if her role in the task force would change because of how she felt about Jason. In a concerted effort to comfort her and reassure her that she was needed the task force, Yolanda was given a long furlough; she took some much-need rest before preparing for her next assignment with a new partner, who happened to be related to Jason.

When she returned to duty, her new partner was Alex Greiker, Jason's younger cousin; he gave her a firm hug and said he didn't want her to blame herself for his cousin's untimely death. He added that he'd have done the same in his cousin's place if he had been there. She felt better about returning to duty, and she and Alex joined the rest of the task force in the hunt for Captain Valeutin Furistahl Bauspeirada.

Hearing that the elusive captain had gone deeper underground, the task force used some new contacts to get a line on where he might be traveling. After talking to some well-informed citizens, the task force learned where Bauspeirada was holed up.

The task force's leaders let Yolanda and Alex handle the search for the elusive captain; they hoped she would be able to overcome her self-doubt. She said she felt up to handling the task and added that Alex was not really needed, but her new partner could come along if he wanted.

Feeling a little hurt by Yolanda's comments, Alex said he had not blamed Yolanda for his cousin's death, so she should not minimize his importance. Yolanda acknowledged that she was wrong in her estimation of Alex's abilities and apologized for her statement.

Alex Greiker accepted Yolanda's heartfelt apology with a firm salute and received the same from Yolanda; Alex now felt like a member of the organization that Jason had been so proud to be a member of. After they gathered the supplies necessary for the task of apprehending the bane of their military experience, Yolanda and Alex went off towards the city of Hassendorf.

When they reached Hassendorf, they went to a local tavern Bauspeirada was said to frequent. The two Madrigald agents went into the bar and waited for their quarry.

After a little while, their quarry arrived, along with a young lady friend. Not wanting to miss the opportunity to arrest the elusive captain for a third time, the two waited until most of the patrons had left the tavern. At a prearranged signal, Yolanda and Alex went over to where Bauspeirada was sitting and pulled out their handcuffs and stun guns.

As he was finishing his beverage, Bauspeirada saw the young man and woman coming over towards his table. When he saw they were carrying handcuffs and stun guns, he motioned for the bartender to hand him his bill.

As the bartender came over to give Bauspeirada his bill, Yolanda stepped in between the bartender and the elusive captain. Bauspeirada reached over Yolanda's head to grab his bill, but then he stumbled and began to fall forward, knocking Yolanda to the floor. She grabbed a firm grip of his sweater vest. The elusive captain tried in vain to get free of her, but before he could escape, Alex fired his stun gun at him, and he slumped to the floor, unconscious. Yolanda slipped out from under the weight of Bauspeirada and stood up.

After thanking Alex for subduing the elusive captain, Yolanda motioned for him to help her pick up the still-unconscious Bauspeirada. After they got him to his feet, Yolanda and Alex warned the bartender and the other patrons not tell anyone what happened. After they made their way through the tavern's door, they could hear a small commotion from back in the tavern.

They looked around for a cart to put the unconscious Bauspeirada in, but there wasn't one in the area, so they dragged him a few blocks to a nearby loading dock, where they found a cart big enough to hold him as they returned to the task force.

As they left with the cart, someone shouted at them that they could not use the cart. When they explained that they were transporting an unconscious war criminal, the man told them they could use the cart. As it turned out, there was a Madrigald Coalition cargo ship in the area, and they took the cart to the dock and asked the cargo ship's commander Thorson Gulper to allow them to bring their prisoner aboard.

This was not easy, because the cargo ship's commander Thorson Gulper did not like having women aboard his ship. However, after promising a large payment for helping them, the ship's commander Thorson Gulper relented and allowed them aboard.

After taking the unconscious captain to the cargo ship's hold, Alex and Yolanda began their journey back to the task force.

By this time, Bauspeirada had woken up. Alex and Yolanda brought him to the Madrigald Coalition intelligence and interrogation units, and he was put on trial for war crimes. His trial lasted for three weeks, and he was found guilty and sentenced to a long term in prison. Meanwhile, a new Fatavian threat arose. This new threat began on the morning of April 16 and lasted for eighty-six war-weary days.

On July 11, after putting the latest Fatavian threat under wraps, the Madrigald Coalition ended their military operations in the Berasculatan region. First, they decided to train small groups of Berasculatan military recruits. The training began on July 15 and continued until the Madrigald Coalition felt they were ready to handle the job of internal and external security. There were some minor drawbacks during the early stages of training, such as forgetting how to dismantle a military blaster. The Madrigald Coalition's military instructors worked tirelessly to correct these problems.

After the military trainers resolved these problems, they decided the Berasculatan Military Service was ready for operations. The next part was to assign the recruits into specific fighting units. These squads then went on a small military mission. The mission began on September 14 and was supposed to last for five days, but that is not what happened. It started out okay but got worse, and a rescue mission was launched on September 21. The rescue team reached the spot where Horse squad had run into trouble, but there weren't a lot of survivors left to rescue.

When he learned that the squad had come under intense enemy fire, General Callison concluded that Dolvan, or another creature like him, was on the loose in the region. Callison asked the Madrigald Coalition high command for another task force to search out this creature and destroy it.

The high command approved the task force, and they got under way. Starting at the bluffs just outside the city of Nieberon, the task force sought the new creature in the war. After two weeks, the task force concluded that a small group of individuals had replicated Dolvan and was using it for its own use.

This news was utterly disturbing to the Madrigald Coalition high command; if a small group of individuals were capable of replicating Dolvan's awesome fury, then the war would become even more precarious. They decided there had to be way of finding these people and stop them, as well as stopping the real Dolvan and his Fatavian masters.

The high command asked for information about people who were sympathetic to the Fatavian Coalition, and the task force amassed a list of names about a mile long. They cut the list down in order to focus their attention on the likeliest suspects.

The task force organized the list into small groups. With these groups, the task force members went door to door, asking people if they thought any of these suspects were up to something fishy.

The respondents identified people they thought were going to do something drastic; these individuals were brought in for further questioning; after weeding out the less dangerous from the list of suspects, the task force was left with eighty-five people who could be the perpetrators of the cloning of Dolvan for their own personal purposes.

The Madrigald Coalition high command decided to monitor the eighty-five candidates with intelligence agents, hoped they might lead the task force to their Fatavian contact and supplier. This monitoring bore fruit on November 11, when Isaiah Norderham made a call to a person identified as Karol Evardarcy. During the monitored call, Norderham asked Evardarcy when his Fatavian replicated robot mercenary would be delivered to his residence. Evardarcy said he would deliver the Dolvan unit to Norderham as had been requested as soon as possible.

It was a challenge to figure out when Evardarcy would get the replicated Dolvan unit Norderham had requested. However, they soon had their answer after a low-level intelligence agent stumbled across the manifest log of a ship that said the captain of the vessel had had fluctuations in his ship's air conditioning unit. The ship was the *Tiger's Claw*; the task force headed for the wharf, and the task force's commander, Lieutenant Hiram Coulovey, asked the wharf master where the *Tiger's Claw* was.

The wharf master told Coulovey that the *Tiger's Claw* had not arrived yet but was due in anytime. After seeing a vessel approach with the flag of a tiger on its main mast, the *Tiger's Claw* had finally arrived in port. A small group from the task force went over to the ship and asked to come aboard.

The next morning, they asked Stanley Grincoeur, the captain of the *Tiger's Claw,* if they could see the ship's cargo hold, and he agreed. The task force noticed huge burn marks inside the specialized container manifold. They told Captain Grincoeur he had been carrying at least two Dolvan units in his hold; the captain said they belonged to Jeffery Coltangius. When the task force told him what was going on, Grincoeur pledged utter loyal to the Madrigald Coalition; he told Waturichan he would do anything to get back at the Fatavian Coalition for damaging his cargo hold.

Waturichan told Grincoeur the Madrigald Coalition would pay for his repairs if he would shuttle the task force back and forth doing their missions. He agreed to this and said if they needed him for personal missions, he'd do that also. His first mission involved investigating an old classmate of his in high school.

The task force was investigating whether Simon Vandergras was a willing participant in Fatavian activities in the Grana Gard region. Upon hearing that he'd be charged as a war criminal, Simon hired Thaddeus Trivaloney, a prominent defense lawyer. Trivaloney argued before the lead judge that his client had been forced into the service of the Fatavian Coalition.

The prosecutor objected, saying that if Vandergras had been truly forced into working with the Fatavian Coalition, then why had they found hidden transmission letters acknowledging cooperation with the Fatavian Coalition? After a brief consultation with his client, Trivaloney stated that his client told him that a Fatavian agent had agreed to pay him to keep these papers.

The prosecutor scoffed at the assertion that Vandergras had decided to work with the Fatavian Coalition for just pay.

After hearing that, Vandergras was overcome by his anger, climbed over the defendant's table, and charged towards the prosecutor. Before he could get his hands around the lead prosecutor's neck, he was restrained by a bailiff and forced back into his chair. The bailiff warned Vandergras that if he attacked the prosecutor again, he'd end up in the jail's main infirmary.

After sitting back down, Vandergras calmed down. Trivaloney began to speak up for him as the lead prosecutor tried to arouse him again from his seat. After several hours of debate between the prosecution and defense teams, the judge in the trial handed the case over to the jury. The jury deliberated for sixteen days and then announced to the judge that they had a verdict.

The jury foreman said they found the accused guilty. The judge sentenced Vandergras to thirty years' hard labor and a $3 million fine. When he heard the sentence, Trivaloney moved quickly to appeal the decision of the court. After submitting the appeal to the court for swift processing, the sentence was left intact.

On March 3, Vandergras went off to prison to begin his long sentence. After a few days in his new surroundings, he began to break down. By the third week in prison, he began to whisper to himself that if he ever got out prison, he would go after Winston Frenkendielon, his Fatavian handler. The Madrigald Coalition high command had placed an informant in a nearby cell, and he told them they needed to hunt for this Frenkendielon.

The hunt for Frenkendielon began on April 2, and he was captured on August 10. When he was brought into court, he had suffered some bruises while in his jail cell. Not wanting to be construed as being like the Fatavian Coalition, the leadership of the Madrigald Coalition demanded that an inquiry be held to find out if the prisoner had been tortured by his jailers at any point. They decided to give each jailer a polygraph test.

The inquiry began on September 2 and continued until November 21; this gave those participants in the inquiry time to go over what had been said and come up with the proper conclusions about was telling the truth and who lied about what happened.

The final report was submitted on December 3, 2469; not everyone was happy with the findings, but there was no time to dispute them because a Fatavian attack was expected on Madrigald forces at Trikolaner. The attack ended with the Fatavians suffering major losses; sensing that the Fatavian Coalition would be willing to talk after such a loss, a peace delegation journeyed to the Fatavian headquarters at Rolalez.

When the peace delegation arrived in Rolalez, they asked to be led to the command post to talk peace with the Fatavian high command, but instead, they were taken into custody. They weren't allowed to see any of the Fatavian high command until after being waterboarded for five hours. When they objected to this treatment, they were told it was to "cleanse" them of their electric devices. Captain Herman Uzederack, the leader of the delegation, told Captain Cornelius Grissler, the head of the intelligence gathering service, that they didn't have any electric devices; they had been sent on a diplomatic mission.

Not believing what they said, Grissler told Uzederack to shut up and be ready to be processed for military detention. The peace delegation members had their photos taken and their arms and legs scanned and numbered, to determine who the detainees had been in civilian life. Once they were done being processed, the delegation members were split into three groups. Grissler wanted to see if they would try to escape and bring sensitive materials back to the Madrigald Coalition.

When none of the members tried to make a run for it, Grissler decided to let one of his underlings have a crack at getting the information.

Meanwhile, Uzederack could not find out where the other peace delegation members were being kept. Grissler asked the Fatavian Coalition high command to transfer Uzederack to a different location.

His superiors told him he would have to deal with Uzederack for a little while longer, because there was no room for him at the other prison. Grissler then placed Uzederack in solitary confinement.

By this time, Uzederack had found other means to entertain himself. One way was to build a miniature telescope. He also built a miniature compass. One day, he was able to get his hands on a radio. This allowed him to send a message to his superiors, telling them where he was and what was happening.

When General Reginald Buricavi heard his voice for the first time in a long time, he told Uzederack to sit still for a little while longer, and if he played his hand right, he'd soon be rescued. To that end, Uzederack tried to form a bond with some guards so he could find out what was happening. After a few days of being friendlier with some of the guards, Uzederack learned a small offensive was planned to take out as many twelve hundred enemy troops.

Not wanting to have any of his fellow Madrigald troops massacred by the Fatavians, Uzederack decided to warn his brothers in arms using a courier he'd had made friends with. The courier went to the Madrigald Coalition high command and gave them Uzederack message.

For this reason, they were ready to meet this latest foray by the Fatavian Coalition. The Battle of Hockery Hill was fought, and it ended in a Madrigald victory. Soon after this, a search party was sent out find Uzederack and his compatriots in the peace delegation. When they reached the peace delegation, some had died and others were starving to death.

When the search party found Uzederack, he showed them what he had found out. After several days of rest and then a brief debriefing by his superiors, Uzederack wanted to get back to work so he could get justice for all his dead comrades in the peace delegation, but that would have to wait, because he had to get medical clearance to see if he was of a sound mind to return to full duty.

CHAPTER 10

DEFEAT OF THE FATAVIAN COALITION

Major Herman Uzederack waited to be seen by Dr. Oliver Cransandicki, the highly touted psychiatrist who would decide when he could go back to duty. He had to wait because there were many other younger troopers who needed to talk with the doctor. Their first session was on July 28, and it continued until August 6. The two men discovered during this session that they were both married and had seven children.

In their next session, they went beyond these similarities and focused on the real problem. During this session, Cransandicki asked how Uzederack was feeling; Uzederack said he was really missing his family right about now.

Deciding to press on, Cransandicki asked Uzederack how he felt about his dead colleagues in Madrigald Coalition diplomatic corps. Uzederack said he also missed his colleagues and then mentioned that some of his colleagues had been like his brothers and sisters. Cransandicki asked which of them were like his siblings, and Uzederack mentioned all but two of them. When Cransandicki pressed further on the subject, Uzederack said he didn't include the other two colleagues, Major Thaddeus Trikolaner and Major Madeline Jipperoux, because they were like his aunt Mildred and his uncle Oliver.

Cransandicki asked him to explain why these two colleagues were like his aunt and uncle. Uzederack said that Trikolaner and Jipperoux were like an older married couple, always countermanding each other's directives about how things should go in matters of regulations and how the peace delegation should be dressed.

Realizing that if he wanted to continue to help Uzederack find his way back to the field of operations, he needed to understand his daily life, and he planned to meet Uzederack's uncle and aunt. He decided to hold a series of teleconferences with the individuals. To get Uzederack to agree to a couple of breaks in this latest session, he promised they could show one another the latest mail each had received.

Cransandicki made his way to a huge makeshift conference room with two sets of view screens, where he asked a colleague to watch Uzederack while he made the teleconference calls. The colleague said she would do so. Cransandicki contacted Uzederack's Uncle Oliver and Aunt Mildred. They were a wealth of information about why Uzederack had made the comparison about his siblings, but he wasn't able to make a definitive comparison between Uzederack's uncle and aunt and the two dead senior diplomats.

Just then, he got a message from someone called Miniverix. Cransandicki was running out of time because he needed to get back to Uzederack as soon as possible. So, he called the number, left a message of his own, and headed back over to continue their latest therapy session. When he returned to the room where he had left Uzederack, his colleague told him that he was tired of waiting, so she sent him back to his living quarters.

Cransandicki decided to continue their therapy session later. So, with that in mind, he set up another appointment for him and Uzederack to meet. The next therapy session was two days before Uzederack's thirty-fifth birthday. Cransandicki started the session by giving him a piece of cake and some gifts. He asked Uzederack how the presents and cake made him feel. Uzederack said he felt good but he also missed his wife's cooking.

When pressed to describe his wife's cooking, Uzederack said that she made soybean soup with a Caesar salad and sausage and bacon sandwich. Before he could ask him to explain further, all of a sudden, the psychiatrist's pager went off. When he saw the name Miniverix come up on the pager's screen, Cransandicki said he had to make a phone call.

Before letting the doctor off, Uzederack asked him to get some art supplies. Cransandicki told him he'd get the supplies after he was done with the phone call. He didn't want to leave Uzederack alone again, but if he was going to help him get back into service, he had to make this call.

He decided not to use the phone at the treatment center line because his supervisor had complained about the phone charges at the treatment center. His supervisor said that the phone charges were in excess of five thousand dollars. He found a private phone and returned Miniverix's call. They talked for about an hour. Miniverix agreed with Uzederack's assessment of both Jipperoux and Trikolaner. Miniverix also told Cransandicki that if he wanted to get to know Trikolaner and Jipperoux better, he should contact Yves Reinhard Ickelfeld.

Cransandicki decided to do this once this latest therapy session with Uzederack ended. When he got back to the treatment center, Uzederack had left for the day.

The next morning, before he resumed the therapy session with Uzederack, Cransandicki went to the treatment center's makeshift cafeteria to get some breakfast. As he finished his meal, he saw Uzederack coming towards him.

As Cransandicki got up from his seat, he wondered why no one had told him Uzederack had arrived early for their therapy session; in fact, Uzederack came to the treatment center to get some modest reading done before the session. When Cransandicki asked why he could not get reading done in his quarters, he said his new roommate didn't like him reading up on current events while he was undergoing psychological treatment.

Cransandicki told Uzederack that it was all right for him to keep up with current events, and if he wanted to read a newspaper, he could read them during their therapy session, and they'd make an activity out of it. They did this for the next sixteen days, but on October 2, while they were going over that day's newspaper articles, loud gunfire was heard not far from the treatment center. Cransandicki decided to take his patients away from the center to get away from the fighting.

The therapy sessions resumed four days later in a new location. After several more days, Cransandicki determined that many of the patients were ready to head back to their regular duties; however, this didn't include Uzederack, who still needed more therapy.

Unhappy at being kept back in treatment, Uzederack tried to get transferred to another psychiatrist's division. This they said would not be possible, because Cransandicki said some minor issues had to be cleared up before he'd sign off on Uzederack returning to service.

Realizing that he was not getting what he wanted, Uzederack got himself a lawyer to represent him. The attorney Uzederack hired to represent him was Wilbur Wrenicalin, who had been involved in an important case during the early days of the war Their first meeting as client and lawyer was at the time Uzederack's therapy session was supposed to be. When he learned that Uzederack had hired an attorney, Cransandicki called Thaddeus Hereniskelonger, his own attorney, who arrived from Manchu Prime at a very quick pace.

Cransandicki's attorney arrived at three o'clock, as the second half of the session started. As they began, the two attorneys took up their positions on the far side of the treatment room, watching for any hostile action by the opposing client. When nothing happened immediately, they began to chat and then decided to play cards. Their gin rummy game lasted for several hours, even after the session had ended. Eventually, a nurse kicked them out of the treatment center; she was about to close up the center for the night and told them that if they wanted to continue playing their game, they could go to the base's lodging facility. She also told them that she had gotten tired of them arguing over whose bid it was, which they did during every hand they played.

They asked her why this bothered her; she said the lawyers were too competitive with one another. Asked to explain her answer, she said she was almost sliced in the face by one of the cards. Aghast at the suggestion they would harm someone with their card play, the lawyers asked to see the mark supposedly made by them playing the game.

The nurse, Claire Marie Hasopwarich, showed them a small gash covered by a smiley-faced bandage.

When they saw the gash made on Nurse Hasopwarich's face, the two lawyers apologized for whatever pain they caused and agreed to go somewhere else to play. It took them until the next day to find a suitable place to relax while they waited to hear if their services were needed. After a few hours, the lawyers decided to check into their individual hotel rooms and wait for word of when the next therapy session was to take place.

While he was waiting in his hotel room, Wrenicalin learned that one of his clients was planning to do something drastic. Rather than get involved in the situation, Wrenicalin decided to take a short nap.

As he lay down on his cot, he heard pounding on his hotel room door. He got up to see what was going on and was quite startled to see his fellow lawyer, standing there with a bloody shirt.

He let the other lawyer in and asked if he wanted to go to the hospital; the other lawyer said he didn't think he needed to go to the hospital, but he asked Wrenicalin for a place to stay while he recovered. Wrenicalin allowed him to use his cot for the rest of the day, while he tried to find out what was going on. After a little while, he got some things accomplished.

Meanwhile, Uzederack and Cransandicki were planning to set up a time for their last therapy session; because of the attack, they would both be needed in the field, doing whatever good they could do under the circumstances. The session only lasted a couple of minutes, but it was more revealing and productive than the all-other therapy sessions. Everyone now had a chance to get on with their lives.

Now that he was allowed back on duty, Uzederack went out and helped those who had been affected by the attack. The first thing he did was check up on his lawyer, in case he needed help. He went to Wrenicalin's room and found Hereniskelonger there as well. He noticed that Wrenicalin didn't have a scratch on him, but seeing the blood on Hereniskelonger clothes, he asked the lawyer if he needed a doctor. Responding that he was alright, Hereniskelonger became indignant at the next line of questioning. He said that if something was really wrong with him, why didn't he feel like he needed to see a physician?

Cransandicki told him from a psychological standpoint, he had seen a lot of people involved in traumatic events, and they turn a blind eye to the effects of the event. They don't face it head on and try to go on with their lives as if nothing had happened at all.

When he heard that explanation, Hereniskelonger decided to get a second opinion of what was wrong with him. He had decided to transfer his clients to another attorney in his law firm, including Cransandicki. When he heard he had a new lawyer, Cransandicki decided that it might be for the best, but he still wanted to help Hereniskelonger deal with the tragedy that had just occurred. To do this, he needed to enlist the help of his former patient, Herman Uzederack. He found out where Uzederack was; he was working with an investigative team that had been assigned to find the latest bomber.

Cransandicki realized that it might not be possible for him to get to the one person who could help him treat Hereniskelonger from the psychological condition he faced, but he still wanted to help others who had been affected by the bombing. His first new patient was Claire Hasopwarich, who had been physically injured and also emotionally scarred by the bombing. They began their therapy sessions on November 17. Their first therapy session lasted for several days, with some success.

About a week later, Cransandicki got a call from Uzederack, who said he had heard that Hereniskelonger had refused to get treated for depression. When asked how he knew about Hereniskelonger perceived medical condition, Herman said he'd seen Hereniskelonger go off on a higher-ranking officer in the Madrigald Coalition, and the officer was looking into having Hereniskelonger charged with a mild misdemeanor until he could get a physician up to where they were located and examine him.

Cransandicki told Uzederack he had to get Claire Hasopwarich's consent to travel to where Hereniskelonger was being held for questioning. She gave her consent to meeting at the new location after getting word that her sister-in-law, Candrella Anne Buricavi-Hasopwarich, would meet her after the next therapy session.

He told her that he was willing to help get passage to the Treisalvan sector, so they could continue their therapy sessions, after he set up a special therapy session for his friend and lawyer, Thaddeus Hereniskelonger. She said she appreciated the offer, but it wouldn't be necessary, because her sister-in-law and her brother, Colonel Benjamin Hasopwarich VI, could pay the cost of her fare to the Treisalvan sector. They packed their things and left in separate train cars, heading for the Treisalvan sector. The journey took two months. When they arrived, they learned that Uzederack had been wounded by Hereniskelonger when he tried to start a conversation.

Hearing that, Cransandicki and Claire Hasopwarich decided to be cautious about where they went and who they talked to while they waited for Claire's sister-in-law, Candrella, to show before they set up a time for their next therapy session. Around four o'clock, Candrella Hasopwarich arrived, with her children in tow.

They talked for an hour before having dinner. When they finished eating, they discussed when Claire was to have her next therapy session. They wrote down the time for the next therapy session on a piece of paper the waitress loaned them. After they paid the bill, they left the restaurant.

Cransandicki decided to see how Uzederack was doing and get a lead as to the whereabouts of Hereniskelonger; he got on a bus that was supposedly going in the same direction as the hospital where Uzederack was being kept sedated. Unfortunately, the bus wasn't heading to the hospital; instead, it went to a clinic near the hospital, where there was a protest going on.

Cransandicki decided to get off with the other passengers; he cautiously walked away from the protesters, but as he got closer to the hospital, a leader of the protest group spotted him and tried to stop him from going into the hospital. When he saw the protester coming towards him, Cransandicki quickened his pace and hoped to get to the hospital as quickly as possible. Thinking he had made a clean getaway from the protester, Cransandicki headed for the hospital's security station.

As he got closer to the security station, Cransandicki could feel someone tugging on his sweater. Turning to see who was tugging on his sweater, Cransandicki saw the face of the young protest leader, staring at him with an angry look on his face. Not wanting to create a bigger public scene than was already occurring, Cransandicki tried to pry the young man's hand from his sweater. This wasn't an easy task, because in the young man's rush to stop Cransandicki from reaching the hospital, the young man had gotten his belt buckle caught in the doctor's sweater.

Upon realizing that fact, Cransandicki had no alternative but to kick himself loose. It took most of his strength to get free of the young man, who was still hanging on for dear life. With one last kick to the stomach of the young man, Cransandicki broke free. He arrived at the hospital security station and got a pass to see his friend, Herman Uzederack.

They told him to hurry up to the fourteenth floor of the hospital because Uzederack's doctor was going there to see how he was doing. He got onto an express elevator to the tenth floor, but after going up a few floors, the elevator suddenly stopped moving. They used the elevator's emergency phone but only heard static. They decided to pry open the elevator's upper hatch and climb out of the car into the elevator shaft.

It took them forty-five minutes to get the hatch open. After seeing how far they were from the next floor, the youngest passengers were allowed to climb out first, and then the second youngest passengers got their chance to climb the elevator shafts cables. After a while, everyone had made their way to the tenth floor. After saying goodbye and good luck to his fellow travelers on the stuck elevator, Cransandicki sprinted up to where Uzederack was being treated. But when he got to the room, he learned that his friend had been transferred to another hospital.

He asked where this new hospital was, and a nurse told him it was in Banularaskinana. Before going there, he decided to call his wife and tell her how he was doing; he didn't want her to worry about him coming home from the war injured. He then called Claire Hasopwarich to tell her that their next therapy session would have to be in Banularaskinana, because he still needed to know how his friend was doing. She understood that if she wanted to continue her therapy with the doctor, she'd have to go to Banularaskinana to do so, and she decided to go there at her earliest convenience. She left her sister-in-law, Candrella, a note telling her where she was going, and she arrived in Banularaskinana just a few minutes ahead of the doctor.

On the morning of February 11, 2471, Claire Hasopwarich and the doctor arrived at the hospital where Uzederack was being treated. They headed up to his room and arrived just as his lunch was served.

After chatting about some trivial subjects, Cransandicki and Claire began asking him questions, which he answered with as much patience as someone in his current condition could, considering what he'd recently gone through. They asked him where he thought Hereniskelonger could be now. He told them it had been reported that Hereniskelonger had been asked to join the Fatavian Coalition. Then Cransandicki asked if he could be granted access to his medical competency reports to see if that were true; later, the doctor became relieved to learn that he did not cause the distress leading to Hereniskelonger's actions.

As Uzederack was about to say something further, he was interrupted by the sound of his kids screaming, "Daddy, where are you?" and "What happened to you?" and also "When are you coming home to be with us?" Turning to see a beautiful young woman holding the hands of three children, with another child on her shoulders, Cransandicki and Claire decided to give the young family some time to themselves, but before they left the room, Cransandicki asked Uzederack to write him a note about where the initiation was supposed to take place. Uzederack said he'd give it to him before they left the hospital grounds for the day.

As they left to continue Claire's therapy in another part of the hospital, an emergency warning bell went off. Relieved to learn that the bell had not come from Uzederack's hospital room, they tried to find out what the bell meant after the therapy session ended. During the next session, Claire talked to Cransandicki about what was bothering her.

After that had been resolved, they discussed other problems. As they were leaving the room, another emergency bell went off. This one was much louder than the previous bell. Deciding to investigate where this emergency warning bell was coming from, the two went down several winding corridors, and then Claire spotted the origin of the bell.

But before she could call him over, she was knocked to the ground after an explosion occurred, which had been the source of this warning bell. She picked herself up off the ground and went in search of her new friend and therapist, Dr. Oliver Cransandicki. When she found him, she noticed that he had a small cut above his right eye. She walked him over to the closest aid station she could find.

Once he had been treated for the small cut, Cransandicki and Claire asked if they could help any others who had been hurt during the attack. The head physician told them he'd be honored to have them help out. As they waited around to help with the treatment of a patient, Cransandicki felt a tap on the shoulder. When he turned around, he was amazed to see none other than Herman Uzederack himself.

Cransandicki waved Claire over and began to speak to Uzederack; he was trying to have Uzederack tell them if he heard anything more about the whereabouts of Thaddeus Hereniskelonger, the onetime Madrigald Coalition lawyer and now presumed traitor. At prodding by Cransandicki, Uzederack said that he had heard only small bits more of the whereabouts of Hereniskelonger. After Uzederack told him every sordid detail about his old friend and lawyer, Cransandicki said it might be necessary to get Hereniskelonger's older sister, Thelma Hereniskelonger Rakings-Doldrick, involved to help apprehend her brother.

When that option was presented to Uzederack, he told Cransandicki and Claire everything he had learned from his new friend, Colonel Adam Waturichan. He said he had heard that a crazed lawyer had been making maddening statements about trying to exact some kind of justice on the people who had put him in his current state of mind, and that he wouldn't stop seeking justice until the Trangelman Express had gone through with his load and had delivered his special cargo.

At the mention of the Trangelman Express, Cransandicki understood what Hereniskelonger was trying to say; if what Uzederack said was true, he'd have to get into contact with Thelma immediately, before it was too late. However, he first had to get in contact with Waturichan and inform him of the situation so they could come up with a plan to deal with the Trangelman Express, whenever it arrived on the scene.

After informing those two people of what was in the wind, Cransandicki, Uzederack, and Claire waited patiently for the Trangelman Express.

They only had to wait a couple of days before the Trangelman Express arrived; before reaching Banularaskinana, it had briefly stopped in the town of Ruskerdahlham. Cransandicki told his new colleagues not to be afraid of the Trangelman's glowing limbs, because they were just the side effects of a terrible medicinal treatment gone amok. If they stayed calm, they had a good chance of surviving an onslaught, which was more than the town of Ruskerdahlham could do.

They assured him that they were not afraid of facing the Trangelman Express. He seemed to be at peace with the knowledge that they were willing to face a possible life-or-death situation; he tried to convey to those in Banularaskinana what would happen if they failed to contain the hideous creature.

On March 1, those who had been waiting to get a glimpse of the Trangelman Express got their wishes answered. The first casualty of the Trangelman Express's attack on the town of Banularaskinana was a twenty-two-year-old private, Nathaniel Meruscchi, one of the first line of defenders. As he lay dying, Private Meruscchi saw only the glowering greenish-blue eyes of the creature as it passed the first checkpoint. As the seemingly unstoppable Trangelman Express made its way to the second line of defense, the defenders hit it with their laser blasters. However, those defenders also died from the assault by the Trangelman Express.

As the third line of defenders prepared to fire their weapons at the express, they noticed another creature coming down on their right side. The commander decided to split the third defensive line into two groups so they could fire at both creatures coming at them. However, because the third line had so many soldiers in it, it took a long time to get everyone in place and decide who would command the new sections. By the time they got it solved, the Trangelman Express and the other creature had reached their firing line.

In the ensuing mayhem, the reconfigured third defensive line faced a blazing onslaught; the two creatures made a destructive wave through the line, leaving over three thousand of the line's fifty-six-hundred-member unit dead in their wake. The line's commander, Major Horton Galdenson, headed for higher ground to transmit a warning message to the fourth defensive line about the mayhem they just faced; Galdenson told the commander of the fourth defensive line, Captain Matthias Berkindahl, to make sure his men took precise shots at the creatures.

After he received the message from Galdenson, Berkindahl made sure his men were ready for the creatures. The troops of the fourth defensive line soon saw the two creatures that had devastated the first three defensive lines.

Berkindahl decided to open up on the creatures as soon as they were in firing range; his troops didn't know how much damage they inflicted on the creatures due to the cloud of smoke from their barrage, but when the smoke cleared away, Berkindahl was shocked to see that no damage had been done to the two creatures. He told his men to reload their weapons for a second volley, but he could see that this had no effect on the creatures, either.

The commander of the fifth defensive line, Captain Archibald Mantushack, placed his troops in a triangular formation, hoping his men could hold out longer than late Captain Berkindahl had done. If they didn't, he was willing to go out in the same manner as his friend and mentor.

As the creatures approached their position, Mantushack ordered his men to open fire and to continue firing until they were told to stop. For the next ninety-two hours, they unleashed volley after volley on the creatures, but then they ran out of ammunition.

They couldn't fight the creatures with their bare fists, so Mantushack ordered his troops to retreat and get new battery packs to continue firing. Mantushack then ordered his troops to resume firing on the two creatures.

Mantushack knew he had to get his troops resupplied for another possible assault by the creatures. For the next eight days, the creatures didn't come closer than a few miles away. Mantushack was relieved that the creatures had not pushed their advantage, but he also knew this reprieve wouldn't last for very long. He ordered his troops to prepare for a renewed attack. For the next few days, they got regular updates on the positions of the two creatures.

When the creatures resumed their attack, the squad was ready for them. Alpha Team's divisional commander, Lieutenant Roger Thanderbrook, ordered his troops to fire on the creatures when they came closer, and then it seemed like the two creatures slowed down their advance. However, after looking through his special lenses, Thanderbrook noticed that instead of slowing down, the creatures were somehow becoming a single entity.

Puzzled by this fact, Thanderbrook ordered his troops to keep firing, which they did until the next morning; by this time, Mantushack sent a containment team to the region, where they would set up a lab to study the new entity if they could capture it.

The head of the containment team said they wanted to study the new entity to see what it was made of and to see if they could neutralize it without actually destroying it. Mantushack sent a message detailing his concerns with this approach to the Madrigald Coalition high command. In their response, the high command said they understood his concerns about the dangerous entity, but the council believed that if a solution could be found to bring the Fatavian Coalition to the peace treaty table, studying the entity might do the trick.

Therefore, they agreed to send the containment team all the equipment they needed to accomplish their overall objective, which was bringing peace back to the land.

The special laboratory took a long time to build. It was up and running on July 1, 2472. On August 28, the Fatavian Coalition launched a major attack against the Madrigald Coalition. The ensuing battle took place near the new science center, and over two hundred thousand soldiers were casualties.

After burying their fallen comrades, the containment team got back to work. This, however, was hard for most them because of the long battle. Some of the containment team members sought counseling by trained psychiatrists, including Dr. Oliver Cransandicki.

In March 2473, the Fatavian Coalition was in crisis mode after one of their most valued sponsors, Count Furisthal Bauspeirada Sr., died at the age of eighty-eight. After his much-publicized state funeral, the Fatavian Coalition high command began considering holding peace talks with the Madrigald Coalition. This idea was objected to by certain members of both coalitions, who were not ready to give up the fight until the last drop of blood had been spilled on the battlefield.

In fact, by this time, the entity had decided to leave the area near the new laboratory. Everyone in the containment team was shocked by the fact that their lives had been spared; they were amazed that none of the soldiers had been killed by the entity before it left the area. The head of the containment team, Major Franklin Paploskindermaus, asked for a special scientific vehicle to track the entity's i.e., Cloverdan's movements. He got what he had requested, with the condition that whenever they went out in the vehicle, an armed officer had to go with them.

On the morning of March 19, several members of the containment team drove the vehicle towards the reported location of the entity Cloverdan. Suddenly and without warning, the entity Cloverdan appeared before them. Colonel Salvatore Buricavi tried to get some physical contact with the entity; he moved ever so slowly towards the creature. He felt that if he approached it too quickly, it might scare the entity i.e., Cloverdan off.

As he moved into the entity's i.e., Cloverdan's direct line of sight, it appeared that the creature was trying to formulate words for a conversation. Buricavi ordered his top lieutenant to come up with a rudimentary communications device. The lieutenant completed the task and brought it to where the entity was; it moved away from the device, but after several minutes, it moved back towards the device.

Delighted that entity i.e., Cloverdan was ready to speak with them, Buricavi invited it to sit in a special made chair that had been brought from the lab. The entity sat down, and a rudimentary microphone was hooked up to the communications device. This allowed both speakers to talk to one another without being misunderstood.

Once the specialized equipment was turned on, the first conversation with the entity i.e., Cloverdan took place. It lasted for several hours, and when it ended, the two speakers promised to continue the conversations over the next few weeks.

When the containment team got back to the lab, they filled out a report that was handed over to the head of the containment team, who decided how to proceed without causing any more rifts within the Madrigald Coalition hierarchy. Before he made his decision, the two coalitions began a new series of battles.

The first of these skirmishes was the Battle of Trostenwald. It began on the morning of April 4 and ended nine days later. It was considered a Fatavian victory, but even though they won the battle, they lost more men in the conflagration as a whole. Upon hearing of the defeat at Trostenwald, the Madrigald Coalition high command asked the containment team to hasten their efforts and find a solution to defeat the Fatavian Coalition and force them to the peace table.

After being handed that directive by their superiors, the containment team decided to become more resolved in their dealings with the entity Cloverdan. When they began their next meeting, Colonel Salvatore Buricavi and Lieutenant Roger Halkings went over to the entity Cloverdan. As the two men approached the entity Cloverdan, it seemed to be in a dour mood. To lighten the atmosphere, they explained why they hadn't been in the area recently until now.

Accepting this answer, the entity opened up a little bit more to them, telling them he had been sent here for a purpose. He wouldn't be satisfied until he completed his mission. Buricavi asked him why he needed to complete his mission; the entity Cloverdan replied that he had been given life for it, and without getting it done, he'd be nothing.

This answer stunned Buricavi; everyone in the group was amazed that it seemed aware of its existence in the world. Halkings asked if it felt any remorse over all the deaths it had caused.

The lead scientists in the lab analyzed the entity's i.e., Cloverdan's DNA and were taken aback at what they discovered. They learned that the entity Cloverdan had several elements of the Fatavian Coalition's super weapon Dolvan in its structure; the scientists theorized that the Trangelman Express had formed a symbiotic life form love/ hate relationship with Dolvan, and it would take some doing to destroy Dolvan without hurting the new life form as well.

They developed a proposal to create a modified incubator to "hatch" for the new life form from its original host body, but in meanwhile, even as the Battle of Salamander Point temporarily cut communications with the containment team and the specialized lab. The containment team didn't get a response to their proposal for four months, by which time the entity was beginning to regret talking with the members of the containment team.

They finally heard back from their superiors in the Madrigald Coalition that they would get the incubator, along with some special helpers, for their undertaking. Buricavi and Halkings learned that the special helpers would get their own living quarters for the duration of the mission.

Instead of waiting for the Special Logistics in Warfare and Metallurgy Unit to arrive on site, Buricavi asked his engineering section to construct high-rise living quarters on a parcel of land just to the northeast of the lab's location. With both the containment teams' living quarters being just northeast of the lab, the scientific campus was taking shape. When the construction project completed, the new buildings seemed to resemble a snake in form, which people commented negatively on.

To end the criticism, the campus added a gymnasium to the site so the buildings would not look so serpentine. When the gymnasium became operational, some lab personnel promised the head engineer that they'd use it whenever they could, but at the moment, they were trying to capture the entity and extract the new life form from its original host. This was a very delicate operation, and it took them five days to complete.

Meanwhile, the entity Cloverdan noticed that the main doorway had closed. He turned and headed for another door. As he made his way to this door, it began to close, even faster than the first doorway.

The entity Cloverdan could see the men who had led him into this trap smiling; he only shrugged and headed back towards them. He accused them of lying to him about their intentions; he vowed to escape from them as soon as possible.

The team's leader apologized for the deception and promised that they wouldn't hurt him too much; they only wanted to liberate the being inside the entity Cloverdan from its original host body.

The entity Cloverdan disputed the suggestion that there were two separate beings in him, and he repeated that he'd find a way out of the lab, no matter what the cost. When the head of the lab heard this threat, he ordered the entity Cloverdan be put under restraint and kept in the special diagnostic room.

The entity Cloverdan saw slender pieces of metallic yarn stretching out towards him; as the metallic yarn got closer to him, the entity Cloverdan raised his mechanical arms towards it.

Once it was on top of him, the entity Cloverdan planned to send blazing hot fire down on the yarn, but before he could unleash it, the yarn was around his arms and legs. As he struggled to free himself, the entity Cloverdan was being pulled towards the special diagnosis room. Suddenly, he heard several of his opponents scream as they hit the marble floor in front of him. The entity Cloverdan just sighed in regret for those who had tried to restrain him.

The entity Cloverdan prepared for a new restraining technique, but nothing was done by his opponents. The entity Cloverdan wondered why not but then realized that the restraining team had given up.

He looked up and saw someone holding a very sharp knife coming after him. He tried to slink away from him, but before he knew it, the man stabbed him in his shoulder, causing his arm to become detached from his body. As he tried to put it back in place, he lost his other arm as well.

Realizing that the lab people were dead serious, he decided not to resist their demands. A few seconds later, however, both his legs had been severed from his body, and his helmeted head was in tatters on the ground next to him.

Not able to do anything, the entity Cloverdan just went where he was told to go. That afternoon, he was sitting by himself, feeling somewhat dejected by those who had mutilated his body. The entity begged to talk to anyone who would listen to him.

Around eight o'clock, the entity Cloverdan had been contacted via his radio communications unit. When he responded, he heard a smooth-sounding voice on the other end of the line. He spoke with the voice for a few hours. A little before midnight, they broke off their first conversation but resumed talking to one another the next morning at 9:30.

They talked about a range of issues, from what each was going through to what they'd like to do if things were different. The entity Cloverdan discovered that the voice on the other side of the communications unit was a lonely young woman; he promised himself that before he completed his mission, he'd meet this woman.

He offered to continue their conversations in exchange for not unleashing the mayhem on the lab he had promised. At that very generous prospect, the scientist, Dr. Tabitha Cormanday, promised to continue talking to him at whatever cost to her specific priorities with the project.

His captors delivered some food to his detention room through a panel in the door; the entity cautiously moved towards the tray of food. When he smelled the tantalizing aroma, he decided to eat the food; the entity also sensed some outside smells that seemed to enhance the flavor of the food. He took his time eating all the food, savoring every bite.

In the meantime, while the entity Cloverdan was enjoying his first meal in the detention room, the other scientists on the containment team were developing a specialized molecular listening and analyzing telescope.

After a few bugs were worked out, it was ready for action; while the entity Cloverdan rested, workers snuck the specialized telescope into his room. Alerted that it was time to eat again, the entity Cloverdan got up and ate his second meal, unaware of the specialized telescope hidden in the room. He ate this meal quickly, but he was hungry for more.

Before he could get more food to eat, an alarm on the wall sounded, as if something terrible had happened; the entity i.e., Cloverdan asked why the alarm was sounded. He learned that a Fatavian force was attacking, and a Madrigald force was being called upon to fight the Fatavian force with as much firepower as possible. While hoping he'd be being allowed out to help, he asked how Tabitha, his friend, was.

He was informed that Tabitha had been slightly injured early in the battle; while on her lunch break, she was mistaken for a soldier and had been hit in the shoulder by a hydro-electric-powered rocket-propelled grenade fragment.

Upon hearing that his friend had been injured, the entity changed color and really wanted to get involved in the fighting. Seeing that no one from the lab was willing to let him loose from his confinement to let him help out, the entity i.e., Cloverdan decided to act on his own initiative and break the bolts of the door to the detention room with his fists. He broke the first bolt with very little trouble, but the next ones were more troublesome. However, once he got all of them broken, he hit the door with all the force he could, and it fell to the ground in a very big heap. He made his way through the lab to the facility's exit.

Upon learning that the entity Cloverdan had escaped the lab unimpeded, Buricavi concluded that the entity Cloverdan had fallen in love with the female scientist; she seemed to care about his welfare instead of the containment team's. He recommended that Tabitha be kept under close supervision. When she heard that she was being scrutinized by those in charge of her assignment, Tabitha wrote critical entries in her private blog about the government's involvement in the Madrigald Coalition. However, these private criticisms didn't stay private for very long, and just before the containment team discovered how to defeat the Fatavian Coalition, the critical posts were leaked to the public.

Ashamed at the way in which her private thoughts had been made public for any and all to read, Tabitha decided to disappear for a while, until she could return to doing her job. Hearing that she wanted to go away for an undetermined amount of time, Buricavi decided to give her forty-five days to clear her head of any doubts about her mission.

Grateful to the colonel for the time off, Tabitha decided to go to a nearby recreational resort and spa. She packed her things for the nearly two months she'd be away from the lab; she wouldn't miss those who considered her a coward for her critical posts. After waving bye to those who were still talking to her, Tabitha began the long journey down the stairs that led to her makeshift living quarters, stopping occasionally to get some words of warning or thoughtful advice about her long vacation.

The young scientist received her vacation slips from the colonel, who had reluctantly approved of the vacation at the Madrigald Coalition's insistence. Promising to return refreshed and better able to get the job done, Tabitha left the lab and looked for a lift into the town of Beshemal, where the recreational resort was; however, since no one stopped to give her a lift, she decided to walk to the spa, which as only a few miles away.

When she got to the resort, she checked in and received her room key from the clerk; when she entered the room, she began to feel rested and relaxed and joyful as she looked around the big room. However, this tranquility faded after she unpacked her things; she went out onto the balcony and looked down at the grounds, where she saw three familiar faces approaching the hotel.

She recognized the three Fatavian Coalition officers and could tell they were not there for anything good; if they were there for the same thing she was there for, then she would try to sneak away from the resort as soon as possible. After seeing the three Fatavian officers move towards the resort's maintenance shed, Tabitha decided to find out what they were up to. To accomplish this without getting discovered, she recruited a specialized helper. She found this helper down at the resort's pool. His name was Cornelius Balavantish, and in exchange for dinner and dancing, he promised to find out what the three Fatavian officers were up to.

After leaving the pool, she went off to the spa part for a relaxing massage. After that, the young woman headed back to her hotel room to do a cardio workout. After completing those exercises, she headed for the resort's main dining room. Once again, she came into contact with the three Fatavian officers. She quickly ordered her food and took her dinner to go, so she wouldn't have to see them more than necessary. After getting her meal, she took it back to her room.

After she finished her dinner, Tabitha heard a loud banging on her door and assumed the worst. She got up to see who was at the door. But when she opened the door, she found a little girl standing outside her room. She asked the little girl who she was and why she was banging on her door.

Working up the courage to speak to the older woman, the girl said her name was Alice Yankering, and she needed to find her mother and father, for they had not come back to the family's hotel room. Having a kind heart, she let Alice into the room while she called the front desk to see if they knew where the girl's parents were.

As it turned out, little Alice's parents had gone out with some friends. After reuniting the little girl with her two wayward parents, Tabitha decided to have a belated breakfast in her hotel room. After eating breakfast, Cornelius Balavantish arrived and was her guest for lunch. Thus, with the two meals and with Cornelius Balavantish as company, Tabitha listened while Cornelius told her all he had learned about the three Fatavian Coalition officers.

While Cornelius devoured his food, he told Tabitha that the three Fatavian officers were waiting for word of how things were going in the area north of the lab. She asked him if he had learned anything else, and he said he didn't, but he'd be willing to find out more if she was willing to do more than just have dinner with him.

Tabitha began to get worry because she hadn't heard from her colleagues at the lab, but she felt better after hearing from Roger Paleniski, who worked with her at the lab. They talked for an hour and a half about what happened at the lab before she left for vacation, and they talked about what she had heard might be in the wind for those still at the lab. Paleniski assured her that she should not worry about anything, but she was not comforted by this. She pleaded with him to tell the officers at the lab to prepare for what was coming.

Paleniski had a hard time believing her, but he said he'd let the highest-ranking members at the lab know what was going on. After hearing this, Tabitha broke off communications with the lab and her friend Roger for the time being. Feeling like doing something fun for a change, she decided to go the resort's tennis court. Unfortunately for her, at that precise moment, her legs started to go limp for some reason.

She hadn't had any rest, so she decided to take a nap. Her legs became even more limp, so the good doctor crawled into her hotel room. She inched along to the left side of the bed and finally got into it. She was not be able to enjoy it for very long, because a little while later, she heard more pounding on her door. Tabitha knew it couldn't be another child missing his or her wayward parents, so she yelled through the door for the person to go away.

The pounding didn't stop, so Tabitha decided to take action against whoever it was. She picked up the closest object in the room and planned to hit the person with it. She opened the door with a violent thrust and saw three hungry-looking people in distress. She thought that the Fatavian officers had found what room she was in. After she slammed the lamp onto the first one's head, knocking him out cold, the other two pleaded with her not to hit them. When she realized it wasn't the three officers, she apologized for knocking out the first one, whose name, the other two said, was Randall Sershaniniski.

Upon regaining consciousness, Sershaniniski accepted her apology for hitting him; Tabitha asked what they wanted. The three men said they needed a place to stay for a little while, while their rooms were being attended to by the hotel cleaning staff. At first, she said that was impossible, but after hearing that they'd pay her for her inconvenience, she agreed.

Realizing that she could have three new helpers in her quest to find out what was going on with the Fatavian Coalition, Tabitha called the front desk and asked for three cots to be brought to her hotel room. When the cots were delivered to the room, she tipped the porters who brought them, and her three new helpers took to their beds with glee, after ordering a modest meal for themselves and their companion. After finishing her meal, she decided to go to sleep and not think about anything until the next morning.

Unfortunately, the Fatavian Coalition had been planning to attack the hotel and resort, and early the next morning, they unleashed a huge barrage on the whole area.

When Tabitha heard the explosions, she roused her three new friends from their slumber, and they hurried to the ground floor; once downstairs, they looked for anyone who needed assistance; spotting no one in immediate need of treatment, the four made it safely outside.

They found Cornelius outside the hotel. He was helping some elderly residents of a nearby house that been destroyed by the Fatavian bombardment. They asked if he needed help; he said he didn't, but if they wanted to help, they might look for Marcus Philatone, the hotel's manager, who was forming a relief program for all those affected by the Fatavian attack. So, they searched for the hotel manager.

When they found him and offered to help him with his relief program, he accepted their assistance, and they got to work. While helping with the relief program, they learned that the Fatavians had also attacked the lab.

When Tabitha heard that many of her Madrigald Coalition colleagues had suffered greatly at the hands of the Fatavians, she told her new friends that she wanted to get back at the leader of the Fatavian attack force.

When Cornelius heard how angry Tabitha was, he tried to get his friend to think more positively about what she and her companions were doing to help the victims of the latest Fatavian attack. He talked to her after they finished helping the last group of people who needed their assistance. After their talk, Tabitha realized she had to be less angry in her life.

While working on the relief program's next project, she came up with a plan to analyze the items she had found in the rubble. The analysis would be expensive, but all her money had gone up in smoke when the resort was attacked. She needed to find a generous benefactor to sponsor her. She knew she could possibly take from the relief program's coffers, but that wouldn't help her friends who had lost everything when the attack happened. She then decided to get the money by asking Yuri Paschalmeirhoff, her Remigarian uncle, for help.

Her uncle, in fact, was the deputy prime minister of Remigaria. She needs a special phone to reach him, so she borrowed Tobias Leiferman Jr.'s phone and called him.

When he answered, she explained why she called. Paschalmeirhoff was astounded to hear from his young niece and responded with the utmost tact and clarity that he could not assist her. She was somewhat dismayed by this and began to cry; her uncle then changed his mind about helping her, but the call was disconnected.

As he was about to call her back, he learned that she had called him from someone else's phone line. He then decided that whatever Tabitha was mixed up with needed investigating immediately, but with the Remigarian government in gridlock, he couldn't leave his official post. The Remigarian Empire was in utter financial and social disorder. He'd have to wait to investigate what his young niece was doing in Berasculata.

As luck would have it, as he was thinking about this, the prime minister called him into his private office to discuss what was going on. The prime minister told him that Baldanis I, the Remigarian Emperor, wanted to send a delegation to Berasculata to assess if it was safe for his youngest daughter, Princess Emily Marie Ann Sotaurius, to go and live in Berasculata as their new queen.

Paschalmeirhoff was surprised to hear this but said he'd be willing to head the delegation himself. Happy to hear that his friend was willing to go and assess the situation in Berasculata, the prime minister agreed.

The princess and the other diplomats packed their gear and headed over to the *Horned Blue Bear.* She asked how long it would take to get Berasculata, and the captain said it would take two months to reach the Berasculatan city of Mipperolanderik. Hearing this,

Paschalmeirhoff realized that he'd be late in arriving to see what his young niece and her colleagues were up to.

As the *Horned Blue Bear* sailed towards Berasculata, things were happening there that they would not know about going on around the rest of the planet Mulizan until they arrived on March 31, 2474. Upon reaching the main dock of Mipperolanderik, those who were going ashore thanked the captain of the *Horned Blue Bear* for his hospitality during the nearly ten-week trip.

Appreciative of their praise, the captain promised to send some of his security personnel to protect the diplomatic delegation on their way to Iskelvimbarkien, where they hoped to start peace negotiations. As the group began the arduous journey to Iskelvimbarkien, they encountered many people who didn't like their presence in the region. At one point in their journey, one of the Remigarians was accosted by a man who seemed to be very drunk. As the drunk man got closer and closer to her, the female diplomat called for assistance from her team members. Sergeant Cornelius Priperankenasta responded and punched the man on his face.

Feeling the sting of Priperankenasta's punch, the drunk turned and hit the young sergeant even harder than he had been struck, but just then, he was hit in the shoulder by a high-voltage taser shot by Major Kirk Hasenraker. As the drunk moved towards the group again, the major fired his taser again, hitting the drunk in both his shoulders and one of his legs.

Feeling the pain from the taser, the drunken man gave up his attack against the Remigarian diplomatic delegation. The team went on with its journey, arriving at Velausiraka around 5 p.m. They rested in Velausiraka for a couple of hours and then continued to Iskelvimbarkien, so they could prepare for peace negotiations and thus allow Princess Emily to meet her potential husband.

During the last part of their journey, the diplomats met a traffic jam of refugees. There was no way around the traffic jam, so the diplomats just waited their turn. However, after a while, the diplomatic delegation was temporarily split in sections. It would take several more minutes for the diplomats to get back together as one unit. Once back together they'd begin to continue to head towards the capital city of Iskelvimbarkien, so that the princess could meet her future husband Volerick Lobberstein II.

In the meantime, while this was going on, Frintelsham continued his stealthy pursuit of the deputy prime minister. Just as he was about to get close enough to see what he was up to; the other deputy prime minister would change direction and throw his pursuer off his trail. Frintelsham changed his direction as well, so as to make the deputy prime minister less suspicious. After a while, though, both men realized what they were doing, so they had a small conference to clear the air and allay each other's fears about what was going to happen as they got closer to Iskelvimbarkien.

As they grew closer to Ranulaskindargrose, they realized that the others had made it to the city ahead of them. Sven Gorlander, the head of the new security detail for the diplomatic expedition, told them the new security detail and the rest of the diplomatic expedition were on their way to the city of Sanamaphal. They wanted to meet with a fisherman who was willing to ferry them to Iskelvimbarkien for a small fee.

Paschalmeirhoff and Frintelsham hoped to rejoin their compatriots in Sanamaphal. To that end, they sought a raft or some other means of waterway transportation.

CHAPTER 11

SUNRISE TO PEACE

Unable to find further transportation to Iskelvimbarkien, the diplomats faced the dire prospect of not getting to the negotiation table in time to settle the matter of the whole conflict, as well as get their liege's youngest daughter married to the heir to the throne of Berasculata. Suddenly, though, someone looking on saw the situation they were in and offered to help them accomplish their goal; all he asked in return was that they did not get in the way of him earning a living. Agreeing to the terms of the captain, the diplomats boarded his ship, the *Silver Rhino,* on April 22.

Once the ship got underway, the captain, Patrick Treskalingardman, gave the passengers specific and strict instructions about what they could and could not do and what was expected of them during the journey.

However, he did not take into account that there would be raiding parties of pirates that were sponsored by what was left of the Fatavian Coalition. When he saw the pirates approaching his ship, Treskalingardman devised a course of action to deal with them. He ordered his crew to prepare for a long fight, but then he noticed that the pirates were more interested in the passengers than in the cargo holds. Treskalingardman hoped that it wouldn't come to the point of him having to choose between his ship and the lives of the passengers; he offered to let the pirates have what was in the hold.

The pirates did not want his offer of a small prize; Treskalingardman decided he had to do something dramatic to save their lives. He offered to go ashore and fight the pirate's captain. Believing he would have the upper hand in a duel with Treskalingardman, the pirate leader, Artemis Colganifordheart, agreed to the duel. Each man agreed that the duel would be honorable and dutifully watched by the two combatants' declared seconds.

The two men named their seconds, of whom would watch and monitor every move in the duel to make sure the rules were followed. After that, they prepared food and water so as to give each man strength for the duel. Once this was done, the mental part of the training for the duel began. Treskalingardman needed several training sessions to get ready for the duel, for he was out of shape mentally.

Colganifordheart was also ready for the duel, and he told his second in command that the duel should commence as soon as Treskalingardman reached Rivalender Bay Island. His second transmitted those words to the *Silver Rhino* and also stated that the captain of the *Silver Rhino* need not worry for the safety of his passengers, because they would not be harmed until after the duel.

When Treskalingardman heard that, he told his second in command, Arthur Porlenisker, that if any of the pirates came aboard the *Silver Rhino* before the duel was over, they'd get a rude awakening.

With that statement in the back of his mind, Colganifordheart decided to place the men who would go on board the *Silver Rhino* in berth canoes who were to head just south and west, thus making it less likely of them getting of spotted by the work gangs of the *Silver Rhino.* Seeing that the path towards Rivalender Bay Island was clear of any major pirate ship, Treskalingardman ordered Porlenisker to sail to the southeast end of the island and wait there for his return, and if he did not return, Porlenisker should assume command of the *Silver Rhino* and head for the nearest friendly port so the passengers could get off without incident.

When the *Silver Rhino* reached Rivalender Bay Island, Treskalingardman and his seconds got off and headed to where the duel was being held. After that, the rest of the passengers and crew of the *Silver Rhino* set sail and then waited at an agreed-upon spot where they were to meet the captain if the duel went his way. However, if things turned out differently, the passengers and crew would prepare for an attack by the pirates.

They waited for word of how the duel went for hours, but suddenly and without warning, Treskalingardman and his seconds arrived at the ship, uninjured. Porlenisker tried to find out how the duel went, but Porlenisker was only told to move quickly and without any more questions. At that order, he told his gunners to clear their ordinance bays for later service and told the rest of the men to get ready to move. Treskalingardman was already up for further travel, because just as the ship turned towards the open sea, he was on the main deck, barking out orders.

As Treskalingardman yelled for them to get farther out to sea, they heard enemy gunfire off in the distance. Treskalingardman ordered Porlenisker to have the master of arms issue weapons to every one of the crew who didn't have a sidearm and to any passengers who could help defend the ship. Two of them, Wendy Friskel and Thomas Rufeishan, offered to take arms, and they were issued proton dispersers.

Friskel asked the captain if he had tried to spare Colganifordheart's life; all Treskalingardman would say to the two new defenders of the ship was that if he hadn't tried to do the honorable thing and hit the pirate in the shoulder, he and his seconds would not be alive to defend the *Silver Rhino*.

At that response, Friskel and Rufeishan went to their defensive positions, hoping for the opportunity to use their new weapons. They didn't have to wait for very long. Upon seeing the shadowy silhouettes of their presumed enemy approaching at a modestly steady pace, Friskel and Rufeishan would open up on the presumed enemy immediately.

Half-expecting to hear cheers from their new comrades in arms, Friskel and Rufeishan were not acknowledged immediately, but after a few minutes, they did hear some words of praise. They kept aiming and shooting, as they continued to hold their own with their new colleagues. They continued to fire their weapons until suddenly, they were told to hold their fire.

Not immediately seeing anyone from the pirate unit coming at them, it was assumed that it was all clear, thus there would no order to start firing again. But then the pirates returned, and the defenders resumed firing.

As the defenders fired their weapons in short, precise bursts at the pirates, they noticed that even as they were downing one every few minutes, the pirates acted quite jolly; they could even hear someone laughing. They tried to ascertain where the laughter was coming from. Off in the distance, an individual was laughing at their predicament and attired in unusual garments. Friskel could tell her fellow defenders this man was just sitting idly by on a piece of land just east of a honey grove.

Friskel asked for permission to target this man near the honey grove; she was told that they could try it, but they had to find something to fire at him with. When she heard that, both Friskel and Rufeishan slowed down their attack on the pirates to save ammunition. They sensed he was laughing at the ship to make himself an easy target so the defenders would use up all their ammunition.

As he prepared to show them that he wasn't a real threat to their lives, those aboard the *Silver Rhino* decided to take makeshift rafts and go where he had positioned himself. When he saw them coming for him in a not-so-friendly manner, the man decided that since those on the *Silver Rhino* were not ready to make friends with him, he'd show them the full fury of his being. As the capturing party got closer to him, the man began to set up traps and other defensive devices; if his would-be captors got through the traps, he'd give them their just deserts.

Most of the traps were easily defeated by the team sent to capture the man. After they got past the last of the man's defenses, they edged closer, carefully and cautiously. They decided to capture him alone, so they tried to avoid as much direct contact with him as possible.

The man sensed that these pursuers were trying to avoid direct physical and visual contact with him, so he made himself somewhat invisible to them. However, although he hid his physical form, he could not hide his emotions, which seemed to give off a very prominent glow to his pursuers. Seeing that his plan to get away wasn't going as he had hoped, the man decided to try something more dramatic. He had to do it soon, for his pursuers were getting closer; otherwise, he had no other alternative but to surrender and then try to figure something out once he was in their hands.

As he contemplated what he should do, he heard some of the pursuers shouting at each other. He listened to what they said and realized there were some in the group who wanted to capture him and sell him to the pirates in the area; others were having second thoughts about this plan. When he realized this, the man decided not to do any real harm to those individuals.

The man also heard other voices of men who also wanted to sell him into slavery. The man decided to punish them with the full fury of his being. However, as he prepared to unleash his fury, the man was struck by something that hit him before he could react.

His cloaking device had been nullified, and he also lost the ability to move freely, with many of his joints tied up by high-density chains of some unknown metallurgy.

He asked why he had been trapped in chains like he was a slave; a man told him that he was to consider himself the proud and worthy prize of the Cosaverkian People's Alliance. The man asked who they were and what they wanted from him.

The individual only repeated that he was the proud and worthy prize of the Cosaverkian People's Alliance. Still not satisfied with this response, the man asked who the Cosaverkian People's Alliance was and what they wanted him to do.

After hearing the same response to his questions, the man realized that these people had very little respect for the dignity of others. Sensing that the man was not going to listen to any commands to get going towards the ship that he had procured, the individual tugged on the chain until the man came over to where he was standing.

When he reached this individual, the man asked him why he had tugged on the chain so hard. At that question, the individual remarked that it was not the nature of Hashenvendelhorn Prissendorhock to discuss his reasons for bringing his captured bounty to his friends and family with such ferocity, as long as the goods were not damaged in any way and were profitable to all concerned.

The man was amazed that even with his limited intelligence, the individual had been able to capture him without truly understanding what he was doing. The man decided to take pity on the individual, once he showed him some kindness and told his name.

The individual said he already gave his name, and the man understood that Hashenvendelhorn Prissendorhock was his name.

Assuming he would not be given a reprieve from his persistent captor, the man told him his name, Alakona Kristolanger, and said that he had a most peculiar thing happen to him, besides of course becoming enslaved in chains. Hashenvendelorhorn asked what had happened, and Alkona replied that had recently been caught in a stasis cube on Kakoria.

Hashenvendelorhorn believed what he had been told and asked Alakona why he wasn't still there living off the generosity of the populace of Kakoria. How did he happen to appear here at this moment and at this exact spot on the Mulizani world?

Alakona told Hashenvendelorhorn that he wasn't exactly a Kakorian scientist but a Werpian glade cutter. Hashenvendelorhorn laughed at that explanation and said that Alakona couldn't have come here if he were just a simple glade cutter.

Alakona grew upset that Hashenvendelorhorn was laughing at him; he decided he would not speak or move, as Hashenvendelorhorn was trying to make him do. So even when Hashenvendelorhorn stopped laughing and began to move towards the ship, Alakona decided that even if Hashenvendelorhorn tugged on the chain as hard as he could, he wasn't going to move.

When he felt a lack of movement coming from his prisoner's direction, Hashenvendelorhorn tugged even harder on the chain, thus hoping to get his prisoner moving. When nothing occurred, Hashenvendelorhorn wondered if the chain was weakening its grip somehow. He decided to go back and investigate.

He headed back to Alakona, who was holding the main link of the chain; at first glance, he couldn't see anything wrong with the chain, but as he got closer to where Alakona was standing, he felt something very troubling coming from the young Werpian glade cutter (although he doubted this claim).

When he came near Alakona, he asked the young Werpian glade cutter why he wasn't moving. Alakona replied that he did not like being disrespected by anyone, and two, he was doing his cryogenic exercises.

Hashenvendelorhorn seemed somewhat puzzled at that response, and he asked what these cryogenic exercises were and what they had to do with heading to the ship he had risked his life to procure. Alakona decided to tell him what the exercises were all about and why he had stopped walking.

Alakona told him why he had stopped walking and explained about the exercises, which he said he had to complete before they could to the ship. After he completed the exercises, Hashenvendelorhorn promised that he would give him more freedom to move around without pain.

Alakona said he appreciated having the freedom to walk around. Hashenvendelorhorn walked back to the front of the chain and tugged on the binders more gently. Upon resuming their journey, Alakona asked Hashenvendelorhorn if he'd hurt any of his competitors for the rights to bring him back to his home country.

Hashenvendelorhorn told him he hadn't killed anyone back on the hill where Alakona had been waiting, but he had to walk as much as he could with each and every tug on the chain. Suddenly, there was not much of a tug back from the chain, and Alakona decided to investigate. To do that, he had to walk up to where Hashenvendelorhorn had been.

Alakona walked slowly, with less of a wiggle of the restraining chain than normal for Hashenvendelorhorn. Alakona reached where his captor should have been, but he didn't see him. He began to feel alone because even though he didn't like being enslaved, he felt like he was losing a kindred spirit, because Hashenvendelorhorn seemed more like a friend than an enslaver. However, as he began to grieve over the loss of his newfound friend of sorts, Alakona could see people he knew from when he had been on the little hill, planning his revenge for possible enslavement; this made him feel slightly uneasy.

The matter was cleared up a few minutes later. The small contingent of the people were asking one another how to punish the Cosaverkian People's Alliance for their cruelty towards the little guy. When he tried to talk to them about it, they said they'd discuss it with him later.

As he waited for them to talk to him, Alakona hoped that his new friend, Hashenvendelorhorn, wasn't being mistreated physically like he was being mistreated mentally. Finally, they sent for Alakona and asked what he thought should be done with Hashenvendelorhorn. The man asking him this looked like a Remigarian politician, judging by his clothing; he also noticed that his shirt didn't have any army insignia attached to it.

He said that he had no definitive opinion since he hadn't arrived in the area by normal means of transportation. Understanding the whimsical connotations of that response, the man asked for Alakona's opinion again.

After being asked a second time if he had an opinion on the situation in the area, Alakona told the Remigarian politician that he was just a simple Werpian glade cutter who had made a mistake that he was now regretting because of all the trouble he came across because of it.

The Remigarian politician asked Alakona a third time what his opinion was; he felt that this person was just stonewalling him and not giving his true feelings on the matter. Alakona repeated his answer.

The Remigarian politician was surprised that his young guest was not willing to discuss the situation in Berasculata, but he decided to let the issue drop for now. Soon after that, the Remigarian politician left the tent. Once more alone, with no one to talk to, Alakona decided to go on a little scouting trip. To do this, he needed some supplies. However, to get the supplies, he had to find the encampment's supply sergeant.

However, the supply sergeant couldn't help him, because he appeared to be doing something other than supplying the encampment's personnel with their gear. Rather than get involved with the supply sergeant, Alakona decided to go to the makeshift mess tent and get some food.

As he walked towards the mess tent, Alakona sensed something wasn't right. He stretched out his aerocolanginatial sense processors; if anything was slightly off in the general vicinity of the mess tent, he would know of it right away. The processors could not pick out anything amiss, so Alakona went in to get some food.

He walked up to where they were dishing out bowls of food and asked for a huge mashering of everything available. After the servers gave him what he asked for, he went over to the woman who was collecting money for the food.

Alakona realized that he had no money to pay for the food, so he wrote a very long promissory note to the woman. The woman, a stout lady at least fifty years old, accepted the promissory note and told him she expected him to fulfill everything he promised.

He said he would live up to everything he stated in the promissory note, so she let him eat his meal in peace and quiet. Alakona searched high and low for a table where he could sit and eat. He couldn't find a table to sit at; he seemed doomed to eat his meal standing up on his already tired legs.

He stood in the middle of the mess tent, waiting for someone to get up from one of the tables. It seemed no one was in the mood to give up their seat, so Alakona decided to eat his meal before it got cold. As he tried to situate the bowl of food while eating from it, someone came over and said he couldn't eat his food standing in the middle of the mess tent.

Alakona asked the man where he should eat the food; the man, Corporal Atergeld Wagglesmont Jr., said he didn't care where Alakona ate his food, he just couldn't eat in the middle of the dining area, because it would be quite rude to the other diners.

After the young corporal told him what was proper and what was not proper, Alakona explained that even though it might be rude for the people coming into the mess tent to walk around him, he had tried to find a place to eat his meal in peace and quiet, without any success.

The corporal became more abrasive and told the younger Werpian glade cutter that if he had really tried to find a place to eat his meal in, they wouldn't be having this conversation at all. Assuming that young corporal was trying to say that he was a slacker, Alakona took it as an affront to his honor and told the corporal that when he was done eating, he'd be glad to fight for what was right and wrong to say to someone.

When Wagglesmont heard that the glade cutter wanted to duel him over something so trivial in nature, he laughed it off as just false bravado. He then said in a mocking tone that he'd be willing to duel him if he could find a pair of seconds who were as brave as the young Werpian glade cutter and would accept the duel's result, no matter who won. Seeing that the young corporal was trying to say that it would be foolish for both men to fight the duel, Alakona tried to decide what to say to his demeaning comments.

As he considered his answer to the young corporal, Alakona could hear some off-the-cuff snickering from outside the mess tent. Hoping that the snickering was just in his mind, Alakona decided to give a very stout-hearted response. As he began to open his mouth, he heard some loud banging around the mess tent. After it stopped, Alakona began to wonder who was doing the banging.

After finishing his meal in relative peace and quiet, Alakona left the mess tent. As he walked away from the mess tent, he happened upon the young corporal, who was lying on the ground, covered in blood. Realizing that they had been bombed, Alakona looked to see if the young corporal was alive or dead. If he was dead, he would need a quick burial, so as to not let anything disturb the young corporal's ascent to the great barracks in the sky. When he bent down to see if the young corporal still had a spark of life left in him, he discovered he did not.

To his best guess, it had been a short and painless death for the corporal, and he felt it was his duty to bury him with as much respect as possible. Having no digging equipment on hand, Alakona used his arms and legs to begin digging the grave. When he was sure it was big enough to hold the young corporal's corpse, he put the body into the grave.

As he put the corporal into the hastily constructed grave, Alakona felt pity for the soldier, although he had only known him for a short time. He looked at the grave and noticed it didn't have a headstone or marker to tell who was buried there. To show people there was a grave there, he outlined it with sticks and rocks. This part was not to be too difficult, because as luck would have it, there was a granite quarry nearby, and next to the quarry was an apple orchard. The owner of the orchard had scribbled a sign that he was looking for someone to pull out some nasty weeds that were overgrowing the orchard. He'd allow the right person to remove the trees that were rotten out for their own purpose, no questions asked.

This was a good chance to use the skills he had acquired during his time on Kakoria; Alakona decided to take a chance and get the wood he needed for the grave marker. He headed as fast as he could to the orchard owner's residence to see about the weeding job, but when he arrived, he saw several other people with small children waiting outside the orchard owner's house. He was somewhat disappointed that he had not arrived sooner but didn't want to be seen as an ogre by those who needed the work both financially as well as spiritually, more than he needed to build the young corporal's grave. He decided to leave quietly before the orchard owner told them they had to go somewhere else to find food and work, just like he'd been told by many Kakorian landowners that he had to find work elsewhere because there were no jobs in the whole of Kakoria.

But before he got away from the house, the door swung wide open, and an elderly couple appeared at the front step. They called Alakona over to speak with him about the vast number of people gathered around to get jobs and gesturing to him to join those looking for work; he turned and joined a group of people looking to get ready to pull the weeds out of the apple orchard.

After several groups had been formed to weed the orchard, the couple headed back into the house to begin preparing lunch for their newly formed work crews. There were four work crews, and each crew elected a superior officer and an executive committee, who were in charge of seeing that the weeds had been sufficiently removed and determine what maintenance was needed to ensure that the orchard owner and his wife had a weed-free harvest to share with their neighbors.

After getting those issues worked out, each group was given a specific name and designation. Each work group was responsible for a specified area of the orchard, and the other groups were not to interfere with another section unless called to do so. For example, Alakona and his crewmates could not work the weeds in Company Yastenero Section Alpha 1 without their permission. And no one from Yastenero could work on weeds in Company Ziperno Section Beta 1 without their permission.

As the hastily proscribed foreman of the newly formed weed workers unit, Alakona decided to divide the workers into several small groups. As they began clearing the weeds, they heard a terrible rumbling coming from the south end of the orchard.

The workers seemed worried about what was making the noise, but Alakona told them that if there was any danger coming from that area, then those who were attacking the main orchard wouldn't attack them. Agreeing with his logic, the workers got back to their tasks. After they cleared the last remnants of the northern part of the orchard, he called out to other workers, but they did not answer. He got a little worried, but after a while, they chimed in with their responses.

Alakona told them that he'd meet them in their assigned area. They were happy to see him; in fact, they said that without his leadership, the weeding would not have been completed. Feeling honored by what they told him, Alakona promised that if there was any danger from attackers, he would give them whatever protection they needed. When the workers heard that, they promised to make sure nothing serious happened to him. Alakona promised to treat them to a meal once they got back to the main house.

As Alakona and the workers approached the orchard owner's house, they saw several armored vehicles in the driveway; it wasn't safe for them to go to the main house. As they tried to stay clear of the armored vehicles with their weeding equipment, a very stern-looking man appeared and told them to come over to where he was.

They told the soldier, Sergeant Asterrosles Rizzelenicher, they would come over to him after they put away their weeding equipment; Rizzelenicher said he did not care what they were doing, he wanted to talk to them that very moment, adding that he would not be talked back to by a couple of gardeners.

Alakona decided not to correct the soldier about their status as weed workers, but he reiterated that they would talk to him only after they put away their equipment. Rizzelenicher, who was getting angrier by the minute, said he wouldn't let them go until he talked with each of them in turn. Alakona told the soldier that he and his fellow workers had to return their weed whacking equipment before they could talk to him.

Rizzelenicher was now in full rage at their refusal to comply with his orders; he turned to some other soldiers and told them to block Alakona and the workers from returning their equipment to the silo, where it was to be stored until the next harvest time.

Alakona decided they should not get into a fight with these young soldiers, and they turned and headed towards Rizzelenicher, even though they didn't like him very much at all.

The workers passed the young soldiers and arrived in front of Rizzelenicher. They were all smiling, and Rizzelenicher asked why they were smiling. They told him they hadn't seen so many horse buckets in a while. The sergeant was stunned by this cryptic response; he looked around the grounds but saw only his men and their armored vehicles.

When he realized that he was being ridiculed by these men, he told a soldier to find out who the leader of the unit was and strike the man in the face to show that the sergeant was displeased by such disrespect. The soldier, Corporal Slaine Jaurosin, asked one of the workers who the leader of the unit was, but he responded that each of them was the leader in their own right. Jaurosin then told another officer to come forward with a very long metal beam.

The other officer brought over the metal beam, and then Jaurosin threatened to dole out the justice that Rizzelenicher had ordered, to show the workers not to disrespect the armored artillery units of General Ulstanagard Hantabolvia.

When they saw the large metal beam, the eighteen workers said they wouldn't divulge the name of their leader. When they heard that, the Fatavian group leaders ordered his soldiers to put the beam on the arms of the workers, and they wouldn't be allowed to let it drop until they gave their leader's name.

Realizing that if they were going to get through this torment of the large metal beam, they all decided to think about whatever made their life bearable and just concentrate on that. Alakona sent them a signal, and they gave him a wave and a nod of their heads to show they would follow his lead.

The soldiers hoisted the large metal beam onto the workers using a hastily constructed anchoring system. After the beam was in place, Jaurosin motioned for his underlings to move away from the eighteen stubborn men, as he called them.

As the soldiers moved away from them, Alakona and the workers realized that the beam was meant to make them tell who the leader of the unit was and also to see which one of them would be the first to drop from the weight of the beam. With that information in the backs of their minds, they thought hard about their lives before all of this had started. As the minutes turned into hours, Alakona and the workers did their best not to show the anguish at holding the large metal beam in their hands.

In one instance, the beam started to sag at one end of the line of workers; it rose in the middle before drooping again at the other end of the line. Realizing that the workers might need something to drink to keep their stamina up, Alakona pleaded with the soldiers for something to drink. When they did not answer his plea, he decided to shoulder more of the beam on his own shoulders.

Seeing that Alakona was taking on more of the burden, the other workers decided that they could not let him shoulder any more than what was necessary; they appreciated the compassion and encouragement he had shown them during this very difficult and trying time. When Jaurosin came over to see what effect the beam was having on the prisoners, he saw that they were holding the beam up above their heads.

He called Rizzelenicher over to show what was happening with the beam; the sergeant merely muttered under his breath was that it should not be possible for anyone to hold up a three-thousand-pound metal beam without straining. Rizzelenicher decided to add more beams to the weight the prisoners must shoulder.

As they added more beams onto the workers, Alakona and the others used their overall strength to hold up all the beams. Rizzelenicher told them in a mocking way that if they somehow kept this amount of weight up, he might be willing to let them have some nourishment while he thought up some other type of torture to get their respect. After saying this, he told Jaurosin to come over and guard the workers with a blaster, just in case they broke free from the beams.

Jaurosin positioned a trooper to guard the workers and then set up a specialized tent to protect the trooper from the weather while he made sure the workers did not escape.

The trooper, Julius Borenilandoffer, moved under the tent with his field equipment. As he guarded the workers, something happened that he did not expect.

What occurred was that as the eighteen prisoners held the weight of the metal beams without much strain, the anchoring contraption was lifted higher above the ground. It didn't seem to bother the prisoners, and Borenilandoffer told them they shouldn't try to damage the anchoring contraption because of all the work that had gone into its conception. They replied that they wanted to damage it to make sure there were no more means of torture imposed on them; the trooper just laughed and said that if they didn't stop, he'd be forced to shoot them without hesitation.

When they heard that threat, the workers decided that if they were about to be shot at, they would try to pull the anchoring contraption apart anyway.

The trooper looked around to see if they returned the anchoring contraption to its original position, but he saw the opposite. He was amazed that despite his threat of bodily harm, the workers continued to lift the anchoring contraption even higher, determined to put it out of commission.

Borenilandoffer knew he couldn't shoot all of them without putting himself in danger, so he asked his fellow troopers to help subdue the eighteen prisoners.

Initially, no one came forward to help control the prisoners, but after seeing the anchoring contraption rise higher and higher with each thrust from the prisoners, Borenilandoffer grew more worried about what might happen next; if the anchoring contraption was damaged, not only he but all those with him might die in the confrontation.

Borenilandoffer told his fellow troopers that if they did not help him, they might not live much longer. Several of the older troopers came over to see what was going on. Although these troopers did not want to take part in the confrontation at first, they got involved in a most unexpected way, and there was no way for them to back out of it now.

When they saw that the anchoring contraption and weights were being pulled out, the troopers decided to join Borenilandoffer's efforts. They took up positions to help him fire upon the prisoners if things did not return to normal. The breeze began to blow stronger, and the anchoring contraption began to tilt in the wind, even as the prisoners were trying to keep their own composure and make the whole thing a boomerang of sorts to be hurl at the soldiers. Suddenly, the wind got even stronger and more violent, and the contraption began to fall.

Perplexed by what was happening, Borenilandoffer began firing on the prisoners without warning; they tumbled to the ground in varying places. When the whole contraption finally stopped moving altogether, Borenilandoffer felt he and his other troopers had done their duty and hoped the prisoners would stop resisting. Unfortunately, that didn't happen, because just before he discharged his weapon, his commanding officer, Corporal Jaurosin, had walked into his line of fire to avoid the falling contraption.

Distraught at killing his commanding officer, Borenilandoffer hoped he had at least killed or maimed some of the prisoners. Unfortunately for him, only one of the prisoners had been injured in the calamity. Borenilandoffer promised he'd get back at the prisoners for making him kill his commanding officer.

As they moved the wreckage away from where it had landed, Borenilandoffer could see that Jaurosin's wound was visible, and he couldn't let the sergeant see, or else he would tell the general that a trooper had caused the death of Jaurosin, a far distant cousin of the general.

Deciding to do something to make the wound less obvious, Borenilandoffer pulled out a tool and began cleaning up the wound; a fellow trooper came by and told him that while he making the corporal ready for burial, the sergeant had instructed the other troopers to move the prisoners they had captured recently and also the prisoners they had captured earlier. It was rumored that general needed every soldier of his overall command for the upcoming battle.

Borenilandoffer knew he only had a few more minutes to clean up the corporal's body. As he finished, the troopers were ordered to get whatever they needed from the orchard's main buildings and join the general's forces for what was rumored to be a major offensive.

With that in the back of his mind, Borenilandoffer decided he had done the best he could to make the late corporal look presentable for burial. He then gathered what was left of his gear and rejoined the other troopers. After a while, he caught up with his friend, Stroman Silas Paschendelhouser, because as he had quickly gathered up his gear for battle, Stroman had gotten sick after eating too much food.

He told friend Stroman that when they caught up to the others in their group, they could ask the sergeant what had happened back at the orchard. Stroman said he was not worried about what happened at the orchard, but something happened to him in the town of Aperazankiienada.

Silas said that he had gotten into a small scrape with a man who said he didn't like how the Fatavian Coalition was dealing with the Madrigald Coalition. At that revelation from his friend, Borenilandoffer asked if anything else was on his mind. Silas opened up more about how he was feeling about the Berasculatan War.

As they caught up with the others in their group, Borenilandoffer discussed some disturbing things that the artillery units under the general's overall command planned to do with the prisoners if the Fatavian Coalition won the war.

After a while, Stroman Silas said that someone was coming towards them, but he couldn't tell which side he was on.

The Fatavian Coalition troopers moved closer towards the person and tried to see his military insignia. They could see that he had a military insignia, but they couldn't tell from which coalition. They got even closer and half-expected the man coming towards them to tell them to surrender their arms; the two troopers prepared for the moment when they'd have to shoot the person to save their own lives.

Fortunately for the two troopers, the man coming towards them was a friendly; by now, he was waving at them to come towards him Rizzelenicher. Happy that it was one of their own comrades, the two ran towards the man with as much enthusiasm as could be expected, considering the situation they were facing.

When they reached the man, they told him they would be proud to work with him on the Fatavian Coalition's main front line in the upcoming battle. The man was proud to hear that both troopers wanted to be under his command, but he knew that wasn't possible. The Fatavian Coalition had a shortage of able-bodied troops, due to their recent losses and also because there were not a lot of cadets graduating from the academies.

So even though he wanted to have both troopers under his command during the upcoming battle, he could only keep one of them, and the other would have to report to Sergeant Hiram Haspenickhoffercaldot of General Sangeld Kiswather Jr.'s command.

When Borenilandoffer heard that he'd be joining Haspenickhoffercaldot's command, he decided to say goodbye to his friend and give him something to take with him, in case something happened to him. Somewhat taken aback by this request, Rizzelenicher said it would be okay.

After he saw the two troopers exchange gifts in their way of saying goodbye to one another, Rizzelenicher decided to get into the act; he gave Borenilandoffer something to give his wife, just in case something happened to him.

When Borenilandoffer met Sergeant Hiram Haspenickhoffercaldot, his new NCO, he commented on the trooper's unmilitary decorum. Borenilandoffer explained the reason for his unmilitary appearance, and the sergeant allowed him to get cleaned up before the battle. He asked the sergeant where he could shave and change from his dirty uniform.

Haspenickhoffercaldot assigned Trooper Jerome Nawendelhausercan to show Borenilandoffer where he could shave and change his uniform for the upcoming battle. He hoped the rumors of a major offensive were true, since their commander, General Sangeld Kiswather Jr., wouldn't send them to this area unless there was a battle being planned.

Borenilandoffer asked the other trooper to show him where he could change. Nawendelhausercan said he'd show him and also tell him what else needed to be done to become a valued member of the artillery unit.

Borenilandoffer thought that Nawendelhausercan wanted nothing to do with him, but because Haspenickhoffercaldot told him to get cleaned up for the rumored future battle, he decided to wait off to the side while Nawendelhausercan chatted with his pals in the artillery unit. As their conversation continued, Borenilandoffer began to sing a song he learned growing up on the plains of Coerinadakerhaus in Vistrabia.

Immediately after he began singing, Nawendelhausercan broke off his conversation with his pals and said that if he wanted to make friends, he shouldn't keep singing that song, which made them all uncomfortable.

At that suggestion, Borenilandoffer stopped singing, and he then asked if he could get cleaned up before reporting to Sergeant Haspenickhoffercaldot's tent.

Borenilandoffer explained that he was not getting cleaned up for a field parade; he needed to look presentable to the sergeant so he would see he wasn't a bum. He wanted to be given a combat position in the rumored upcoming fight. Nawendelhausercan told him it wouldn't take long to get cleaned up for presentation to the sergeant for inspection.

However, as he was getting cleaned up, word came down that the battle had begun. There wasn't time for General Sangeld Kiswather Jr.'s troops to prepare for the long trek to the site of the battle for control of Berasculata.

Nawendelhausercan told Borenilandoffer to hurry up so they wouldn't be late for formation to begin the march towards the battle site. When Borenilandoffer finished getting cleaned up, he left the tent before buttoning up his uniform. A few onlookers came by and pointed out that several of his buttons were undone. After he buttoned them up, Nawendelhausercan asked Borenilandoffer why his uniform's buttons were not fully buttoned up.

Borenilandoffer said he didn't want to seem like a mother hen. He also didn't want to feel like a fool by telling a fellow trooper how he should dress himself. At that response, Nawendelhausercan told his new comrade that if they ever saw one another on the street back home, they wouldn't make eye contact with one another, because he didn't like someone making him feel like a fool in front of others.

Borenilandoffer said he was sorry for being such a burden to his new comrade and he hoped they wouldn't be assigned to the same spot in the line; if anything happened to either of them, he wouldn't expect them to help one another out in the battle.

Unfortunately, they were assigned to the same point in the line of battle formation, and they were forced to look out for one another.

As the battle got under way, their side launched the first salvos in an attempt to draw out the Madrigald Coalition's calvary and the infantry units of General Benjamin Hasopwarich. Under the command of Lieutenant Isovennoblia Waturichan, the calvary and infantry units of Colonel Gustavus Nawanki met the threat of the Madrigald gunners and tried to take them out. Unfortunately for him, they couldn't get to the Madrigald gunners because of the arrival of Remigarian calvary.

When General Furisthal Bauspeirada III saw the Remigarian calvary on the field of battle, he became confused, because they had been told that the Remigarian Imperial Armed Forces would not be involved in this military operation. However, they suddenly showed up, and then it hit him like a bolt of lightning: The Remigarian emperor wanted to his youngest daughter to marry the rumored new king of Berasculata, Volerick Asthonincald Lobberstein, the great-great-grandnephew of the late king. If that were the case, he'd have to do something dramatic as more soldiers appeared on the side of Hasopwarich's forces.

Bauspeirada did not want to be defeated by a force of newcomers to the war, so he asked General Sangeld Kiswather Jr., his family's long-established friend and comrade in arms, for help in trying to dislodge the Remigarian calvary from the field of battle. Kiswather said he would do as much as possible. To do that, he had to move one of his artillery units to support their advance on Haspowarich and the Remigarian calvary to get close enough to launch his assault.

Not mincing words, the general told his friend and comrade in arms that if he wanted to do something spectacular, he needed to protect their joint advance right away, because he would order his troops into the field battle when the need arose. At that mild tongue lashing by his friend, General Furistahl Bauspeirada III did as directed and called up the artillery unit to help support Haspenickhoffercaldot's advance.

When he was informed that his artillery unit was to help in the advance of the assault being directed at the forces of Hasopwarich and his Remigarian reinforcements, Haspenickhoffercaldot took it all in surprisingly good spirits. He told his lead deputy, Corporal Aulden Friskendahlabermback, that all of the troopers under their command would meet the enemy head on; they were to face their fate with as much grit as possible.

Friskendahlabermback had little military experience in the field of battle, so he told his troopers to only bring their field packs with them and not the heavy cannon, because in his opinion, they would not need it all. He believed there wouldn't be time to bring it up and get into position. So as the overall commanders in the assault looked on from the heights where Hasopwarich was positioned with his men and their Remigarian reinforcements, Colonel Waturichan's artillery units prepared to fire on the Fatavians; thus, the battle began.

The assaulting group was greatly decimated by huge amounts of firepower being lobbed on them by the Gorgadalian gunners. When Bauspeirada saw that he could not win the fight, he ordered a general retreat, but he told Haspenickhoffercaldot's artillery unit to stay and cover the retreat. He realized that he needed their expertise if they were to survive the war. However, he didn't know that the sergeant had fallen in the battle; as he was positioning his men to fight, he had been killed by an enemy sniper. Even so, Haspenickhoffercaldot's troopers began firing their weapons in a show of force. Unfortunately for them, a larger force was heading their way, and this army had more men than they did.

Not wanting to be slaughtered by this larger force, Borenilandoffer ordered his fellow troopers to surrender to the new unit coming towards them. Not knowing if they should follow this order, many good troopers died in the minor skirmish that followed. However, as their numbers dwindled, the rest of the artillery unit surrendered. They were told that they would be surrendering their arms to the Berasculatan Royal Armed Forces of King Volerick Lobberstein II.

CHAPTER 12

BEGINNING OF THE RETURN TO MONARCHY

After they that is the former Fatavian forces surrendered to the forces of the Berasculatan Royal Armed Forces, Trooper Julius Borenilandoffer and the other members of the artillery unit were marched off to their prison camp to await word of what was to happen to them. As the day wore on into night, without anyone telling them what was happening, there was a sudden series of movements coming towards the prison camp's metal fence, which had been set up to make it hard for the incarcerated troopers to escape.

As the movements got louder and came closer to the prison camp, the incarcerated troopers half-expected to see a firing squad approach the prison camp and call them into the field and shoot them dead for their actions in the war. Fortunately for them, there was no such firing squad.

Instead of a firing squad, the soldiers were escorting a group of civilians over to the main gate of the prison camp; the gate opened, and the people came in. After the civilians made their way into the prison camp, the gate was closed. Borenilandoffer wondered where the civilians would reside, as the huts they lived in were all full.

He decided to investigate the matter. He cautiously went over to the civilians, who were gathered in a circle near the prisoners' huts. He asked the civilians why they were near the huts he and his associates had been assigned, and one of them said that was the order of the prison camp commander, Lieutenant Atermis Sawenikford. It seemed that

Sawenikford wanted to be able to talk to the civilian prisoners from time to time, and this way, they'd be near his own living quarters. This appalled Borenilandoffer, who asked the civilian prisoner where the military prisoners were supposed to live. Naturally, he didn't know; he only knew where his fellow prisoners where to reside.

After hearing that answer, the young trooper headed back to the rest of his group. As he walked, he noticed someone in Madrigald Coalition military fatigues moving towards him. He assumed the man was a guard and moved a few steps to his right to get out of his way.

He was about to say something friendly to the guard, but then the guard spoke to him in a not-so-friendly way. He told the trooper that he had no right to talk to the civilian prisoners without permission. Doing so could get all the military prisoners confined to their huts, and they could be further punished by not getting any nice care packages from their loved ones.

At that threat, Borenilandoffer asked the guard why they would keep the military prisoners incommunicado from their loved ones.

The guard's threat made him only more determined to get whatever was coming from his loved ones. He told the guard that he wanted to tell his fellow prisoners what he had said, and he asked if he could tell them in private.

The guard, whose name was Private Calvin Rensolanderminda, agreed to let the prisoner have a private conversation with the other former troopers, but he said that he'd return when from his superior, Corporal Matthias Bindelhaven, ordered him to. At that assurance, Borenilandoffer said he would not do anything to make the private look derelict in his duties.

When he heard this, Rensolanderminda headed away from the trooper, who finally made it back to his fellow prisoners.

Upon hearing that the other troopers were willing to do whatever it took to make life in the prison camp more comfortable for both them and the civilian prisoners, Borenilandoffer promised that if they made it through the final weeks of the war, he'd arrange it that those who had surrendered with him wouldn't suffer any dishonor at the hands of their superiors in the Fatavian Coalition. The other military prisoners said they'd do whatever he asked them to do. Amazed by their loyalty to him, Borenilandoffer said he'd be only too happy to accept their kind help, if necessary.

Little did they know that they'd have to help one another sooner rather than later, because while they were discussing what they were going to do about the emotional conditions they faced, they still had to resolve what they were going to do about their physical living conditions while in captivity as prisoners of the Madrigald Coalition and their royal Berasculatan allies.

To that end, the camp guards were to lead the military prisoners to their new living quarters on the other side of the compound. As they were being led to their new quarters, one of the troopers remarked to Borenilandoffer, "Even as we are being herded into our new quarters, we can't forget that even though our old living quarters were not lavish, at least we are to be shown how to be pigs on stilts because as you can see from being marched over here by these Madrigald Coalition hyenas, our new quarters are downright awful."

After seeing their new quarters for the first time, the other troopers felt the same. Once again, Borenilandoffer stepped forward in his leadership role and told his fellow troopers that if they were to survive this ordeal, they should try not to look at the current conditions of the new living quarters; instead, they could fix up their quarters as best as can be, so that if they were able to escape, they might get away and head back to their individual homelands.

At that suggestion, the troopers who were now prisoners of the Madrigald Coalition promised to do what he asked, thus making a very peaceful transition to the current situation; they all hoped they'd have a chance to achieve that goal at the end of their individual incarcerations.

When he heard that the prisoners wouldn't try to escape from their captivity, Sergeant Thibbel Sanderankin tried to get the work crews special tools to beautify the area where they lived. It took a while to hear back from the head of construction assigned to clean up the area.

The sergeant told the guards they should gather the military prisoners near the new living quarters while they clearing, painting and rehabbed the area. To that end of thinking, the guard told the sergeant that they would set up the military prisoners in a spot where there was sort a channel near it; they wouldn't be able to trudge very far through the channel because the water wasn't deep enough for them to swim away to freedom.

As the guards put them on long, thin logs in the channel, the military prisoners could see large vehicles approaching the site of their new living quarters. As the sergeant had said, the vehicles carried work crews who would do what they could to make their new living quarters suitable for the housing of military prisoners.

After several minutes, they found out why these military transportation vehicles had brought fighting troops to where the new living quarters were being set up: their sole purpose was watching the troopers captured in the latest battle.

After conferring with his direct supervisor, Lieutenant Sawenikford, about what he was told by the officer in charge of the convoy of military vehicles, Sergeant Sanderankin ordered the guards to lead the military prisoners about three-quarters of a mile away from their new living quarters. When the guards said they had to move again, the prisoners said they were really not pleased about leaving the area.

The sergeant led the new detail of prison camp staff and their captives three-quarters of a mile to a small farming village. At the far southeastern edges of the farming village, the prison detail again built new living quarters for the sentries and the military prisoners.

The head of the construction consortium told the sergeant that while he had been informed about their latest relocation, it would take some time to assign work crews to the task, because the original crew had been ordered to build a maintenance depot as soon as possible.

Sanderankin asked when the work crews would arrive.

Sensing that the sergeant felt that his fellow guards and their prisoners were being given the shaft, the construction head said that he would try his best to get the original work crews assigned to the tasks of constructing and rehabbing the land of the military prisoners and their guards' living quarters as soon as possible, but he couldn't promise that another project wouldn't take precedence.

Grateful for the kindness that he was being shown, Sanderankin replied that he and his fellow guards and their prisoners would be only too happy to receive the work crews as soon as they were in the new location.

He headed back to the prison camp detail after making it known to the construction head that even though they had been forced to relocate their Fatavian military prisoners to this spot in the outer hinterlands of the Berasculatan countryside, they too needed a place to reside, while formal negotiations were under way to seek a peaceful end to hostilities.

While he was walking back, he was struck on the back of the head and lost consciousness for a short time. When woke up again, someone was looking down at him, holding a farm implement in a threatening manner. When he asked the farmer why he was doing this to him, the farmer's wife said her husband was upset because the sergeant had trampled over his visenark spud trees.

Sanderankin asked the farmer's wife when he had done this. She told him it happened when he and his men had trudged through the forest after leaving the channel on their way to their latest living quarters.

The sergeant apologized and promised to make restitution to them as soon as they got word that the war was over.

When he offered restitution, the farmer backed away from Sanderankin, who stood up from where he had fallen after being hit. Once he was standing, he thanked the farmer for allowing him to get up. Not knowing if the sergeant was serious or just being coy, the farmer nodded his head in reply.

Acknowledging the nod from the farmer, Sanderankin decided to return to where the others in the detail were waiting for him. But when he arrived at where they had been, there was only one guards left, and he told him the prisoners had escaped; the sergeant found this very disturbing, given that they had pledged that they wouldn't escape custody while peace negotiations were in the offing.

Sanderankin asked the lone guard on duty, Private Charles Ockenwalder, to tell him what happened. Ockenwalder explained that a riot had ensued after one of the military prisoners had seen a beautiful young woman.

After hearing that, the sergeant asked Ockenwalder to continue his narrative and inform him of which direction the escaped prisoners had gone. Ockenwalder next told the sergeant what the military prisoners had said about him, which put him in a heated rage, Sanderankin then calmed down and told Ockenwalder that if they were going to recapture the prisoners, they needed to go in the same direction that the prisoners went.

Ockenwalder understood the sergeant's motives for recapturing the prisoners, so he started off down the path he had seen the prisoners take. Sanderankin followed the young private down the path, hoping they might see one of the other guards so they wouldn't have to track the escaped prisoners by themselves.

They did see another guard, but unfortunately, he had a huge hole in his body. Taking into account the position of the hole in the guard's uniform, they surmised that the guard had been fatally shot by a projectile from a prisoner's weapon.

They decided to bury the dead guard. First, however, they'd needed the tools to begin digging a grave. They also had to find a place to bury him; as they were about to collect his corpse from the pile of stones where he had fallen, a farmer showed up with his animals, who wanted to graze near where the guard had fallen. Taking the hint that the animals were very fond of the stone pile where the young guard had died, Sanderankin and Ockenwalder began moving the late private from where he had landed.

As they were in the midst of lifting him from the stone pile, someone came by with a wheelbarrow and shovel; he offered these tools to help bury the soldier. Sanderankin and Ockenwalder tried to thank the man for his kindness. However, before they could thank him, he disappeared from sight. They asked around and found out that his name was Heurakistal Ninawardekmann, and he lived in Lauveronismald, a town not far where they currently were standing.

They finished digging the grave and worked on getting the deceased private interred. Sanderankin said he would unload the private from the wheelbarrow, if Ockenwalder made sure that the crowd, which had gathered while they dug the grave, didn't get in his way.

Ockenwalder told the sergeant that he'd try his best to keep the crowd back; Sanderankin began to move the wheelbarrow towards the grave. But as he approached the recently dug grave, a young man came out of the crowd and moved to block the sergeant's path. Sanderankin told him that unless he wanted to start something he didn't think the young man could finish, he should get out of his way so he could do his duty and honor a late comrade in arms by giving him a proper burial.

The young man, Horace Miskellanderick, became indignant and asked the sergeant why it was so important to bury someone in a grave that was hastily made by two people, neither of whom had seen before now. The sergeant explained to the young man that they were doing it this way because while he may prefer to put the private in a marked grave in an area cemetery, they proudly buried him on this particular parcel because it was where he died.

Miskellanderick decided that the soldiers were right to bury their comrade in this place and moved away from the grave. When he stopped blocking his path, Sanderankin moved the wheelbarrow into position and let the corpse slide out of the wheelbarrow and into the grave.

The onlookers headed back towards where they were going in the first place. Sanderankin and Ockenwalder finished working on the grave and then went off to talk in private.

They overheard a fierce group of men planning to do something to them, so the three new compatriots decided to fight back against whatever these men did. They moved into position to prepare for an assault by the men, hoping they could have a slight advantage. But the assault they expected did not happen. This was because as the new compatriots prepared to do battle with the group, something was hampering the group from the other side.

The new compatriots hoped that whatever was hampering the fierce group of men wasn't some monster; they moved off towards the group, which was slowly dispersing. Suddenly, something got closer to the fierce group of men, who fled in haste. Upon seeing the men leaving with their tails between their legs, the three new compatriots could tell that whatever attacked them was not a benevolent being, and they should be afraid of it. They moved cautiously towards it, but the being moved away from them and headed back in the direction it came from.

The trio was not sure why the being moved away from them; they wanted to show it their gratitude and offer it their friendship for helping disperse the fierce group of men. However, as they walked towards the nearest town of Lauveronismald, they came upon an agricultural co-op with a nearby harbor; as they came closer to the farm, they saw damage they assumed was done by the being. They asked the village mayor how they could help, and he said they could capture the entity, which was a weicandrostrampericus.

They told the mayor they weren't there to capture any entities, so he said they should continue with their journey. They did not want any outsiders who weren't willing to put an end to the weicandrostrampericus before it harmed another village.

Sergeant Sanderankin asked if the hyper bus station was still operational so they could get tickets to Lauveronismald. The mayor said the station had been spared and showed them where it was.

When they saw the station, the three men were surprised that it was still in working order; despite the damage it had suffered, there were huge crowds of people gathering in its main hallway. After waiting several hours, they bought their tickets, which were stamped with a special code. Sanderankin asked a clerk at the station what the special coding meant.

The clerk said the code signified which hyper bus they were to get on. Sanderankin noticed their tickets had different codes and said they were going to the same destination. The clerk told them she understood but the Six Ostrich Hyper Bus Company would not change its policy. At that, the three compatriots said they would try to meet up again at Lauveronismald and then proceed to where Heurakistal Ninawardekmann resided so they could return his wheelbarrow and shovel.

They found a map of the town and picked a place to meet: the Blue Crocodile Restaurant, in the eastern part of the town. When the hyper buses arrived, they each found their bus, climbed inside, and sat down.

As they travelled, the road went through several large forests. Suddenly, as the hyper buses came out of the last forest, the hyper buses were attacked by a band of assailants, who claimed they were part of the true Berasculatan Liberation Army. Hoping to get a glimpse of these assailants, Sanderankin could only see the barrels of blasters being pointed at the windows of his hyper bus.

When he looked at the leader of the assailants, Sanderankin recognized him as Christopher Vaskendahlingdora, one of the escaped military prisoners. When he realized that, he wanted to get his hands on the man for what he and his compatriots had done to Private Jasenias. He told the other passengers they should just give the assailants what they wanted, and that they might leave the convoy alone.

Vaskendahlingdora then told his ragtag team to order the passengers off the hyper buses. That order irked one Wendell Goulanderham, who had run out of patience.

The passengers realized they were being used as hostages to the true Berasculatan Liberation Army's goal of rising to power. To that end, Sanderankin, Goulanderham, and the others decided to help their fellow passengers get safely off their respective hyper buses.

Vaskendahlingdora also ordered the drivers to get out of their vehicles. Sanderankin informed the drivers of their plan to deal with the assailants.

The drivers agreed to follow the plan, as long as no one from the outside got wind of what was going to happen. As luck would have it, as Vaskendahlingdora decided what to do next, a group of armed men began to move into the area. Vaskendahlingdora ordered his underlings to shoot all their hostages, but this barbarous attack wasn't fulfilled, because the armed men began firing on the assailants.

Vaskendahldora saw that his underlings were dropping like flies, so he decided to escape before he was killed or captured. Unfortunately for him, he was wounded by a blaster bolt from one of them men.

When Sanderankin and Ockenwalder saw the former Fatavian trooper laying on his back with a hole in his shoulder, both Private Charles and Sergeant Thibbel also noticed a member of their former prison camp detail standing near the wounded rebel.

Sanderankin moved towards Vaskendahldora to make sure he was completely disarmed. He didn't see anything in the wounded man's hand, but as Vaskendahldora was falling to the ground, he pulled a knife from its sheath and hid it in his sleeve. As the sergeant began to lift up the rebel leader, the blade slipped out of its hiding place. Sanderankin knocked the blade out of Vaskendahldora's hand.

Vaskendahldora sensed that he had no other choice but surrender; he decided not to pull any more tricks and gave up all his weapons. After finally subduing the former Fatavian trooper, the three Madrigald Coalition soldiers lifted him up and carried him from the field.

They decided to bring him with them to Lauveronismald to get medical treatment. They also wanted to return Ninawardekmann's wheelbarrow and shovel, and they needed to compensate the farmer whose plants were trampled as well as the people from the agricultural co-op.

The three Madrigald Coalition soldiers got on the same hyper bus with their recaptured prisoner and started again for the town of Lauveronismald.

When the hyper bus reached its main terminal, the three soldiers got off with their wounded prisoner and headed for the Lauveronismald Municipal Hospital. The doctor there told them that the war was over. They didn't believe him at first, but then they heard that the war was indeed over.

The new royal government in the capital city of Iskelvimbarkien made an announcement that both sides should forget the past wrongs done during the war.

CHAPTER 13

EARLY STORM CLOUDS FORMING OVER REMIGARIA

Planning to do as the new Berasculatan monarch said, the three former troopers decided to return the wheelbarrow and shovel, and then return to the Madrigald Coalition's former front lines to be discharged from their military duties. They checked on their former prisoner, and a nurse told them he was resting comfortably. The three former Madrigald Coalition troops then headed for Heurakistal Ninawardekmann's home to return his tools and thank him for kindness.

Unfortunately, when they arrived, they learned that after he had given them the shovel and wheelbarrow, Ninawardekmann had been killed by his neighbor, who didn't like him. The neighbor was under arrest for murder.

After leaving the Ninawardekmann residence, the three men went to the bank, which wasn't that far away. When they entered the bank, they saw someone they recognized from all news reports; it was Valeutin William Wyclef Bauspeirada, and they assumed he was trying to withdraw money from an account that did not belong to him.

Not wanting to make a scene, the three men went over to a security guard and said something was up with that customer. The guard, whose name was Frinwalker Basenthaler, said he'd look into the matter. At that, they went off to do their own banking business.

The security guard noticed that the customer was acting funny towards the teller and decided to move near the suspicious man.

The security guard continued to observe Bauspeirada, who was taking a banking slip from a teller after concluding his banking business. As Bauspeirada turned away from the teller's window, he noticed that the security guard was now right behind him, and he seemed interested in him. Hoping to avoid direct physical contact with the guard, Bauspeirada pivoted around to his right side to avoid a collision.

After showing the guard he wasn't in the mood for any contact, either physical or visual, Bauspeirada asked the guard what he wanted to talk about him. Frinwalker asked why he had been acting strangely. Astounded by this question, Bauspeirada tried to come up with a plausible excuse for why he had acted peculiarly.

The account he had made a withdrawal from wasn't his own account; it belonged to an acquaintance of his, and this friend was allowing him to withdraw amount from it, without question or harassment.

Frinwalker did not believe for an instant about that this was true; he told the man to give him another story to believe, or else he was planning to arrest him right now for bank robbery.

Bauspeirada tried to come up with a more compelling story to tell the security guard, but the security guard said he was under arrest.

When Frinwalker tried to detain him, Bauspeirada charged the guard and tried to take away his service blaster. Unfortunately for him, Frinwalker knocked him out with one strong punch.

When Bauspeirada woke up, he was handcuffed to a steel pipe, which was near a row of phones. Not seeing the security guard, Bauspeirada wondered where his presumptive jailer might be. As he was wondering this, Frinwalker returned to where Bauspeirada was handcuffed and explained that he had called his superior officers. They told Frinwalker that a police vehicle would be coming to pick up the suspect, and he should take him outside in a few minutes.

As Frinwalker lifted his prisoner up, Bauspeirada reached for the guard's service blaster; unfortunately for him, Frinwalker had moved his blaster under his uniform. After that, Bauspeirada didn't try to grab the blaster again.

As Frinwalker led him out of the bank, Bauspeirada saw the three men who had been in the bank before he had been arrested; he wished he could get his hands on them for letting the security guard know what was going on. When Frinwalker realized that the people his prisoner was sneering at were the men who had told him something was up, he asked them what they were doing. They told him they were waiting for transportation to the town of Hedagordemasmilsan.

Frinwalker told them they were waiting on the wrong side of the transportation stop to get to Hedagordemasmilsan. He told them they should cross the street and wait at the stop outside the bakery. The three men said they were very grateful to him for pointing out their error.

The trio warned Frinwalker to be careful with his prisoner. He said they had nothing to worry about because he had tried something already. The three men waved their hands in acknowledgment of what the security guard had told them and went across the street to wait for their bus.

Frinwalker saw them wave their hands and waved his hand back in acknowledgment. Taking in all the waving hands, Bauspeirada was glad to see the approaching police vehicle, not that he wanted to go to jail, but because maybe someone in the police vehicle would be less careful with their service blaster. Unfortunately for him again, the police that arrived were as smart as Frinwalker. In fact, they either put their service blasters under their uniform shirts or locked them in their vehicle.

They put Bauspeirada into the police vehicle and drove him to the jail. In the back of the police vehicle, he noticed one of his colleagues, who was not just handcuffed but also shackled by his feet as well. He hoped he would not get the same treatment, but he did.

By the time the vehicle reached the jail, the three men had reached Hedagordemasmilsan. When Bauspeirada saw the jail they were to occupy, he remarked to his colleague that it looked like a dump. His colleague, Bicandrolis Egintolmanshack, nodded his head in agreement.

One of the police officers in the paddy wagon heard the two prisoners complaining about the conditions of the local jail; he told his fellow officers that they should do something to make the prisoners know who was boss. Therefore, as the prisoners were being led into the jail, they were struck with a baton to show them that while they were incarcerated, they should not talk about how the jail looked.

After being hit, Bauspeirada and Egintolmanshack understood they weren't allowed to talk about what happened to them or complain about the jail. After that, the guards split them up so they couldn't come up with a scheme to break out of jail.

Egintolmanshack was more of a threat, so he was placed in the maximum-security section of the jail complex; Bauspeirada was placed in minimum security.

Bauspeirada objected that if they were good enough to be traveling partners, they should be in the same cell. The guards said they didn't consider him much of a threat. When he heard that, he said that if he had been given a chance, he'd have tried to crash the paddy wagon on the way to the jail.

They repeated that he was not considered a major threat. Hearing his again, he started to repeat what he thought about doing to the paddy wagon, but before he could say a word, he was hit again. However, unlike the first time, he was hit with a tranquilizer dart. When he woke up this time, he was already in his cell.

Bauspeirada introduced himself to his cellmate, and they got to know one another. His new cellmate, whose name was Burchand Yiruchandrasha, said the guards had brought him unconscious into the cell and placed him gently on his cot. When he asked when they could see their lawyers, Burchand told him tomorrow at three o'clock.

Bauspeirada then asked when the court hearings began. Burchand told him it was shortly before that. Bauspeirada knew he'd have to find a way out of the jail before he went mad. Just then, he and Burchand were called out of their cell for supper.

When they got on line for supper, Bauspeirada noticed how long the line was and hoped they would their food soon. Their turn finally came, but when Bauspeirada saw the food, he wasn't too eager to eat it.

However, when he saw how excited Burchand was about the food, he decided to try it. He asked his cellmate why he liked the food, and he responded that he didn't know; he just loved it. He and Bauspeirada looked for a table to eat at. They sat down after spotting one in the corner of the lunchroom, and then they were joined by a very beautiful young lady who said her name was Binderaskandellia Noreliskerunta.

After returning her greeting, Bauspeirada and Burchand started to eat. While they ate, they noticed that she was staring at them. They decided to talk to her; as they spoke, they learned a lot about one another. After a while, the guard on duty in the lunchroom told them to shut up and finish their meals because it was almost time to go back to their cells. The three prisoners told him they'd try to finish quickly.

After they finished eating, the three new friends left the table. They gave Binderaskandellia a slight head start on her journey back to her cell, and then the two men headed back to their cell.

When Bauspeirada and Burchand got back to their cell, the guards on their floor told them to go right to bed and not ask any questions. They didn't feel sleepy at all and asked why they were being sent to bed so early. One of the guards told them that if they didn't do as they were told, there would be trouble. After hearing that, the two men decided to go to bed immediately, without any further debate.

After a relatively good night's sleep, the two men asked the guards if they could eat breakfast early. The guards said no, they could not eat breakfast earlier than everyone else; the prisoners were supposed to attend church services first. Bauspeirada told the guards he wasn't really religious.

The guards said they didn't care whether they actually participated in the service; the prisoners had no say in the matter. Deciding not to fight over it anymore, Bauspeirada and Burchand agreed to go to the jail's chapel. As they prepared to leave their cell, they heard which guards were to be leading them to the services. When Bauspeirada saw the guard assigned to him, he joked about how big and bruising his guard was.

When his guard heard this, he commented that it would be a pleasure to watch them during the services. At that rebuke, Bauspeirada told his cellmate he must have touched a nerve.

The guards said it was time to go to the chapel. As they got underway, the two men saw a familiar face, Binderaskandellia, who they didn't expect to see this early in the morning. She was wearing a stylish outfit, so they assumed she was going to have a role in the services.

They hoped they could talk with the young lady before she headed off to the chapel, but the guards told them that wouldn't be possible. She wasn't allowed to speak to anyone who might help her escape before her court hearing, which was in a couple of days.

Bauspeirada told the guards he did not care and would be willing to undergo whatever punishment they'd give him, if he could only talk to the girl for a moment. The guard who was escorting him to the chapel said that if he wanted to feel a severe shock to his body, then he should go over to the lone female prisoner. Bauspeirada was not afraid and wasn't sure that the guards would follow through on their threats of bodily harm, so they moved towards the young lady.

The guards did indeed follow through on their threats, and despite being struck with large bolts of energy from the guards' proton shock poles, Bauspeirada felt even more dedicated to the task of talking to the girl.

Upon seeing how much her fellow prisoner was willing to risk to talk to her, Binderaskandellia told the guard prodding her into the chapel that she would go inside freely if they stopped hurting her two friends.

At that request, the guards leading her into the chapel motioned for their own counterparts to stop what they were doing to their prisoners and let the three go into the chapel. The guards leading the two male prisoners turned off their proton shock poles. The prisoners weren't allowed to talk to one another, and the youngest guard of each detail watched the prisoners carefully to make sure nothing escaped their view. As the guards led them into the chapel, Bauspeirada and Burchand cautiously moved towards Binderaskandellia.

As the group continued their journey into the chapel, they came upon another group of guards in a half-circle, holding their proton shock poles at the ready. The other detail's leader said that he and his men had been forced to take down their prisoners, without much regard for their safety.

The leader of the jail guard detail asked the other leader if any of his men needed medical attention. He responded that none of his team needed medical attention; none of them had been injured in the latest incident, but he added that it should be noted in the logs that both prisoners taken down with proton shock poles were on their way to the jail's main infirmary, wanting treatment for their wounds.

The head of the newly formed jail guard detail said he'd note it in his log, and he'd be willing to personally vouch that the guards had been forced to use force against the prisoners to keep them in line. The detail leader thanked his superior for his kind gesture.

After seeing Bauspeirada and Burchand follow their friend's advice and stop what they had been doing, the detail leader told his fellow guards to lower their shock poles and take the three into the chapel, without wasting any more time. The chapel service was expected to start soon, if the chaplain was on time. After being led into the chapel, the three prisoners were taken to their individual seats; their seats were far apart from each other.

Because of the distance between their seats, the three prisoners realized they could communicate with each other through a pipeline of people sitting between them. However, they decided not to activate the pipeline for fear of retaliation from the guards.

They tried it later, but it was the wrong time, because as luck would have it, one of the members in the pipeline dropped the note in her possession. She failed to recover it, and it was picked up by a guard. He asked her where she got the note, but she wouldn't not say. Instead, she stated that she would rather be sent to solitary confinement than name any of her fellow conspirators. Since she had been caught red-handed with the note, she should be sent to solitary.

The guards said to her that if she wanted that, then she was going to get it. She replied that it wasn't what she wanted, but since it was what it was, she was willing to take the fall. To that, the guards said there must be something or someone she had feelings for on the outside. She replied that there was no one she had feelings for on the outside. Not believing her for an instant, the guards tried to get her to open up about why she said she had no one on the outside once she was freed.

She said she didn't have to reveal anything to them, and she wanted to go to solitary confinement immediately. At that brazen statement, one of the guards said to her that if she wasn't willing to reveal anything about her personal life, she should at least tell them who had given her the note she had dropped by her seat.

She said she got the note from Jasper Nigelonbanterick. When they heard that, the guards went to talk to Nigelonbanterick, who told the guards he had gotten the note from Brenda Bildoreskandathorn.

They went to Bildoreskandathorn's seat, and she said she had gotten the note from Williard Tripperangeld, who had threatened to harm her family unless she became a pawn in his scheme. Tripperangeld denied that the scheme was his and said he never threatened Bildoreskandathorn's family.

Due to the efforts of Nivalon Brismer, the plot started to come apart. Brismer told his immediate superior that he had a feeling something was going to happen during the service. At first, he didn't take him seriously, but after the service began, things started to happen. Now choosing to believe him, he told his fellow guards to be ready for anything.

The plot was discovered when another woman let a note slip through her fingers. They asked her where she had gotten the note, and she said she received it from Miskelish Mautismal. When they found him, he said he had gotten the note from Kireshonald Niperonishcan, who claimed she got the note from Binderaskandellia Noreliski, who said that while she had written the note, it was for everyone who wanted freedom from enslavement.

The head guard in the chapel then told her that if she and her friends wished to do something wrong, the guards would help them in some way. Binderaskandellia used her facial expressions to let her accomplices know that the head guard was going to have them do something terrible to get them to turn away from their evil ways. To that, Bauspeirada and Burchand cringed at what they would face for trying to accomplish their dreams of freedom.

When they heard that they would be moved to a new jail cell, Bauspeirada and Burchand wondered if any of their fellow conspirators would be coming along. They learned that they weren't. Burchand and Bauspeirada were heading into their new jail cell blind. When they got to their cell, they noticed some of their fellow conspirators' former colleagues were in the cell with them. Bauspeirada asked which bunks were theirs, and they were told that the bunks facing the guards' monitoring station were to be theirs, for the time being.

Bauspeirada asked his new cellmate why he had said "for the time being."

The man, known as Thaddeus Kippergaun, told Bauspeirada that he didn't think they had long to live in this jail cell.

Bauspeirada replied, "If that's a threat, don't expect to see us frightened by that."

Kippergaun said, "Good, because my fellow prisoners and I don't mind being in a cell with stout-hearted fellows, because that means they have some very fine prey to hunt in the morning, before it's time to go to the courthouse."

Bauspeirada headed back over to his bunk, where Burchand had positioned himself on the upper bunk. Burchand asked Bauspeirada what he found out. He said it was just as their new cellmate told him. Somewhat taken aback by this, Burchand went over to the new cellmate and asked if it was true.

Bauspeirada and Burchand began developing a new plan to get out of jail before their new cellmates killed them. When they were called for their first meal together, Bauspeirada and Burchand would get the group's silverware. They did their jobs very well. In fact, they did it a little too well for the guard's taste. The Kakorian-born guard, Nivalon Brismer, told them to return the overabundance of silverware.

They replied that they did not understand him. He responded by saying he understood their situation, but the extra silverware wouldn't get them the freedom they sought. They asked how he knew what they were planning to do with the silverware, and he explained that he had a special gift that told him things of great importance. Not exactly believing him, the two continued to hoard the silverware. He told them again to put back the silverware. They didn't comply, so he told them that if they didn't do so by the time, he counted to three, he'd tell the other guards what they were up to. They replied that they didn't care what he told the other guards; they wouldn't give up their stockpile.

He decided to tell his fellow guards what they were doing. As he went back to the guards' table, he begins to feel something coming towards him from behind and to the right of him. Reacting instinctively, Brismer blocked the plate with his forearm. He knocked it to the floor, but several fragments flew away. He turned around to see if the two male prisoners had been harmed by the debris, but they were okay.

He spun around and went directly to the guards' table, where he told the leader what the two male prisoners were planning to do with their silverware. Taking him at his word, the head guard in the cafeteria, one Michael Mininiski, ordered two guards to go over with Brismer and dissuade the two prisoners from their plans. Brismer was grateful that Mininiski sent these guards to help him deter the two male prisoners.

Brismer and the other two guards went over to Bauspeirada and Burchand. Before they got there, Brismer could see with his telepathic awareness a single blue reverberation that became a double blue reverberation. The two other guards, Thaddeus Posler and Manuel Spalonerback, asked Brismer if he was alright because of the change in his suit's color; he told them he was alright, and they should deal with the current situation facing them. Not wanting to offend him anymore about how he was feeling, the two guards just moved to his side as he moved towards the table where the two prisoners were sitting.

Upon seeing Brismer, Bauspeirada and Burchand had gotten their own silverware as well as sets for the others in their group. Brismer told them he and the other guards were standing at their table so they didn't try anything foolish, like starting another riot.

At that response, Bauspeirada said he didn't know they had started a first riot.

Seeing that they were trying to make him seem like a total idiot, Brismer said to them that they could not deny that they were principal architects of the riot in the chapel. They were surprised that he had figured that out and did not want to let him know they were planning something for later on; they told him he was very much mistaken about their role in the chapel riot.

Brismer then told the other guards that they should start to move in on the two prisoners so they could not begin what they were planning for later. As the two younger guards started towards the prisoners, a wave of uncertainty crossed Brismer's face, and his uniform began to change color from a double blue shade to a double purple red. When the young guards arrived at their seats and saw the prisoners were only eating their meals, they looked back towards their superior.

Seeing his uniform change color and noting the dour expression on his face, the two younger guards asked him again if he was alright. Brismer claimed he was alright and said they should focus on their current subjects. They continued watching over the prisoners. But just as they resumed watching them, a sudden, mysterious rush of air filtered into the cafeteria.

It did not take long for them to figure out where the mysterious air was coming from: It came from an area next to the dining table they were watching. Telling their fellow guards to come over to where the mysterious air was coming from, they tried to peg the exact source. But as the young guards sealed off the vents in the area, a new threat seemed to be coming for Brismer.

Not wanting to let the prisoners escape their notice for very long, without much fanfare, the new threat against Brismer unexpectedly show its physical presence in the cafeteria. As it approached the table, Brismer realized that he was the target of the whole prism of threats and activated his quantum refraction balls. Unfortunately, the threat struck at Brismer's heart with ionized crystal daggers. As the daggers pierced his heart, he dropped to his knees; as he died, a glow emerged from his body covering the whole cafeteria.

Seeing their dead comrade on the ground before them, Posler and Spalonerback attacked the threat that had killed him. Seeing those who had been with his rival coming after him, the threat backed out of the cafeteria. The assailant was not able to leave, because as he was backing away from the table, where his rival had positioned himself to stop others from leaving, the two who had been with his rival hit him in his midsection. He couldn't stop the pain from the blows he suffered from his rival's two counterparts, because even as he tried to stop the throbbing pain, they continued to strike him.

A gust of wind blew through the cafeteria; Bauspeirada and Burchand could not fathom where it had come from. However, by the roar it was making, they knew they had get away from it and fast. Unfortunately, they couldn't get away from it, and it seemed that the wind was trying to pull them towards the guards; it also seemed to be pulling their fellow cellmates.

Upon seeing their cellmates again, this time with their own hastily fashioned weapons drawn, Bauspeirada and Burchand constructed weapons of their own. To their dismay, as they prepared to rush in for their own private combat, they saw the guards who had been watching them preparing to fight with the threat near where their late former colleague's body had fallen. They wondered if the remaining guards would come over to where they were now and try to stop them, but it seemed that the guards were busy defeating the thing that had killed their colleague.

However, when the guards didn't come over to where Bauspeirada and Burchand were, they discussed which side each of them was to handle and headed over to their opponents.

They moved to strike at their chosen foes, but the two guards they were fighting got caught up in a cloud of mysterious energy. Not knowing what to expect as the mysterious cloud closed around them all, they fought until their numbers were cut in half. When the mysterious cloud of energy opened up again, the eleven survivors found themselves on an island.

They decided to stop fighting until they could assess the exact position of the island; they soon found out that they were not on any of the islands that belonged to Berasculata. Hoping to find any markings to determine whose country the island belonged to, they soon realized they had ended up on Crunaosila Island, which belong to the Remigarian Empire. In fact, it was off the southwestern edge of the mainland of Remigaria itself. With that in mind, it was up to Posler to check in with the Remigarian authorities on the island.

Leaving Spalonerback with the other surviving prisoners, Posler headed northwest towards the main city of Mireucandolsarmat. It took him several hours to get there, and he found the main administrative building.

Posler began walking up the long, steep steps to the top of the main administrative building complex. When he got to the main door, a security guard asked what his business was. When he told them the whole story of how he and the others came to the island in a whirlwind, the whole security detail broke out in laughter before asking him why he didn't bring the rest of his party with him to confirm the tale. Posler said it wouldn't have been possible, because several of them had been part of a violent criminal organization in Berasculata.

After hearing that, Vakeral Bitulandos, the head of the security detail at the main administrative building, asked why they were brought to Remigarian territory. Posler said that they did not exactly bring them here to the island but were in fact somehow teleported to the island.

Bitulandos asked who among their party was a teleporter. After thinking about who could be the teleporter, Posler decided there was only one possibility of who could have teleported them to the island.

After hearing what Posler said could be the only possible way they could have been teleported to the island, Bitulandos said he'd send out a search party to find any signs of Kakorian teleportative residue where Posler said his party was currently located. Posler was grateful to the security head and tried to shake the man's hand. Not certain if he should shake the hands of someone he didn't know, Bitulandos quickly moved his hand away.

After Posler dropped his hand to his side, a group of men in battle fatigues appeared. Figuring this was the search party, Posler asked Bitulandos where he could sleep.

He told him to go to the Lasomatriamorcum and offered to have his aide show him the way. At that, Posler thanked him.

The aide and Posler left the main administrative building for the Lasomatriamorcum. Simultaneously, the search party left to find Posler's group. But when they reached the spot where Posler said he left his group, what the security detail encountered didn't match up with what Posler had told Bitulandos. Instead of seeing ten people waiting on the beach, there were six, and instead of Kakorian teleportative residue on the beach, they found residue from a Gruckelian device. They sent word back via radio to Bitulandos.

After being roused from his bed, Posler was brought back to the main administrative building. When he got there, Bitulandos accused him of duping them about his party and said he should confess to knowing they used Gruckelian teleportative. Bitulandos told Posler that he was crazy if he felt these facts were true.

When he heard this, Posler told Bitulandos that he was crazy, and if there were teleportative in the area, they were not Gruckelian teleportative.

"They must have been teleported here while protecting us from a creature of some sort," he suggested, "who tried to killed them but killed their friend instead."

Bitulandos then asked, "Then how come the search team that I sent out to your de-embarkation point only found six people instead of ten?"

Posler said he did not know why the search team found six people instead of ten, unless four escaped while Spalonerback wasn't looking.

Bitulandos then called Victor Feulinsatrokis, the head of the search team he had sent to Posler's de-embarkation point, to find Spalonerback and ask him what happened.

When Feulinsatrokis responded to the call from Bitulandos, they got talking and couldn't stop. Bitulandos asked if there was a man there named Spalonerback. Feulinsatrokis said he thought so but would go and find out. A few minutes later, Feulinsatrokis came back on the line and told Bitulandos that there was a man named Spalonerback in the group, but he had been injure. Bitulandos told Feulinsatrokis to bring him to the local hospital.

Following Bitulandos' directive, Feulinsatrokis spaced himself and the nine others under his direct command so as to make sure that the five remaining prisoners didn't do anything foolish; he didn't want to have to stop them by force of numbers, and he didn't want to have to call for backup while carrying the group's most prized cargo, Manuel Spalonerback.

They reached the hospital in two hours. Once inside, Feulinsatrokis asked for a nurse to send for a doctor to see to the man on the stretcher. When the doctor arrived, he said that Spalonerback needed to be in a treatment room immediately. The nurse got several orderlies to help get Spalonerback off his makeshift stretcher and onto a gurney; they took him to the nearest treatment room.

After working on Spalonerback a few minutes, the doctor told Feulinsatrokis he couldn't save his life.

Feulinsatrokis told the doctor that was not possible, since Spalonerback only had a twisted ankle and some bruises.

The doctor said that once they began to treat him, Spalonerback started to convulse in very strange ways. It seemed to the doctor that something had crawled inside Spalonerback, and when he tried to fight back, the thing decided it didn't want an unwilling host.

When he heard that, Feulinsatrokis called Bitulandos and told him what happened. Bitulandos realized that if he didn't act, things could get worse. After hanging up with Feulinsatrokis, he began to call the territorial governor, but then the prime minister of Remigaria called and told him to get down to the capital, pronto. Surprised that the prime minister would contact him personally instead of going through the chain of command, he called for a ship to sail to Casulimatron, the capital of Remigaria.

When the ship arrived at the port he had designated as the pickup point, Feulinsatrokis brought with him his whole team, Posler, and all of Posler's surviving prisoners. After arriving on the mainland, a specialized shore patrol led Bitulandos, his team, and all of his guests to a special warehouse. Once inside, they were told a special representative would be there to greet them and take them to the prime minister's office.

After telling them this, the shore patrol left. As they waited intently for the special representative to arrive from the prime minister's office, they began to guess who it would be. The game became very educational for them to learn some things about one another. They learned, for example, that Burchand had once been part of a theatre troupe. When pressed about why he'd been locked in a jail cell, he began to respond when the special representative from the prime minister's office walked in.

The representative was a very beautiful young lady, and the six men stopped listening to Burchand and paid attention to her instead. She said she was Special Representative Selena Miltenrich and asked which one of them was Bitulandos. When Vakeral heard his last name mentioned, he raised his hand.

After confirming Bitulandos's identity, Miltenrich explained what had happened and why the prime minister wanted to get him personally involved. Bitulandos asked what his team was supposed to do. He said he would not do what the prime minister wanted until he knew what his team was to do.

Miltenrich called her boss and asked what she was to do. She was told to transport all the prisoners they had in their custody to a local jail and then take the others to a local hotel.

Bitulandos was conflicted about this, but he decided to do as instructed. After deciding to do as he had been instructed, Bitulandos gave his former troopers one last command: to be very vigilant with the remaining prisoners. They all promised to do as he commanded. After listening to them give their last oath of fealty, he sent them on their way to the closest jail.

As they marched out of the warehouse center, they waved at him and Posler, signifying how much fun they had during their brief time together and also how close they had gotten. Once they left the warehouse, Bitulandos and Posler headed to the closest bus stop, but on the way to catch the bus to Casulimatron, they were accosted by some drunken villagers.

They told the drunken villagers that they were not in the mood to hear any of their ramblings, but they continued ranting nonsensical things until they reached the bus stop. After the last of the drunken villagers had left the bus stop area, to keep both his sanity intact and to also punctuate the boredom of waiting for the bus, Bitulandos broke out into song. Unfortunately, as he was in the midcourse of his song, Posler indicated he wasn't in the mood to hear him song any more than the drunken villagers.

He asked Posler why he didn't like the song, and Posler remarked that he didn't feel like celebrating anything yet because he missed his beautiful girlfriend and her children, his possible future stepchildren. Bitulandos asked him how many children there were, and Posler said there were five kids: three girls and two boys, ages eight to fourteen years old.

After hearing this, Bitulandos told him all about himself. When Bitulandos had finished speaking about his home life, Posler asked him when he thought the bus would arrive. Bitulandos said it should be there very shortly. When the bus arrived at the bus stop, several passengers came off it, and then Posler and Bitulandos got on board. After paying their fares, they headed towards the back of the bus.

In the back of the bus, they noticed that some of their fellow passengers had decided to place their goods on the seat next to theirs. They tried to get some cooperation from these passengers, but they wouldn't remove their goods from the seats. Deciding not to rock the boat, the two men stood for most of the journey to Casulimatron.

When they got off the bus, the two men hailed a cab. After giving the cabdriver the address, he sped off into traffic and soon dropped them off at the Slocken Parrot Arms Hotel. They walked into the hotel to check in. Posler let Bitulandos go through the main doors first. Thanking him for let him go in first, Bitulandos told Posler that he should check in at registration desk before he forgot.

Posler thanked him for reminding him to check in and said he'd only be gone for a few minutes. Bitulandos said that while he was checking in, he'd wander around the hotel.

As Posler was waiting in line to get checked in, Bitulandos called the prime minister's office. During their call, he told the prime minister about the current situation facing the Remigarian Empire. The prime minister asked him if he did what was requested. He said yes, and the prime minister asked him one more thing: "Is the guest someone we could trust with a key part of the objective when we propose our solution to the crown prince?"

Saying he thought they could trust the guest about what they were planning to propose to the crown prince, the prime minister added that as soon as the guest was checked in, he'd bring him to the prime minister's office so they could discuss the situation.

As luck would have it, as they were finishing their conversation, Posler appeared to the right of Bitulandos. Somewhat startled that Posler was standing right next to him, Bitulandos asked if he had checked in. Posler said yes. After hearing that, he told Posler they would be leaving the hotel for a while.

Not sure what to make of this, Posler asked him where they were going.

Bitulandos said that for the moment, it was a need-to-know thing, and he did not need to know. Posler said then why should he be forced to go after just checking in.

Bitulandos told him if he wanted to avenge his friends' deaths, then he should come with him.

Not wanting to seem like a coward, he decided to follow Bitulandos wherever he was going in order to avenge his friends' deaths. He told Bitulandos he would go along with whatever he had in store for them. After Posler said he would go with him, Bitulandos called for a cab so he and his friend could go to the main administrative building in the capital city.

After a few seconds, the hotel staff called for a cab to pick up the two men (one of whom had officially registered as a guest of the hotel) to take them to the prime minister's office. When the cab arrived, they got in it and headed to the prime minister's office.

The cab drove them to the prime minister's office. After paying the fare, they walked into the building where the prime minister's office was. Once at the entrance of the building, Bitulandos opened the door for Posler and then followed him through it.

As the door closed behind him, Bitulandos instructed Posler to walk slowly so the security personnel knew they weren't there to do the prime minister any harm. Unfortunately, Posler couldn't restrain himself and decided to run towards the security desk to get his visitor's pass. When he reached the security desk, they told him that he wouldn't get his pass until he showed some decorum in the office of the prime minister of Remigaria.

Posler apologized for running up to the desk and asked again for his visitor's pass.

Sensing that he was truly sorry, the head of security for the prime minister's office, one Archibald Henshenshedo, gave Posler his pass. As he put it on, Posler was asked why he was at the office of the prime minister. Not knowing exactly what to say, he waited until Bitulandos came over to the security desk. When they saw Bitulandos coming to the security desk, Henshenshedo asked why he wanted to see the prime minister. Bitulandos said the prime minister had asked them to come and talk about what the country was facing from an unnatural enemy.

They were told that it wouldn't be long until they could see the prime minister. Henshenshedo invited them to wait in the main anteroom of the prime minister's office.

After going inside, the two thanked Henshenshedo for letting them in. He replied that as guests of the prime minister, it was his job to let them in. At that, they offered him a salute.

Henshenshedo returned the gesture and then told them that if they wanted anything, don't hesitate to ask for it. He then left the anteroom and headed back to rejoin the rest of the security detail. Soon after that, the prime minister of Remigaria showed up.

He asked them if they had been waiting long for him, and they said they hadn't been waiting too long.

He asked if they had been seen to by his new brother-in-law and head of his personal security detail, Archibald Henshenshedo. They asked him how he knew it had been Henshenshedo who taken care of. At first, he told them he was intuitive, but then he said he had seen Henshenshedo leaving the area they were now in. After exchanging pleasantries, they got down to business about what was happening in Remigaria.

They talked for an hour about what was happening in the Remigarian realm and how an unnatural enemy might be involved with the whole thing; the prime minister said that to get what they needed to fight this new threat, they needed to get the crown prince's personal approval.

To that, Bitulandos asked the prime minister how the crown prince was doing.

"Well, Vaskeral, with what he has had to deal with lately since the son- in- law of his father i.e., King Volerick Lobberstein II i.e., his brother-in-law and his sister, the new queen of Berasculata, aren't not doing so well both physical and thus so far matrimonial, his and his father's enemies are mounting heavy challenges to the House of Sotarius's rule of governing the empire."

Upon hearing that, Posler asked the prime minister if there was anything he could do to help.

The prime minister replied, "Well, yes, Thaddeus, if the crown prince asked me to do something, I could, but so far, he has not asked me to do so. Until he does, I am powerless to act, even as prime minister of Remigaria."

Posler asked him, "Then why don't you try to get him to ask you to help him out?"

The prime minister said he could not force the crown prince to ask him, because if he did, the crown prince's foes would see him as more than just a humble servant of the people but as the prince's chief puppet master.

Posler said, "Just because you would be forcing the crown prince to ask you for your help in his problems, how could that make you his puppet master?"

The prime minister said, "Even though I wasn't within the crown prince's inner circle, people would say because of my many years of service, I had influenced him into doing something he didn't want to do."

Posler asked, "Why would that be a bad thing, if it helped him right the wrongs of many of things that were happening in the country now?"

"Because the crown prince already has people who are telling him what to do and think and how things should be," said the prime minister.

"So, what if he does have people telling him what to do and think, Prime Minister, sir?" Posler said. "You could at least work with these people instead of being on the sidelines doing nothing but just talking about doing something.

At that, Bitulandos told Posler he was out of line and said it wasn't up to him to say what the prime minister should or should not do.

Posler replied that if the prime minister wasn't willing to force the crown prince to ask him for his help in solving his problems, then why not work with the people who were telling the crown prince what to do?

When he heard that, Bitulandos said he wished that he had not brought Posler here at all.

Posler told Bitulandos, "If you did not want to take me here in the first place, why did you make a huge fuss about me going to my hotel room at Slocken Parrot Arms Hotel?"

"Because I thought you'd be a big help in trying to solve the problem the prime minister called about," said Bitulandos.

"Well, that's what I've been trying to do," Posler replied. "I've been trying to show that if the prime minister isn't willing to do what is necessary in getting what they need to fight this new enemy, then how could anyone expect the regular citizens to do something, when he can't do something as the crown prince?"

Bitulandos told Posler that he didn't make any sense at all.

After hearing what Bitulandos said, the prime minister said, "That's true because by using reverse psychology on me, Vakeral, Thaddeus has shown that by not taking charge of some of the things crown prince is facing, I'm not being as effective as I should be."

Surprised to hear this, Bitulandos asked the prime minister if he was willing to do what Posler had suggested.

The prime minister said that he was, and he would call the crown prince as soon as the head of his personal security detail got him a line to the crown prince's private residence. Henshenshedo then got a line to the prime minister for his brother-in-law.

Unfortunately, after getting on the line with the crown prince's private residence, the phone was answered by one of his top handlers, Zesauralin Eserperalkinder, a man the local press said had just downed a very long drink and then belched the empire's national anthem in four burps. The prime minister, Quelan Doserbick, didn't think he had a prayer to talk to the crown prince at all. However, he soon heard the voice of the crown prince on the phone, and they had a long conversation.

They talked for almost an hour while the prime minister laid out what he, Bitulandos, and Posler had been discussing. The crown prince asked if the prime minister had any proof of what they suspected was happening in the realm.

To that, Prime Minister Doserbick said, "Not exactly, but how else could these people get here from Berasculata without using a boat or plane?"

The crown prince asked who had traveled to Remigaria from Berasculata without boat or plane.

The prime minister mentioned the name of Thaddeus Posler.

Upon hearing Posler's name, the crown prince asked if this Posler had a relative named Walter.

Thaddeus told the prime minister his uncle was named Walter. After confirming this information with the crown prince, the prime minister asked the crown prince why he had wanted to know this. The crown prince said he had been reading an article about a Berasculatan man, Walter Posler, who had been stabbed to death by a knife-wielding maniac on his way to work.

When Posler heard this, he knew it had to have to been his uncle who had stabbed to death. Now even though he did not much care for his uncle Walter, he did have a fondness for his aunt Natasha and his younger cousins, Valerie, Nicholas, and Nicole, and thus he told the prime minister to tell the crown prince. After hearing that from the prime minster, the crown prince said that he would like to meet and then console the young Posler.

Thaddeus said he'd like that, and if possible, he'd like to catch and then punish whoever was responsible. The prime minister told Thaddeus that the man who killed his uncle was named Charles Augustus Aloysius Kiswather Polchansway Sr. After briefly crying about his uncle, he asked to see the crown prince right away. After some doing, the prime minister brought him and Bitulandos to the crown prince's residence.

They arrived at the crown prince's private residence on the morning of July 3, 2474; they each had much to discuss with the crown prince, including how to get the necessary equipment needed to defeat the threat they were sure was coming and also to find, capture, and punish Charles Augustus Aloysius Kiswather Polchansway for the terrible things he had done in his life.

After thinking on all the things brought to his attention by the three men, Crown Prince Rawenthantoriska Yerberan Sotarius consulted with his whole staff and then called for the Remigarian legislature to pass the Beutarionona Accord. After getting certain guarantees from the crown prince, the legislature voted on the accord. It passed by a slim majority, but it passed nonetheless, 3,245,980 to 2,975,120.

After the accord passed, the head of the legislature told the crown prince of the decision, and he in turn told the three men.

That the hunt would in earnest soon for Polchansway and all of his criminal associates.

EPILOGUE

Now as the weeks went by and as the newly formed Berasculatan/ Remigarian Special Intelligence and Special Investigative Services Alliance or also known as "Berremspinseal" was getting its "feet" proverbial wet and thus coming up without nothing concrete as to where Polchansway and his associates were, the hope was fading fast as to where they that is Polchansway and his criminal associates might make their first strike since the killing of Duke Walter Posler III, a staunch alliance friend and the warmest, kindest of uncles to Thaddeus and siblings and also the kindest kind of father to Thaddeus and sibling's cousins could or should have in their lives. Suddenly and without warning there would be news some good and then some not so good news. The good news was that the new Berasculatan king Volerick Lobberstein II and his wife the new queen of Berasculatan were doing much better and were expecting their first child soon but that was the end of the good news, the bad news was that there had been still hadn't been any sightings of Polchansway or any of criminal associates and that was troubling especially since the alliance had spent so much time and money looking for them so long now. Now as the hope of finding Polchansway and his criminal associates was seeming to be fading as the weeks continued to go by without any sightings of them i.e., Polchansway and his criminal "buddies" or what they might be up, then suddenly a tip would come through to the hotline that had been set up by the alliance's leaders that Polchansway and his criminal "buddies" were in the city of Tolagurichia Minor, which was the very edges of the Tolagurichian-Vueckakolchiniska Plain of which sat on the "terraces" of the Zetatolagurichian Valley of the Cizetatolgurichian- Detavueckakolchiniskasan Desert or also as the "Kids" Desert.

However, upon arriving in the area and after going over several possible siting places, they that is the team that he that is Thaddeus had been working with on the case in the growing search for Polchansway and his criminal "entourage", they'd find nothing linking him to the area except the word of one Auberon Askerdarishimendozakian of whom had said he had seen them i.e., Polchansway and the "entourage" in the area. Now not wanting to not believe him i.e., Askerdarishimendozakian, but also not wanting to be lead on a wild goose chase as they that is the team had been lead on it seemed at the moment, Thaddeus and Colonel Cimbarius "Cimbros" Heuradokiman would ask Mr. Auberon Askerdarishimendozakian some most poignant and pressing questions, one of which was how do you know it was them i.e., Polchansway and his "entourage" and Auberon Askerdarishimendozakian would say that he knows it was Polchansway and his criminal "entourage" because of the way in which they "carried" themselves inside of the marketplace store of which he that is Auberon worked. Stating that how they that is the group that he Auberon saw them acting didn't make them Polchansway and his criminal "entourage" they that is Thaddeus and Colonel Cimbarius Heuradokiman would thus ask Auberon Askerdarishimendozakian to describe the people saw more furtherly and so he that is Auberon would and after this furtherly descriptions they'd know at least some of those of whom Polchansway was supposedly "allied" with were in the group that Auberon had seen but as for if the "leader" of the group that Auberon saw in the store he worked at, could have been anyone and so they'd ask for confirmation details like: describe the physical features of the "leader" of the group you saw inside your store?, and so Auberon would begin by describing him i.e., the "leader" of the group that he that is Auberon saw inside the Gilded Guppy as a man in his late forties with a wolverine tattoo that ran elongated around the corners of his face and also having a couple of firebreather tattoos run horizontally down each of his hands and also having a couple of falcon tattoos running the length of his legs. Now somewhat agreeing with what Auberon was saying about the "leader" of the group that had been seen inside the Gilded Guppy department store but they still needed to know the height of the man and weight and also eye color to be positive that it was indeed Charles Augustus Aloysius Kiswather Polchansway Sr. before they i.e., the team moved on the tip, and so after stating that the man i.e., the "leader" of the group was at least 6'9" in height weight at least about between 250 and or 260, and also had greenish blue eyes with a volcano-like hairstyle and also a harpsichordian – like voice and with that last bit the team i.e., Colonel Cimbarius Heuradokiman, Thaddeus and the others with them would begin to concur that the person i.e., "leader" of the group that had visited the Gilded Guppy department store was probably Viscount Charles Polchansway Sr. and they then ask to see what he that is probably Polchansway and his associates bought at the store and so Auberon would lead them to the store and thus begin to show them i.e., the team all of the items that the group had bought with their ill gotten gains and thus upon seeing the registry of the items that they that is group had bought they'd had determined that the group was probably going towards one of the resort towns on the edges of the outer purview of the Remigarian Empire but to find out to which one of the resort towns and or islands the criminal organization was headed would take some time to figure out and they'd have to figure it out soon before a major crime happened that could have major international implications.

Now not long after teletyping a message back to the R.I.S.S. office of which they that is the team i.e., Colonel Cimbarius Heuradokiman, Thaddeus and the others with them had found out about what Polchansway and his criminal "buddies" had purchased at the store i.e., the Gilded Guppy department store, did the R.I.S.S. office and its current office manager respond back that there had been some rumors of a large group of men and women and children having been seen looking at the Zecarodisembarasocolari Zoo and Resort on the island of Zester Prime. Now not wanting to chance it, both Colonel Cimbarius "Cimbros" Heuradokiman and Thaddeus would ask the current office manager Lieutenant Jesserally Juckson to have finer "gander" of information before send them i.e., the team over there i.e., Zester Prime and thus after having that finer "gander" of the information reported to the R.I.S.S. office, Lieutenant Juckson said that yes he could most definitely confirm the that information was just rumor anymore and that they that is "Dragonfly" Squad should head over to Zester Prime before the group left the island with their "trinkets" and or some other event happened and so with that "Dragonfly" Squad would leave immediately for Zester Prime and once there i.e., Zester Prime would begin to canvas the in and around the zoo and thus the surrounding resort any sign or other clues about the large group that Polchansway was supposed to be leading and upon not exactly finding any signs or other clues about the group would assume that the group had left the island of Zester Prime but as to where they that is group had gone immediately after leaving the island of Zester Prime until there was a report of a disturbance being reported on and around the island of Abethechanali – Frezzalenkindarishimidoslarbend or also known as the island of "Angel Hearts" and it would be there that the team's hunt would begin anew for Polchansway and his criminal associates and or "buddies"

The End.
Read further in Ridges for the Wise: The Remigarian Ruse.

Printed in the United States
by Baker & Taylor Publisher Services